Tales From The Dark Tower

Illustrated by Joseph Vargo

Monolith Graphics, Cleveland, Ohio
Edited by Joseph Vargo and Christine Filipak

PUBLISHED BY MONOLITH GRAPHICS
CLEVELAND, OHIO
www.monolithgraphics.com

Cover and Interior Artwork by Joseph Vargo
Graphic Design & Photography by Christine Filipak

Publisher's Cataloging-in-Publication Data
Tales From The Dark Tower / Illustrated by Joseph Vargo
Edited by Joseph Vargo and Christine Filipak
ISBN: 0-9675756-0-5   LCCN: 99-075958
1. Fiction—Horror   2. Vampires—Anthologies
3. Ghosts—Anthologies   I. Vargo, Joseph

Revised First Edition
Printed and Published in the United States of America

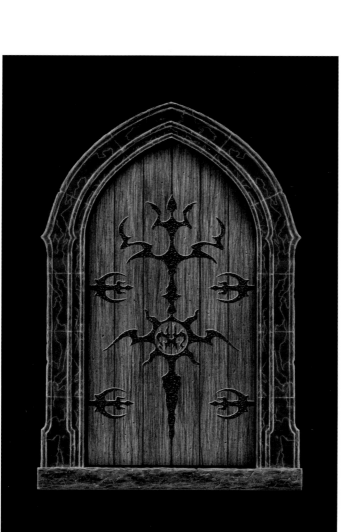

~ Contents ~

The Dark Tower

JAMES PIPIK AND JOSEPH VARGO

In an instant, the battle erupted. The clash and clang of metal resounded like thunder and the knight's camp was now the heart of the storm. Appearing like frightful spectres out of the darkness, the Turks were upon them from all sides. It was an ambush and the trap was well laid. Cut off from retreat, Brom saw comrades fall on each side of him. Frail flesh gave way to cold, sharpened steel and bones shattered beneath axe and mace. Death screams of crusaders were drowned out by the shrill battle cries of Turkish warriors.

All hope was lost this night. To stay and fight meant certain doom. The sacred oath that Brom had sworn, to give his life for God and country, gave way to a deep and primal instinct to survive. Slashing and parrying his way through the onslaught, he formed a desperate plan. If he could reach the horses, he might evade the slaughter and escape through the dense forest. As he advanced, cleaving a path through Turkish flesh and bone, an arrow bit deep into his shoulder while another found its mark through his chain mail shirt. A sabre glanced off his sword, tearing open his thigh. As he hesitated in pain, an axe crashed across the visor of his helmet and knocked him off his feet.

Laying on his stomach, Brom glanced upward. A lone figure cloaked entirely in black stood amidst the havoc, untouched by sword or lance. Blood pulsed from the knight's forehead, obscuring his vision. Brom threw off his helmet to wipe his eyes, and looked again toward the grim shadow. The dark figure now stood directly before the fallen knight, peering down upon him. Though its face was masked by darkness, its eyes reflected the firelight of the massacre. Brom was certain that Death had come for him. The thunderous sounds of the battle fell quiet, and the figure stood in silence over him. Blood streamed from the crusader's wound, blinding him once again, and once again he wiped away the veil of crimson. When he reopened his eyes, the dark visage was gone.

Brom awoke suddenly from the nightmare. It had been less dream than memory and it left him shaken. He lay covered by thick blankets in a dimly lit room. His head throbbed. He tried to rise, failed and then lay still.

"You are awake," a soft voice whispered from the darkness beside him.

Brom turned his gaze toward the voice, but his eyes could not focus in the dimness. He saw only the silhouette of someone sitting beside his bed. The knight's throat was raw and dry, yet he struggled to speak. "Where... where am I?"

"This place is called Vasaria," the soft voice replied. "It is my village."

Brom could now detect that the voice was that of a woman. "I was... pursued," he recalled.

"Rest your worries," the voice continued in a soothing tone. "You are safe now." Brom felt a small hand rest gently upon his shoulder and fell strangely at ease. He closed his eyes. He dreaded further nightmares, but could not stave off his weariness. He soon fell into sleep and dreamt no more.

When Brom awakened next, he was alone. Weak daylight filtered in through the shuttered windows. Opening his eyes only a fraction, he peered around the room. Surveying his surroundings, he found himself in a small bedchamber. The only prominent furnishings were a low table, a single chair, and the bed he lay in. A simple fire hearth was recessed into the far wall. Its grate held only ash and smoldering embers. The room was cold. Beyond the foot of his bed, a single wooden door had been left slightly ajar. The chamber was sparsely adorned, save for strings of dried herbs and the knight's own belongings. His helmet and sword rested upon the narrow fireplace mantel and his boots lay in the corner. On the wall next to the door, his chain longshirt and crusader's tunic hung from hooks.

Brom stared at the tunic, now bloodstained and tattered. He could no longer distinguish the bright red cross from the white fabric it was sewn upon. Memories of the battle slowly crept back to him and he shuddered. Pain shot from his injuries as he struggled to sit up. When he examined his battle scars, he noticed they had been tended. The arrow wounds in his shoulder and side had been neatly bandaged. He pulled back the wrappings on his thigh and discovered that the deep gash had been sewn closed with needle and thread. The wound in his forehead, which had seemed serious, was already partially healed. He began to wonder how long he had been here.

Brom threw off the covers and sat up on the edge of the bed. The crucifix he wore around his neck fell loose from the long nightshirt he had been dressed in. The room spun wildly for a moment and he closed his eyes, then he forced himself to his feet. Lightheaded though he was, it felt good to be standing upright. He put weight on his right leg and felt a jolt of pain, but he found it could support him. He hobbled to the window and drew back the bar to open the shutters. He ran his fingers through his long, black mane and looked out upon a row of small buildings along a meager cobblestone road. Towering trees surrounded the village on all sides. He wondered how he had ever chanced upon this remote place nestled in these thick woods. The road straggled uphill into a dense knot of trees. High above, a tall, dark castle overhung the village. It appeared to have been chiseled from some enormous, black stone upthrust from the forest.

"You should not be on your feet," spoke a soft voice from behind him. It was the same voice he had heard in the darkness.

Brom turned and saw a young woman standing in the now open doorway. She walked toward him and set a loaf of bread and a bottle down on the table. Her face was smooth and pale. Her dark, almond-shaped eyes drew up slightly at the outside corners and seemed to reflect a hint of sorrow. Long hair, black and lush, hung loosely about her shoulders and down onto her back. She wore the blouse and skirt of a Romany peasant over her light but ample frame.

"You speak English," Brom said with slight surprise.

She nodded.

"Who are you?" he asked.

"My name is Rianna," she said, smiling shyly. "I tended you."

"I see." Brom returned her smile. "I am greatly in your debt for all you have done for me," he said, bowing his head before her. "I am Sir Brom of Falkirk from the isle of Britain, Knight of the Scarlet Cross." Glancing upward, he could see that his lengthy title evoked no reaction from the girl. She simply stared at him curiously. He remained quiet for a moment, taken by her innocent charm, then raised his head and asked, "How long have I been here?"

"You came here three nights past," she answered.

"Three nights past?" he wondered aloud.

"You should not recall any of it," Rianna assured him. "You were badly injured and lay in sleep since then."

Brom stared blankly past the girl, returning his gaze to the battle-torn tunic. Now the memories flooded back to him and he began to recount them out loud. "My regiment had been among the crusades throughout the Holy Land. After three long years, we were finally returning home. All looked forward to seeing kinsman again." He paused for a long moment, as if in deep thought. "We crossed the Danube, upriver from the Iron Gates, and made camp in the vale of Olt. We thought we had left battle far behind us."

The knight steadied himself on the window sill and drew a deep breath of cool air. "In the dead of night we were set upon by the Turks. Caught off guard and heavily outnumbered, we stood no chance. It was a massacre. My fellow knights... my friends... dead and dying all around me. The battle was beyond hope. I escaped the slaughter on horseback with four riders in pursuit. I drove my steed hard that night and all the next day through rugged mountain forests. I was desperate to elude them, but there was no escape. Like wolves that had tasted blood, they would not relent until they had made the kill. Exhausted and near collapse, I came upon your village."

Brom turned and looked out the window to the village street. "I saw the distant castle and hoped it might offer sanctuary, but my vigor had been spent and I knew I could not reach it before being overtaken by my pursuers. My final hopes rested in the mercy of your villagers. I reined my steed and called out to any who might aid me. An old man appeared beside me and helped me from my horse. Another villager guided me to a house... this house. The old man swatted my horse, sending it into a gallop toward the castle. I heard the hoofbeats that had followed me for hours ringing on the bridge that led into the town. I peered out through the cracks of the window shutter as the Turks rode into the village. The old man remained standing in the road. The riders surrounded him with their horses, nearly trampling him. They shouted at him fiercely, gesturing menacingly with their scimitars. The old man said nothing. He simply pointed up the road toward the castle. One of the Turks brandished his sword in the old man's face and spoke quietly, then all four turned and swiftly resumed their chase up the castle road."

As he finished his story, Brom's eyes followed the cobblestone path and came to rest on the towering keep. "What is that place?" he asked, turning to face Rianna.

Her innocent expression turned to one of dire concern. "It is the Dark Tower. It is an accursed place, haunted by the souls of the dead. No one who enters ever returns."

Brom put little credence in her response, thinking it to be bred of unfounded rumor and superstition.

"And what of the Turks, the soldiers who chased me?" he asked.

Rianna looked downward to avert her eyes from his, then answered in a solemn tone, "They will not return." This was all she said on the matter. She turned and stepped to the doorway, stopping there only long enough to say, "You lost much blood. You must eat, then rest to regain your strength." She then left the room and pulled the door partially closed behind her.

Brom cast his gaze again toward the mysterious keep and wondered what secrets it held. He did not know what to make of it. All he knew was that three days had passed and, for whatever reason, his pursuers were gone. He felt safe here.

Brom put a fresh log on the grate and stoked the embers, then sat down on the bed. He made a quick meal of the bread and mulled wine which Rianna had brought for him, then lay back on the straw mattress and rested. He drifted in and out of sleep until late in the day when hushed voices from the next room roused him to wake.

Brom sat upright and listened intently to the whispers that filtered through the door. He could hear Rianna conversing with a raspy-voiced man in their native tongue. Though not fluent in the dialect of the region, Brom understood a few of their words. They used the term *Anglander*, most likely referring to Brom, and more than once spoke of *der Barone*. Then the raspy-voice uttered a word that made the knight's blood run cold. *Wampior.*

Brom was well-versed in the folklore of the Germanic tribes. He knew well the legends that ran all through the Carpathians of wampior or vampyre, creatures of unholy origin who prowl the night, thirsting for human blood. They were nosferatu, the undead. Demons who feasted upon their victims, stealing their lives and their very souls.

The hushed conversation ended. Brom heard the outer door open and close as Rianna's visitor left. With a slight limp, the knight crossed the room and crouched before the hearth. He placed the last log on the waning fire and prodded it with the poker until it caught flame. The door opened and Rianna entered the room. She was surprised, almost distressed to see Brom awake.

"We have had a visitor?" he questioned.

"Yes, one of the elders," Rianna said.

Brom squinted. "The elders?"

She nodded, then said, "They are wise, though fear burdens their judgement. They say we are at great risk to shelter an outlander."

"At risk? From whom?"

She would not answer and tried to turn away.

Brom caught her arm and asked, "The Baron?"

Rianna's face grew pale at the mention of his name. "They fear he watches. They dread his wrath."

"Is he lord of this realm?" Brom asked.

"He is lord of the keep, though few have seen him, and only then as a shadow among the ramparts of the tower."

"Do you believe he is... wampior?" Brom asked.

She looked away and hesitated before speaking again.

"I do not know what he is. Some say he is our protector. Others say it is he that stalks the night." Turning back toward

Brom, she warned, "Of late it is not safe to venture out beyond dusk. Something waits in the darkness. Several have been lost in the night. The elders say it is wampior. They tell us the cross will protect the innocent." She pulled on a thin braid of leather that hung around her throat and withdrew a crude, wooden cross from her blouse. Rianna clutched the holy ward to her bosom as she gazed at the crucifix that hung from Brom's neck.

"Could not the wolves of the forest be the cause of your strife?" Brom asked. "How can you be certain that this Baron of the keep, if ever he existed, is to blame?"

Rianna stepped to the mantle and stared into the fire. "When I was very young, soldiers came to our village. The Avar, the Magyar, I am not certain of who they were." Gazing deeply into the flames, she drew a long breath and continued, "They rode in on tall horses, armed with swords and spears. There were many... fierce, cruel men. They killed three of our elders before they spoke a word. They plundered our homes, savaged our women and murdered any who opposed them. At dusk, a raiding party set off for the Dark Tower, but a few of them remained here in the village."

Rianna's voice was now shaking around ragged breaths. "That night I heard the screams and cries of men in the streets and thought that surely the next day would be my last, but when the dawn came, the soldiers were gone. All that remained were their horses and weapons. No other trace of them was ever found, and those who ventured to the Dark Tower were never seen again." She stood before the hearth, her eyes transfixed upon the fire. The flames lapped like serpent's tongues around the burning timber.

"I have heard such stories before," the knight responded, trying to dismiss what she had said. "Many towns and villages concoct dark tales of terrible things that have befallen plunderers to their homeland. Some are driven off by angels, others by demons, yet the moral is the same."

Rianna turned to face him, tears welling in her eyes. She trembled as she spoke. "Believe me sir, when I tell you that every word I relate is true. For when the soldiers came that day, they murdered my mother and father in this very house... and I was witness. Since that day, when soldiers and marauders find their way to our village, we point the way toward the Dark Tower, as we did with the soldiers who pursued you, good sir. For those who dare to venture within, never return. I assure you that they who pursued you three nights ago are now three nights dead."

As she finished speaking, tears ran down her cheeks. She made no effort to wipe them from her face.

Brom took her gently by the shoulders. "Rianna..." He drew her close to still her trembling. She held herself taut and rigid, taking no comfort from his embrace. Then she melted and clung to him, sinking deeper into his enfolding arms. They stood thus entwined as her breathing became more steady and her trembling eased.

Even then she did not move away. She pressed her face close against his shoulder and he smelled the sweetness of her hair and felt the warmth of her breath upon his neck. His hands explored the soft strength of her back. She put all her weight upon him and he held her almost aloft, then lowered his face to hers and brushed her lips with his. Her hands rose into his hair and she lifted herself to him, her mouth on his, yielding all.

Brom awoke with the dawn. Rianna lay next to him, still fast asleep. Streams of sunlight filtered through the window shutter and came to rest upon the soft contours of her form. He watched the ribbons of light rise and fall with each breath she took. Brom gently brushed her hair aside and gazed upon her fair face. Radiant as any angel, even now as she slept, she was truly lovely to behold. Thoughts of taking her away from this strange place and spending the rest of their days together brought a wistful smile to his face.

As his mind wandered in daydream, his eyes came to rest upon the chamber door. It was now fully opened into the room and Brom could make out something crudely etched into its outer face. Three curious words were roughly carved into the knotted timbers... *Sanvi, Sansavi, Semangelaf.*

Brom rose, then commenced to dress himself, putting on his black tights and tall boots. He inspected his tunic and assessed the damage to the tattered garb. Thoughts of the battle, his fallen comrades and the ominous shadow from his nightmare all raced through his mind. In the background of his thoughts, the image of the Dark Tower was ever present.

Rianna awoke, then smiled, playfully tousling her hair as she stretched. She ran her eyes along Brom's profile as he stood naked to the hip before her. His shoulders were broad, his chest and arms well-muscled and his waist lean.

"Might you have something I could wear?" asked Brom.

She flashed a playful grin and said, "I might," springing out of bed with the sheet wrapped around her. She picked up her garments where they lay before the hearth and went into the outer room. She returned fully dressed a few minutes later, with a vestment of black draped over her arm.

"I have fashioned you a new shirt."

Brom took the garment from her and pulled it over his head. It fit snugly and hung below his hip. Rianna nodded approvingly and left the room again. He finished dressing as she busied herself preparing a meal of dried meats and bread. When Brom emerged from the bedchamber, his sword was at his belt and his helmet beneath his arm. He wore his chainmail shirt over the black tunic Rianna had made for him. Rianna's broad smile slowly faded.

Choosing his words carefully, Brom began to speak. "I have thought long and hard of my calling in this life. Since my childhood, I have been taught that we all serve some purpose beyond our mere existence. I feel mine, still unfulfilled. It beckons me... from the tower."

"No!" Rianna cried out.

Brom crossed the floor, reaching out to console her. Taking her small hands into his, he said, "Of all the knights who were caught in the ambush, I alone survived, and through dense forest in the dead of night, somehow my steed found its way to your village... a village that dreads sundown and the unholy terror that lurks in the darkness. I was spared and led here for a purpose, and this purpose I must fulfill before I can share my life with you. You must believe me, Rianna, I am torn... torn between my duty as a knight of the scarlet cross and my feelings for you. If this Baron of the keep is some mysterious protector of Vasaria, then I will come to no harm. But if indeed some demon dwells within the Dark Tower, then it is my mission to rid your village of it."

Rianna clasped Brom's calloused hand. She turned it palm upward and fixed her gaze upon it. She surveyed each line and crevice, tracing them with her fingers. As Brom watched her, he surmised that her action was no mere caress, for it was said that those born of Romany blood could foretell a man's destiny this way. She studied his hand for a long moment, then without a word, she let it drop. Her head remained lowered. He was curious as to what she had seen, but did not allow it to distract him from his decision.

"Where is my steed?" Brom asked.

"Beyond the house across the road, there is a stable. You will find your horse there," she said, then turned her back to him.

Brom tried to comfort her, "Rianna..."

She would not turn to face him. "Go," she whispered.

"Rianna..."

"Go!" Her voice quivered as if she were crying.

Brom did not want to leave her this way, but could think

of no other words to comfort her. He turned and walked out her door.

Though the winter's snow had almost entirely melted, in areas, ice still clung from roof's edge. Brom could see his own breath in the brisk mountain air. He crossed the road and came upon a stable. He found his stallion tethered there, well kept and rested. Four other horses ran freely in the corral. All four were marked with the same brand, a crescent moon encircling a dagger, the mark of the Turkish elite guard. He thought back upon Rianna's tale of how the marauders had vanished but their horses remained.

His horse's saddle and bit hung on the wall of the stable. Brom took them down. As he fastened them in place on his steed, he turned to find an old man standing silently behind him. It was the same old man who had helped him when he first entered the village. His gaunt face was lined and weighed down by a lifetime of cares and doubts. A jagged scar ran down the length of his left cheek. Brom attempted to speak with him in his native tongue, but all efforts were in vain. The old man did not respond. He only stared blankly at Brom through dull eyes. The knight led his horse from the stable and the old man lingered behind him. Brom now turned his gaze toward the castle which looked menacing, even in the daylight. The old man followed his stare, then looked back to the knight. Reaching out with one gnarled hand, he clutched Brom's arm, then uttered a warning in broken English, "To go there is to die."

Brom held his unwavering gaze a long while, then mounted his saddle and rode out of the corral. At her house, Rianna stood in the doorway. He trotted his horse to a halt before her and declared, "Be it humanly possible, I shall return for you. I swear it. But if I do not, know this... that my feelings for you are strong, and even beyond death, I shall love you." He reached into his saddlebag and withdrew a rosary. He handed it to Rianna, saying, "Be this a token of my love and promise of my return."

Rianna took the rosary from him. The dark red beads draped between her pale fingers. She removed her simple cross and donned the rosary in its place. Not another word was spoken between them. He turned his steed toward the castle road and began his way out of the village.

Brom let his horse set its own pace as he steered it up the road. Here and there one of the villagers stood in the street, watching him pass. Others peered from windows and doorways. All had looks of some unknown sorrow on their faces. Some held their hats in their hands in front of them, as if attending a funeral, while others blessed themselves with the sign of the cross as he passed. The knight shook his horse's reins and spurred it to a trot. A mist lingered at the mouth of the woods ahead and the horse hesitated, but Brom urged him on. As he entered the forest, Brom looked back over his shoulder. The old man stood alone in the road, still watching. Then the village of Vasaria vanished in the mists.

The cobblestone road climbed steadily, snaking its way through the dark wood. The trail was overgrown with bramble and wandering roots. Thick vines twisted and clung around misshapen trees. Gnarled branches bearing long, black thorns reached out from either side of the path and entwined overhead, shading the sunlight to a gloom. There was an unnatural stillness and absence of forest life. Brom's horse stirred uneasily.

In time, Brom spied a single raven perched upon a branch overhanging the road. First one, then another, soon the surrounding canopy of withered and twisted limbs was filled with the ominous birds. They silently watched his passing through cold, black eyes. The knight remembered seeing such scavenger birds descend on the carnage left on fields of battle to pick the flesh from men's bones. Ancient tales portrayed these black-plumed creatures as omens of ill fate, while there were some who believed that the ravens themselves were the harbingers of doom.

Warily, Brom marched his horse along the winding path. The birds, which had been deathly still, now slowly began to flit from limb to limb. Suddenly, one of the overhead ravens let out a single caw, breaking the silence of the forest. The ghastly sound echoed through the trees. Shortly thereafter, more birds began their croaking call from deeper in the woods. Eventually, the knight was surrounded by raven's cries which seemed to announce his arrival.

Ahead now, Brom could see daylight, but the mist obscured much else. As he emerged from the forest path, the fog relented and he beheld the foreboding tower, now looming directly before him, with both awe and dread. Though still some distance from the sinister keep, he had to tilt his head back to see the tops of its black spires. Without realizing what he had done, he drew back the reins of his horse, bringing it to a dead halt. The knight sat before the ominous structure which emerged from the shrouding mist. Tall and black it stood, like some arcane monument to evil.

Every warning and omen, and now some voice from within, told him that woe would befall him if he were to proceed. His good sense pleaded with him to turn back now, but he did not listen. Instead, he drew a deep breath of the cold air, then started his horse on the final ascent up the narrow mountain path to the castle.

Brom marched his steed slowly and watched as the ravens flew from the forest to circle above the tower as if following his progress. The cobblestone path rose steeply here, and in certain areas, came treacherously close to the cliff's edge. When the castle was nearly upon him, he passed through the remains of some ancient gateway. To his right, marble columns and crumbled stone lay in ruins. On his left, the structure remained intact. The columns formed three archways. The middle arch was open, while the ones to each side of it were closed off with elaborate wrought iron gates adorned with garish stone faces. As he passed through the gate ruins, a cold wind picked up and began a mournful howl.

While his horse hesitantly trotted the last few steps to the keep, the knight's eyes scanned the tower's sinister architecture in full detail. The main structure loomed tall, with watchtowers rising from each corner and ascending high above the battlements. The masonry was so weathered from enduring the ages that the stone now appeared black. Mystic sigils and arcane runes covered the tower's lower facade, while gargoyles leered from every niche and ledge high above. Stone creatures, bat-winged and horned, glared down from the battlements. Their distorted faces held the countenance of men and beasts. Their mouths gaped wide, howling and bearing fangs.

And now, the ravens circling the tower began to land and perch among the gargoyles. Black talons clutched and clung to the monstrous guardians of stone, and the whole malevolent edifice seemed to come alive as the ravens began to shriek. It was as if a legion of demons had taken sanctuary in this forsaken place and were jeering down upon him.

When he had reached the base of the wide stone steps leading up to the castle's entrance, he cautiously dismounted and tethered his steed. A surrounding wall, two stories tall, met with the front of the keep and stretched out to both sides of the plateau. A large set of heavy doors were recessed into a central archway at the top of the entrance staircase and provided the only possible access within.

With a slowness that was perhaps more trepidation than limp, the knight made his way up the stone steps. Two massive doors towered before him, framed within a tall arch. High above the foreboding archway, an inscription appeared to be written in English, though frost and ice had settled into the chiseled letters obscuring the message. The only word Brom could decipher appeared to read "hope," but he took no comfort in it.

The doors of the keep were of heavy, dark oak. Each bore half of a huge, strange symbol of wrought iron so, that when closed, the rune was whole. It was formed of sinuous strokes and serifs, swirling polished spikes rising out of a central circular pattern. Though Brom had seen the scripts of tongues from the Celts to the land of the Egyptians, this cryptic letter, if letter it was, remained unknown.

Brom peered through the narrow crack between the doors. All within was dark. He tested the door lightly at first, then with more force, but it did not move. The base of the door was flush with the uneven granite slabs of the portico. Finally, he put his full weight behind it and ground it noisily over a high spot on the walk until it swung free with a loud groan of rust-locked hinges. Daylight fell over the threshold into a short foyer. Beyond, Brom could see nothing but shadow. The bitter wind swept past. He left the light behind and entered the Dark Tower.

The knight passed below the heavy blocks of the arch and then felt a great, black space open above him filled with cold currents of trapped, stale air. He pressed on into the dim corridor which passed under another arch and into a larger hall. His eyes adjusted slowly to the dim light filtering in from behind him and from several narrow windows above. The room opened before Brom into a broad hall, the walls supported by tall sets of columns rising up into shadow. Twin staircases of dark marble swept up along the wall on either side to meet on a balcony above and directly ahead of him. There, doorways led out into higher regions of the keep.

Below the balcony, an archway mirrored the one through which he had just passed; beneath it, chiseled steps dropped steeply into darkness. Bits of fallen stone lay undisturbed here and there upon the dark marble floor. Brom could easily have believed he was the first person to enter this room in centuries.

The wind hissed through the tall arches and sounded like the echo of whispers caught in the confines of the heavy granite walls. He stood for a moment, staring into the darkness overhead, listening to the wind mimic the murmur of voices.

He trod carefully as he made his way to the stair on his left. High up on the wall, torch sconces hung at odd angles, rusted and empty. The marble banister curved to follow the arc of the stair, its once careful elegance now pitted and cracked. As he climbed the steps, he could see that the columns supported a vaulted ceiling in the darkness high above. Near the tops of each pillar, winged gargoyles sat haunched upon ledges, their gazes fixed downward upon the entrance hall. Between the columns, other grotesques peered out from shadowy alcoves around the hall's perimeter.

Atop the balcony, Brom looked down over the marble ramparts and imagined for a moment this room as it might have been centuries before: filled with the warm light of many torches, radiant banners suspended from the window ledges, a proud lord and his lady looking kindly down on the line of brightly costumed guests winding their way up the stairs.

The vision faded into a pattern that, from this height, Brom could now discern in the colors of floor stones below. He knew it for the very rune that stood on the front doors to the tower, the rune without meaning that filled him with dread. The hall seemed now a pit where the warriors of antiquity battled to the death for the amusement of ravening caesars.

Brom turned to the doorway leading beyond the balcony and stepped within. He found himself in an enormous hall, its high ceiling supported by two rows of great, stone columns. The light of the westering sun streamed in at an extreme angle through the tall windows along the south wall. Wind-tattered tapestries were draped across the window arches. On the far side of the hall, a short flight of wide stone steps rose to a dais before the western wall.

The wind bellowed through the tall windows, tossing the tapestries and filling the great room with a haunting moan. It sounded to Brom like the lament and wail of lost souls. He crossed the hall slowly, stopping before the entablature. A single, tall throne occupied the dais. Once the grand hall of some forgotten lord, Brom decided, the chamber now stood abandoned, though he could not call on his imagination to make sense of it.

Brom crossed back through the room and returned to the balcony overlooking the entrance hall. Twin stairwells rose from both ends of the terrace and led to regions above. He entered and made his way up to the next level of the keep. Here, he found room after room of abandoned living quarters. Lush curtains hung in tatters, and though the furnishings remained intact, they lay beneath a thick coat of dust and cobwebs. The beauty of the decor was still evident, yet fallen to decay. He explored the entire floor, finding all the chambers in a similar state of deterioration. Upon ascending to the next level, he found more of the same. The once extravagant and sumptuous rooms were now derelict and deserted, and showed no trace of recent occupancy. As he walked along the hallway, looking into the cobwebbed chambers, he wondered what tragedy or catastrophe could have befallen the inhabitants of this place, causing them to vanish.

Just then, a great bell sounded, shattering the silence of his contemplations. Its toll was deep and hollow. Its loud clang emanated from somewhere above and filled the halls with a resounding echo. Brom hastened to the stairs and bounded up them, ignoring the pain from the wound in his leg. As he rounded a blind corner of the staircase, he was met by a towering form on the landing. The sight of it startled him momentarily. The knight put his hand to the hilt of his sword and drew back, then he recognized the thing for what it was. A monstrous gargoyle, more beast than human, crouched

upon a large, stone pedestal. Its horned head bore the semblance of a man, its face contorted and frozen into an anguished howl. Its forepaws came to rest upon a human skull. The beast's stone claws clasped tight around the skull with talons dug deep into the eye sockets.

The bell tolled again, breaking the gorgon's spell, and Brom raced up the last flight of steps. He emerged through a door at the top of the staircase to find himself outside, above the castle. All was silent now.

A narrow walkway extended around the castle within the perimeter of the battlements. At each corner of the keep, turrets rose. The two at the front of the keep were fortified to serve as watchtowers, having narrow slits for windows. The two rear structures had wide, arched openings at their peaks. While the one to the north stood empty, the southern tower housed a great bell.

Brom strode warily to a doorway at the base of the belltower. He entered and made his way up the narrow stairs that spiraled around the inside of the shaft. At the furthest heights of the castle, he reached the belfry. Here, an immense bell hung motionless and silent. The hammer swayed not an inch. He reached out and touched the cold metal, but felt not even the slightest vibration. Suddenly, an eerie feeling fell over him and some unknown sense caused him to turn his gaze upward.

There, he saw the bats. Hundreds of them filled the belfry roof. They clung to the beams and hung there inverted. Large as rats, their dark fur matted, their leathery wings folded, they slept undisturbed. It made no sense to Brom. Surely, the bell's toll would have awakened these loathsome things from their slumber. Wary not to disturb the sleeping horde, he retreated down the winding stairs.

At the base of the belfry, Brom looked down over the back wall of the castle. Far below, in the rear of the keep, he saw headstones and monuments forming a graveyard within the confines of the surrounding parapet. Here, statues of angels read from tomes and prayed over the graves. Beyond the encompassing wall, the cliffs dropped steeply to the valley below, making the fortress impenetrable from this approach. For as far as the eye could see, thick, pathless forest covered the surrounding mountains.

He crossed the walkway to the front of the keep. Brom stood atop the battlements which crowned the castle's facade, surrounded by the demons and beasts of stone. Here, the gargoyles had stood watch for ages, their weathered surfaces pitted and cracked. Born of phantasm, then conjured forth from the realm of nightmare, they had found a fitting resting place here. Brom looked out over the thick forest and toward the village beyond. Thatched rooftops marked scattered dwellings. It looked mundane and small, though he could not view it in any great detail from this distance.

The sun was low in the sky and the chill of the waning day was growing upon him. Brom hastened to make his way back through the castle. As he descended the time-worn staircase, he was again met by the gargoyle on the landing, but now the expression of the beast had changed. Its face no longer howled in torment, but instead seemed to be laughing as if to mock him. Some play of light, Brom thought, or perhaps his memory had played tricks on him. Brom's gaze fell again upon the death's-head in the clutches of the great, stone beast. So intricately carved and polished was the skull, that he could not be sure it was merely a chiseled effigy. He did not turn his back to the thing and shuddered as he passed it.

His eyes now came to rest upon a candelabra. Draped in cobwebs, it rested upon a sconce. Three candles remained held in place by cured drippings of wax. Remembering the stairwell that descended into pitch below the main hall, he picked the candelabra up and took it with him.

Making his way cautiously down the massive staircase, Brom returned to the entrance hall. He stood before the dark archway, opposite the castle doors. He looked down into the blackness of the stairwell that led somewhere below the grand hall. He was almost certain that it would lead to another level of abandoned and deteriorated rooms, but thought it best to conduct a thorough investigation. Brom withdrew a flint and tinder box from a small pouch on his belt. He struck a flame and lit the candles. Standing within the arch, he held the candelabra outstretched before him and peered into the dim stairwell. The staircase reached its end somewhere beyond the meager light of his candles. He descended slowly into the dank confines of the castle's lower regions.

At the base of the stairs, narrow corridors branched off to the right and left. Brom followed the hall to his right. A dozen strides along, the corridor turned at a square angle to the left. This hallway was considerably longer. The wall on his right featured several tall, pointed arches like the windows of the grand hall above, but these arches were bricked over. The masonry differed from that of the surrounding walls and the mortar work here was crude. Further along, the corridor turned back toward the center of the keep and Brom knew he was circling some enclosed space.

As he suspected, some twelve strides along the hall he came to a pair of arches, one on either side of the hall. The archway to the left led somewhere within the space which Brom had just circled, deep within the castle's heart. The supporting pilasters were exquisitely carved in the likeness of skeletal angels, their arms folded across their ribcages in a graven repose, their long wings drawn back behind them. Beneath this arch, though, was no door, as far as Brom could discern, but a solid block of wood without handle or hinges. It resisted his attempts to force it. If it was an entranceway, it was not meant to be opened from this side. Elaborately carved into the heavy wood was a familiar inscription: *Sanvi, Sansavi, Semangelaf,* the same three words that had been crudely etched into Rianna's chamber door. Brom began to back away, then noticed another inscription chiseled into the marble above the archway: *Noctem Aeternus.* He roughly translated the Latin phrase to mean *eternal night.*

Brom turned to the opposite archway that led toward the outer reaches of the keep. Twin doors met in a point beneath the arch. Each had a great ring affixed to its face. Brom pulled the heavy doors open.

The first thing he saw of the room beyond was color. Rich purple and blue hues shone forth from the stained glass windows, bathing the room in a melancholy glow. The room was a chapel, small but exquisite, in all its beauty and majesty rivaling the finest churches and cathedrals Brom had ever seen. He removed his helm and set it and the candelabra on a small table beside the door.

The black stone here was carved into ornate filigree, opening into alcoves, within which stood statues of prophets and saints. A great mosaic, as of an elaborate labyrinth, was laid into the floor.

But more than all else, Brom's eye was drawn again and again to the windows. Five of them marched along the walls on either side. In each window, circles crowned a central image, while along the base, a series of bizarre figures stood in mute witness. Though he had been enraptured by windows such as these in his youth, Brom recognized none of the figures. The two travelers were not on their way to Emmaeus, for they met not the risen Christ, but a young woman clothed in scarlet. The warrior who met the beggar on the road side was not St. Vincent, for he gave the man not his cloak, but the sharp end of his sword. The stories were strange and cruel, yet Brom found it hard to look away.

The sanctuary was almost sacrilegiously dark. The floor

was of black marble and the altar of obsidian. Brom could barely look upon it. Though it had at first enchanted him, the chapel now seemed blasphemous and grim. He could not deny that it was beautiful, but its beauty was lurid and sinister.

A single vigil light encased in red glass burned above the altar, suspended by chains from the ceiling. It should have lifted Brom's heart, keeping hopeful vigil even there in the chapel of this forsaken place. Instead, a dreadful realization struck him. He was not alone in the keep. The light shining through the stained glass became suddenly a ghastly blood red. Outside, the sun was setting. Brom shuddered and felt unease gathering in his breast like a murder of crows stirring from their rest.

He heard a long, low creak behind him, as of a door being forced open against age-worn hinges. He strode quickly back across the chapel and retrieved the candelabra. With one hand on the hilt of his sword, he crept cautiously back into the hallway beyond.

The doorway beneath the arch of the skeletal angels now stood open. Brom lifted the candelabra high and peered into what seemed to be a vast library. Shelves of books lined the walls on both sides of the room. A narrow balcony encircled the room's perimeter, giving access to the higher shelves. Close to the center, a kind of den had been created of plush, cushioned chairs and low tables. At the far end of the room, a large, heavy table held stacks of books and scrolls.

Curiosity gnawed at Brom, but he was more concerned with discovering who else was in the keep with him. He left the room and proceeded back the way he had come. He came quickly to the stairs leading up to the entrance hall. Though he suddenly remembered that he had left his helm in the chapel, he began immediately upward, then stopped cold in his tracks at the top of the stair.

In the foyer opposite stood a shadowy figure, silhouetted

against the velvety blue of the evening sky beyond. The knight kept his eyes fixed upon the shape and slowly set the candelabra down on the floor beside him. The figure stood motionless. It stirred within Brom the memory of the grim visage from his nightmare.

It spoke. "How pleasant that we have a visitor. What brings thee here at this late hour?"

Brom stared and said nothing. The mist had found its way through the open door and now crept silently toward him, blanketing the floor of the entrance hall.

"It matters not, for thou art welcome." The voice was low and echoed through the empty hall. Though it spoke in English, the accent was thickly Romanian.

Brom stood in the shallow pool of light and slowly slid his hand to the hilt of his sword. "I am Brom of Falkirk, Knight of the Scarlet Cross."

"Well met, good sir," the shadow said. Though it spoke in the voice of a man, somehow Brom could not wholly think of it as human. "Who knows what bonds thou and I shall form in thy sojourn here?"

"Are you, then, the Baron?"

It made a noise that might have been laughter.

"The villagers yet speak of the Baron? Their memories are long. And what wouldst thou with the Baron, good knight? His legend is black, his name venom, his very existence, a plague upon the Earth. Better thou go thy way and let such things be."

"I seek him."

The shadow slowly stepped toward him. "Indeed? Wouldst thou take his treasure, mayhap, and hie back to England? Thou wouldst not be the first to make the attempt."

"I seek no treasure," Brom said, "only the truth."

"And, if the truth be something more grim than thou hast imagined, what then?"

"If indeed some vile devil resides within these walls, then his day of reckoning has come and he shall answer for his deeds."

"How so? What form of penance shall be suffered upon him?"

"He must pay with nothing less than his life."

"With his life, thou sayest?" the thing questioned mockingly. Brom heard the fall of heavy boots as the figure stepped closer. "Art thou the man to take it from him?"

The knight stood in silence and gripped the hilt of his sword tightly.

"Hear me, then, Brom of Falkirk. I am lord of this castle and of all Vasaria. As such, I offer thee the freedom of the realm. Thou may go now, noble sir, and take thy leave of my keep and my domain. Take the fair child of the village who has lent thy tender mercies to thee, if it be thy will and hers, and leave without fear. Go wither thou wist in all of Christendom. Live a life long and plentiful and think never of Vasaria again." The figure stopped just beyond reach of the light. "Or stay and make thy stand against the Lord of the Dark Tower. But know this, if thou stayest, thy suffering shall be beyond compare."

The knight stood within the candelabra's halo and slowly withdrew his longsword.

"Ah... my son," the shadow whispered.

Brom lunged forward, swinging his sword down on the dark form. Almost too quickly for Brom to see, a pale hand rose to meet the descending sword. He felt the blade bite hard into something, but it did not seem that it was flesh. The hand closed around the blade and wrenched the weapon from his grip. It tossed the sword aside and it clattered off into the shadows.

Brom tried to back away, but again the shadow moved with unnatural speed and caught him from behind, a hand at his throat, another clutched the knight's long mane and yanked his head back. Brom struggled to escape. The grip on his throat tightened and Brom relented, gasping for breath.

The pale hand crept from Brom's throat and sprawled its clawed fingers across the silver crucifix that hung upon the knight's chest. He felt cold breath on his neck and a coarse voice whispered, only inches from his ear. "I see thou wearest the cross of the Christ," it said, lifting the cross with a taloned finger, "though alas, not the ward thou hadst hoped." The hand withdrew from sight momentarily. "For see, I wear my own." The skeletal hand now held a crucifix just within the edges of Brom's vision. It was chained to the shadow behind him. Though tarnished almost to black, the cross was ornate, bearing the crucified likeness of Christ.

As Brom gazed at the crucifix, the thing behind him drew its head slowly forward over Brom's shoulder and into the light, revealing the face of the dreaded Baron. Gaunt and ashen, it looked upon Brom with eyes, lifeless and black. Its head was completely shaven and its ears were pointed like those of a bat. The thing drew back its lips to expose a jagged line of teeth pointed and sharp as daggers. The countenance resembled that of a grimacing skull.

The low voice whispered, "Thy destiny is sealed, my son." Its jaws gaped wide and then Brom felt its teeth tear into his throat. A pain unlike any battle wound he had suffered pierced him. He tried to pull away again, but though the creature no longer held him fast, Brom felt his strength desert him. He could not move, as though his will, his very life were ebbing away. The light from the candelabra grew dim and then all was darkness.

His next awareness was of a pain that ran through his whole body. It coursed through him like venom in his veins. His arms and legs curled in against his torso in spasms of cold burning. His chest contracted around his heart, suffocating him. He knew nothing of his existence but pain, not even where or who he was. He could not even gather the strength to cry out.

How long he lay upon the cold marble floor, he did not know. At length, though, a presence seemed to settle in behind his eyes and he regained his perceptions. Though the pain did not actually abate, he found he could will himself into motion despite it.

Brom opened his eyes. The entrance hall around him was bathed in shades of blue light. He could now see to the full heights of the vaulted ceiling. Surrounding the vast space, clamoring at the tops of the columns, the gargoyles and grotesques glared down upon him from their perches. Like some macabre audience lusting for more, they seemed to relish in his torment. He rolled over onto his knees.

The Baron stood below the arch that led down to the chapel. He took up the candelabra, now blazing with light, and extinguished the candles, one by one, with long, black talons.

Brom struggled to speak around the pain in his throat. "What have you done to me?"

The creature looked at him with its soulless, black eyes. "I have tasted thy life, and passed on my legacy to thee."

"What do you mean?"

The Baron stepped slowly, circling the fallen knight as he spoke. "Thy faith is no matter of mere coincidence to thee. It walks with thee, its seat in thy heart, its strength in thy arm. Thou dost act on what thou dost believe. Of a time I was much the same. Thou shall understand all soon. My treasure, such as it is, lies within the library, my inner sanctum. Now it is thine. When thou hast done with me, seek thy answers there."

"You have... bitten me." Brom touched his neck, finding blood there.

"I bore this burden as long as I was able and then beyond. Now it is thine to carry. My life is strained beyond enduring. All that remains is to finish it." The Baron stopped, his booted foot on the blade of Brom's discarded sword. "Even hadst thou not been a creature slow and clumsy, thy blade could scarce have troubled me." The Baron drew back his cloak to reveal an ornate sword in his hand. "A century and more ago, before the

First Crusade, three knights came to this keep. Poor, pitiful creatures, even as thou had been, but they came well armed." He lifted the blade, slowly turning it to admire its honed edge, "In all my years, I have never seen its equal. It is said to have been wielded by seraphim to cast out the fallen ones. I have used it but once, and it hath served me well... as I pray it shall serve you." The Baron offered the sword, hilts first, to Brom. "I have cured thy weakness; now I gift thee with a weapon befitting thy nature and thy mission."

The knight staggered to his feet and took the sword. The pommel and the hilt glistened with dark jewels. It felt strangely alive in his hand.

The Baron knelt before Brom. "All thou hast said of me is true and worse," he said. "I slew all who ventured into my lands without my leave. I drank their blood and their lives. I consorted with powers and demons. I have borne this burden long enough and now I shall be rid of it. Kill me now, lest I cannot fight this hunger one more night."

Brom felt now a strange sympathy for the pitiful creature kneeling before him. The Baron bowed his head and began to recite a Latin chant. It sounded to Brom like a prayer. The knight could not bring himself to strike the fatal blow.

The Baron looked up again at Brom, tears of blood streaming from his black eyes. Almost shrieking now, his voice resounded through the great hall. "End it now! Free me from this darkness, for I am no longer its master." The Baron bowed his head again and resumed his arcane prayer.

"... In nomini patris..."
   Brom lifted the sword.
"... et fili..."
   He clenched the hilt with both hands.
"... et spiritus sancti."
   He brought the blade down swiftly.

The sword tore through the creature's neck. The Baron's head rolled free and his body crumpled to the ground, a withered corpse. The blackened crucifix fell clear of the severed stump into a pool of blood. Brom picked it up. Suddenly, a great wind swept through the keep, driving the knight to his knees and engulfing him in howling darkness.

Brom stumbled to his feet. Light fell over him in strident waves and he could barely see. Beyond the open door, dawn broke over the mountains. He dragged himself to the doorway and looked out at the rising sun. The world seemed to go up in a blaze of light, so pure and intense that he could not take it in. Even with his arms shielding his face, the sunlight blinded him. He fell back into the tower, dragging the door shut behind him. Light streamed down from the windows in thick beams. It illuminated the rune laid into the floor to a brilliant scarlet.

He retreated through the arch and down the stairs trying to escape the light. It seemed to pursue him down the corridors, pounding on the bricks of the sealed windows. Brom came at last to the chapel. He entered and threw himself upon the floor, the crimson labyrinth almost searing his naked hands. The windows that had once cast a somber glow, now burned like some lurid, fevered dream. The figures leered and ogled one another with lewd abandon. Even the obsidian altar now shone with brilliant reflections of the garish colors. "My God," Brom said, "what has happened to me?"

He backed out of the chapel and turned now to the library. He plunged through the archway and into the shadows. He slammed the door that had once been too heavy to even move behind him with a mere gesture. He fell back against the door, finding sanctuary at last in the library's cool silence. No light from outside penetrated the heavy stone walls, yet Brom could see clearly in the darkness, though his vision was again tinted blue. The knight sat on the cold stone and reflected upon all he had encountered in these last few days of his life. He knew that the man he once was no longer existed.

As night fell over the mountains, Brom emerged from the inner sanctum and returned once more to the battlements of the tower. He looked out over Vasaria as he did only a day ago, but all was changed. He could see the village clearly and in full detail, the firelight of the houses, the last villagers scurrying to the safety of their homes. As he watched, a light appeared beneath the forest canopy below, making its way slowly up the road. Brom waited patiently as the torch came closer, weaving its way along the winding path. Brom watched as the old man from the village emerged from the forest path and approached the castle on horseback. He passed the ruined gates and proceeded to the tower, stopping before Brom's tethered steed. The old man looked up at Brom, the same grief-stricken cast to his eye as the morning before. Brom now understood the nature of the dark legacy he had inherited. He realized that his destiny did indeed lie within this forsaken place. The old man took up the horse's reins and turned back toward the village. Then he proceeded into the forest and did not look back again, the torchlight receding into the night.

Brom stood upon the battlements, a thin shadow among the gargoyles, and looked out over the realm. The ice, which had obscured the inscription in the castle's facade below his feet, had melted. The warning chiseled in the black stone above the entrance to the Dark Tower was now plain to heed...

ABANDON HOPE ALL YE WHO ENTER HERE

I have since given the Baron's remains a fitting resting place in the graveyard within the parapet. I have begun to explore his library sanctum, and only now do the secrets of the Dark Tower begin to unfold.

All this I relate to you and swear it to be the truth as I take quill to parchment and begin the first of my own journals as lord of this forsaken place.

— *Sir Brom of Falkirk*
Knight of the Scarlet Cross
In the Year of Our Lord 1192

My predecessor wrote obsessively. The shelves of this room, his library, contain volumes filled with research, philosophy, history, theology, scrolls of ancient mythologies and lost civilizations, even his ruminations and musings, all maddeningly mixed in nearly impenetrable Latin or archaic English.

He wrote repeatedly that he was providing a legacy for posterity, but his prose is so intense, so dense, I cannot help but suspect that something more drove him, as if he busied his mind with endless words so as to avoid something else, something too dark, too painful to contemplate.

I do not know thee, faithful follower, but I know that if thou hast chosen this, thou hast a special brand of courage. And that if thou art truly wise, then thou wilt scan these pages further, and list attentive to my tales. I have been ear to ghastly griefs, but with the darkness that engulfs me hast come a kind of knowledge. Wisdom, gleaned from ancient scrolls, gathered and bound in these tomes, I now bequeath to thee, true heir, to use and learn from better than I have... Faint candles in the gloom to guide thee throughout the long and trying nights.

I have entered into a new existence, one unimaginable to the man I once was. He thought he didst know his enemy well. Only now do I see how mistaken he was, how mistaken I was.

I begin with the cross. Many believe it a ward 'gainst the unholy, that it doth possess power over them. Is it not so in blessings and exorcisms? The Name and the cross fendeth off evil spirits, but not so these creatures. I have seen them laugh at the cross without fear, take it up without pain, and though many of them deem the cross blasphemous, as their faith doth lie in other gods, other powers, that hath been ever true of heathens and infidels. Though I am one of them, I myself wear the cross without pain, little though I deserve the honor.

My senses are changed, heightened. Odors are strangely distinct now. Like a hound, I know people as much by scent as appearance or voice. I feel the most slight change in temperature, though I myself remain cold ever. I hear the smallest sounds over great distances. Even now, the keep doth settle about me with groaning of old stone, the wind doth rustle a tattered drape in an open window high above, bats stir in their uneasy sleep in the bell tower, an animal prowls the grass at the edge of the forest. At night atop the balustrades, I hear voices, even from the distant village. And as slight sounds are clear to me, loud noises hath become deafening. And so it is with light, my true bane.

I know true darkness no longer. I can see even in a completely sealed room, the world seen as through a blue gauze. I can read comfortably in the most meager candlelight, and colors are again clear and bright. At night, the stars doth shed light enow for me to see clearly and moonlight is as full day.

But the day... The light of the sun blinds me. Its heat doth wither my cold flesh. Things such as I seek sanctuary from the sunlight. I retreat to my windowless sanctum, to my books, to the darkness, to wait out the long, dead days, listening to the world outside, waiting for the heat of the sun, dimly discernible even here, to fade to the cool of night. Were I to bind my eyes and cover my skin, I might endure some measure of daylight, blind and burned, but I pray I never have need. I have seen what the dawn can do to the unprotected.

I am now a night creature, however, I do not sleep away the days, entombed in the earth. Indeed, I no longer sleep at all.

Weariness is unknown to me, save a certain lassitude of the soul.

The power... We knew, when we hunted, that our quarry were possessed of strength and speed far beyond us, but we had no idea the true power they didst possess. Men are slow and weak, pitiful, helpless. They are naught but need and struggle. To dominate them would require but little effort. If my hunger were given its way...

For that is the one great truth of my existence — hunger. I yearn not for food, nor for drink such as I once needed. I do not age or grow weak for lack of such things. I may now live without limit, for I have passed beyond natural death into an unnatural life. I still breathe, aye, and blood doth flow through my veins, as should not be true of the dead. If that

breath be stilled, if that blood be spilled
— and it doth require no sacred or
blessed weapon, no matter what legend
may say — I will expire, though what
may become of my soul, I know not.

I need nothing to maintain my life,
yet the hunger is with me always. It doth
burn within me, unsated, but I dare not
quench it. Its shadow enfolds me within
its dark embrace, holding me captive as
within the coils of a constricting serpent.
Should I surrender and warm myself
with the heat of mortal blood, it would be
as if I gasped for breath, and the
darkness would tighten its unrelenting
grip around me all the more, and I would
fall and fail again and again, until at last
all that I once was would be dead and I am
irredeemable and damned.

Born of the Night

ERIC MUSS-BARNES

Upon the wall of the library sanctum, there hangs a singular tapestry, exquisite and hypnotic. I do not recognize the period or the region of its origin, but the fabric and condition of the weave alone dictate that it is ancient, perhaps centuries old.

There are numerous works of art, paintings and friezes, among the countless shelves filled with tomes, yet as beautiful and intriguing as they might be, it is this lone tapestry which truly captivates me. Again and again, I am drawn to it, spending long hours gazing upon it, studying it, trying to decipher the story behind it.

The tapestry depicts a horned man with dark wings outstretched in mid-flight before a beautiful woman who reclines seductively upon a crescent moon. She bears angelic wings and is draped in a flowing gown of white. Winged faces, lurid yet beautiful, leer from each corner, surrounding the two central figures. Of what legend it truly represents, or what mythical deities it portrays, I am uncertain, but there is almost something familiar about it.

Among the Baron's research, I came upon a tome, much larger and older than his leather-bound journals. As I leafed through the tattered and yellowed pages, I discovered strange sigils and detailed drawings depicting angels, devils and unnatural beasts amidst texts written in some unknown, arcane language. In the midst of the book, a piece of parchment lay folded to mark a specific page. Here, upon the pages of the book, I found a drawing, beautifully rendered, of the tapestry which had intrigued me so. The page opposite held only text written in the same long-forgotten language. I unfolded the loose parchment which kept the page and discovered prose written in the Baron's hand. He must have translated the text which accompanied the rendering.

For countless ages, Night longed for the Moon.

Night bided deep in caverns, submerged in his darkness, surrounded by demons and the dead and wraiths of darkest dread. Far above was the Moon, aloft in the heavens, bright, yet elusive. Entranced and held captive by her luminous spell, Night languished, spinning dreams and illusions of love and, as Day mounted heavily upon Day, passion became fever.

Night gazed to the Moon, longing for the embrace of her icy hands. A single touch. The lightest whisper of her flesh upon his. So lustrous was her skin, sculpted of starlight and ivory. Frosted wings were a crescent of moonglow across the heavens, her silver glow the canopy of a succubus bed. She radiated not the harsh, blinding, scalding light of Day, but a light pure, exalted, immaculate. No creature of darkness could resist her. Every authority, every strength Night possessed, faded when she appeared.

Overwhelmed by her perfection, enraptured and enchanted, so completely consumed by her was he that Night began to question his own power, to doubt all he was.

For if she held dominion over him, was he true darkness?

Or was she?

Perhaps he possessed no dark magics. Perhaps he was as weak as any mortal man, seduced by demoness beguile.

Looking upon her, his rage and pain and passion plumbed depths beyond all comprehension. To be denied her was anguish. Night could bear it no longer.

For aeons he had kept to his subterranean shadow while the light of Day held the Moon. No more.

Cursing or vowing to worship any god or devil, by the fate and will of any evil or light, it mattered not. He would fly to her.

And so, through sheer will and the pure conviction of his longing, Night spread wide his dark wings and took to the skies. Night rose from his ancient caverns, darkening the vales and forests, the oceans and mountains in his flight, and drove Day from the sky. For every hour that the Moon shone, Night held dominion over the heavens.

At last, Night came to the Moon and found her awaiting him, as enslaved by love, as tortured by the centuries of longing as he. Her ages of desperate beckoning finally answered, she reached out her alabaster hand, kindled with desire on the cusp of fulfillment.

No words were spoken. No words were required.

None but she could quench the Night's desires. None but he could charm her. And of none but the other would either ever dream.

At last, they touched. A tender caress. Softly. Gently.

Darkness entwined with moonlight, the fire of their passions, at long last unleashed.

Their lovemaking bore them the darkest of things strange and beautiful. Serpentine medusas, cursed of vain beauty, devil-horned satyrs who revel to fulfill lusts insatiable, skeletal legions of the dead who stand guard at the threshold of darkness, and fierce beasts, savage and ravenous, who tear through the heavens with thunderous roars. On dark wings, their offspring took flight to the four corners of the earth. With each dawn, they sought sanctuary, retreating to the dim recesses of the world, yet still they arise from the shadows as darkness descends, these children, born of the Night.

I can only wonder as I stare again into the tapestry, was my predecessor drawn to it and mesmerized by its strange beauty as am I? Did he, too, find it distantly familiar? Did he share the same maddening visions in his seclusion here? The answer to it all eludes me, and I am plagued by the unknown.

Madness incarnate, laughter outside my chamber door. Madness has a form. Twisted and deranged with a harlequin smile. I find my quill trembling as I write this. I know not why I bother to put these words to paper. For the benefit of what soul do I perform this act? Ah... the scratching again, the sound of claws scraping against stone... and the laughter. Low whispers and childish giggling. Maniacal, terrifying laughter... Yes. That is why I write this. To stave off my own insanity...

Strange dreams have come to me again, visions which lay thick over my waking mind. I no longer sleep. It is not in the nature of the creature I have become. And yet, somehow I still dream. The solid reality of my sanctum fades and time passes in a haze of vague memories and images which I am not certain are entirely illusion. Of late, I am haunted again and again by one recurring dream, one which truly disturbs me and which I am compelled to relate.

It begins in the grand hall. There is a masquerade ball being held at early dusk. The tower looks so different in this dream. There is a warmth to it, an atmosphere of comfort and elegance. Torches ensconced along the walls fill the vast room with an amber glow. The music of minstrels resounds throughout the hall. Hundreds of costumed guests are in attendance and the revelries stretch down into the gardens outdoors, gardens that do not exist in the waking world. People seem to recognize me as I pass, raising a cup to my health.

I wander to a place in the recesses of the castle and find myself before a gateway. Beyond the gate is only darkness and I know something waits there, something cold and cruel. The gate seems somehow familiar, but before I can recall where I have seen it, a servant in a pale mask with bleeding eyes motions me away and ushers me back to the ball. A shadowy aura has befallen the revelry, and the ball is suddenly dimmed and ominous.

And now the queen makes her entrance. Her presence brings a hush upon the room. She is costumed in an elegant, flowing gown of black satin. An ebony crown adorned with dark jewels rests upon her head and sleek bat wings extend from her back. Behind her, three shadows move as one.

A sea of revelers parts in her path and I alone stand before her. Without a word, she extends her hand to me in an invitation to dance, her long fingernails sharp and black as a raven's talons. Her face is exquisitely sculpted, smooth and pale with high cheek bones. For a moment, I am about to decline. She is so beautiful, I avert my gaze. As I look down, I see I am clad in gleaming, black armor. It is far more majestic and intricate than any garb I have ever owned.

I accept her outstretched hand and we dance. Her dark eyes hold me rapt. Her hand rests lightly in mine, the other demurely lifting her gown from her feet. As we turn, the revelers spin around the periphery of my vision and I now notice three pale figures adorned in armor similar to my own. They stand motionless in the hall, opposite the three shadows.

The queen addresses me as "Lord Brom," although I do

not recall introducing myself to her. Each time she says my name, the shadows whisper something I cannot understand. She says my name again and again, and with each word she seems to recede, to fade into a dark mist. Then without warning, I find myself before the gateway again. Alone. It is a mausoleum gate, the entrance to some ancient crypt.

Parts of the dream vary each time I have it, but not this part. So real is this part that I often wonder if it is merely a dream, for I recognize this gateway. It is within the graveyard of the keep. I know it well... the textures and hues of the wrought iron, the intricate artistry of the twisted metal, the sculpted stone guardians, and the large cross set into the gate's center. Does it act as a ward to protect the spirits of the dead as they slumber eternally? Or is it a sacred seal, a talisman put here to prevent some thing from escaping the crypt?

Every instinct tells me not to open the gate, yet every impulse demands that I do. Slowly, I lift the latch. The chill of the metal is cold in my palm. With a begrudging creak, it edges open. And what lies beyond is not something I expected at all.... no devil awaits to pounce upon me, only a dank stone stairwell leading into... nothing.

A dozen and one steps slink down into the gloom and stop at a stone wall. A wall with something scratching on the other side. This sound alone terrifies me more than any ghoul I could have envisioned. Because, somehow, the claws resonate as if scratching within my skull instead of behind the wall.

Suddenly, I am back in the ballroom again, but everything has changed. There are fewer guests. Night has fallen. The tower itself is in ruins. Dust and cobwebs cover everything and yet the oddly-masked souls continue to dance to silence. I have changed as well. My dark armor is gone and I am left standing unclothed. Spying my hazy reflection in a mirror, I now see that a pair of curved horns protrude from my head and black feathered wings arise from my back.

For some reason, this frightens me more now as I write this than it does when I see the vision in my dream.

The queen stands before me and she too has changed. No longer draped in ebony-black, her gown is now a sheer, white silk. A misty cloak falls light as fog over her shoulders. Barely covering her at all, her dress is translucent as spider-strings, loosely fitting over voluptuous breasts and long, ivory legs. The wings upon her back are no longer the leathery wings of a bat, but are now the smooth, pale wings of an owl. Her icy demeanor has melted away to reveal a creature of unbridled seduction.

All that remains of the guests are a group of four hideously costumed creatures bearing demonic wings and unsettling masks—masks which seem to change and blend from plaster into their true faces and then back again. Their costumes seem more flesh and bone than fabric and paint. An impossibly muscular, lion-like demon with monstrous wings moves aside as the queen approaches me. Two of the other creatures, a horned, bearded devil with falcon wings and a bat-winged medusa, take their places in opposite corners of the ballroom. The fourth, a skeletal warrior with raven's wings, seems to leer at me as the queen leads me in an eerie, musicless dance.

So perfect and flawless is her beauty, like a porcelain statue come to life. Every movement is dreamy and light, like the fading sensation one feels when mere moments from awakening. As the scene unfolds before me, it seems strangely familiar. It is as if my dreams and memories are woven together like the threads of a fine tapestry. The tapestry, yes, that is where I am. I have become a part of it. I am the dark being, enraptured by the moon goddess.

The four creatures stand guard in the corners of the room, surrounding us as we dance. Her cloak twirls and arcs through the air, encircling us both in a crescent of glowing white. With every step, I feel I am floating above her, held aloft by her slightest touch. I close my eyes and can hear the darkness call. The night summons like an unquenched love, beckoning with the promise of dark desire.

She speaks to me. "Come to me, my love..."

And now, I hear the whispers of the grotesque entourage, words sighed so lightly they could be the sound of my own breath, "Come to us... stay with us."

I begin to fall. Downward I plummet through a seemingly endless cavern. Tortured screams and lamenting wails echo as the walls rush past.

When at last I strike the ground, the stone beneath my hands is rough and solid. Cold. Damp. I can smell the mildew and feel the sandy grit on my cheek. I look upward, my breath steaming on the chill air in a shrinking shaft of light. I find myself at the bottom of a flight of thirteen steps. Before I can retreat, a huge stone door slides closed above me.

I am engulfed in darkness, darkness such as I have not known since I became what I now am: true darkness, black as pitch, that no nocturnal sight can penetrate. I proceed slowly, my arms outstretched before me, blindly feeling my way through winding tunnels.

Now a faint red glow emanates from somewhere deep within the maze. Slowly, the dank walls become visible. Some are adorned with intricately carved reliefs, while others contain niches holding human bones and skulls. I am lost within an immense labyrinth of ancient catacombs, crumbling and decayed.

The crimson light leads me down a long passageway flanked by skeletal columns. It ends abruptly at a solid stone slab. It is the entrance to a tomb. Above it, a solitary word is inscribed as the epitaph for that which lies within. The inscription chiseled in the granite reads, "LILITH".

I stand before the heavy stone which seals the tomb. I dare not cross this final threshold, yet I fear that I am destined to venture beyond it. The skeletal figures on either side turn their heads ever so slightly and grin malevolently at me. I know not precisely what lies within this forbidden crypt and yet I do. It is she, evil incarnate. And now, from beyond the door, the scratching begins again. The sound of fingernails clawing desperately against the stone.

That is when I awaken. Yes. I do think it was more than a dream... a premonition, perhaps. Day. Night. Darkness. Shadow. The hours of dusk and black pitch all blend together in this tomb. There have been times when I know sunlight has touched this land. Days of glorious beauty like those I had seen when I was a child, but now such memories seem like a cruel torture. Visions of an imaginary time in a promised land which never truly existed at all. Now, when sunlight touches Vasaria, I move within the deepest confines of this dread place, continually masked in shadow and gloom.

Noctem aeternus... indeed. So it was written. So this place has become for me. Has madness truly come to take me? And if I already be mad, how would I be able to know it? And when will this accursed laughter cease? But wait. It has stopped. And now instead... What is this? Behind my chamber wall, I hear scraping... clawing which resonates as if scratching within my skull, instead of behind the stones.

Her hair shines like ebony in the moonlight. The scent of lilac is in the air as she draws near. She touches my face, gently caressing my brow, my cheek. Her fingertips lightly wander to my lips. I close my eyes and pull her close, her skin soft and warm against me. I feel her beating heart keeping time with my own...

I awake slowly from my reverie and feel the chill of the autumn wind as it rises above the parapet. The scent of lilac still lingers from my dream.

Vampire's Kiss

CHRISTINE FILIPAK AND JOSEPH VARGO

Rianna stepped swiftly as she traversed the worn forest path. Though the moon shone bright and full overhead, only thin shards of its light trickled through the dense canopy of branches and vines. She had seldom ventured this deep into the woods, and never by night. Opaque tendrils of mist stretched across the ground and slithered like serpents among the gnarled roots, threatening to coil around her ankles with every step she took. She lifted her dress to her shins and hastened her pace up the road to the castle.

In her village, she had heard whispered tales of the shadow in the tower. Some said it was the dreaded Baron, that he still held dominion over the realm as well as the Dark Tower, but the elders said that the Baron was no longer lord of the keep. Perhaps, Rianna surmised, this mysterious shadow was the Baron's ghost, for she had heard tell that long ago he lost his mortal soul, and was thus cursed to haunt the tower for eternity.

The elders had lifted the curfew and declared that it was again safe to venture out of doors beyond dusk, yet they still warned those who did to wear a cross as a precaution. Rianna touched the rosary she wore around her neck and clutched the crucifix in her hand. She had not removed it since the day the outlander, Brom of Falkirk, had bestowed it upon her.

It had been many months since her beloved knight ventured boldly up the forest path to the tower, never to return, long, anguished months filled with loneliness and remorse. She felt responsible. She had to know his fate.

Rianna reached the wood's edge and stood panting just within the shadow of the trees. She tried to slow her breathing as she squinted and surveyed the sinister mass of black stone that loomed before her. Though she had lived in fear of the tower her entire life, she had never fully realized how foreboding and oppressive it truly was. Clouds swept across the full moon, taking on the appearance of writhing spectres, momentarily adrift upon the wind, before returning once again to the fathomless depths of night.

Peering out from the cover of twisted bramble, she noticed a crumbling structure in the midst of the open grounds that lay between herself and the keep, a series of stone arches which stood to one side of the path. Spying no signs of life, she ran to the archway and clung in shadow there. She again looked toward the castle, now noticing the elaborate detail carved into the facade. Grim gargoyles peered down from the castle's heights. Graven images of demons and beasts lined the battlements. Keeping their vigil over the tower, they sat silent and deathly still. As Rianna took a step toward the keep, one dark figure raised its head and turned its ashen face toward her.

Rianna turned and fled, running as fast as she could, back along the twisting forest path. She stumbled over moss-covered cobblestones and thorny bramble, yet never slowed her pace. She did not stop to catch her breath nor turn to see what might have followed her. She rushed to her home and bolted the door behind her.

Later that night, as she lay in bed, she wept and cursed her own fear for causing her to flee. She would not rest easily until she returned to find the answers she so desperately sought.

Many weeks passed as she weighed her decision, all the while, plagued by her fears and haunted by thoughts of Brom. Tears came unbidden to her when she collapsed into her bed at night. Dreams that she could not recall upon waking left her feeling hollow with longing. When the moon was once again full, she had finally gathered the courage to return to the tower.

As night enveloped the sleeping village, she bathed and washed her hair in water scented with lilac oil, then dressed herself in a silken gown. The sheerness of the fabric temptingly revealed her shapely form as it clung to her damp skin. She closed her eyes for a moment and summoned the cherished image of Brom from her memory, then drawing a deep breath, she slipped silently out of the house and away from the village.

Once again, Rianna ventured up the forest path to the tower. The trees seemed to float upon a murky sea of mist, their thorny branches and sinuous limbs reaching outward as if to ensnare her in their grasp. The fears that had plagued her during her first journey to the tower were still lurking in the recesses of her mind, and were beginning to surface yet again. However, she was resolute. There would be no turning back this night.

As Rianna neared the end of the overgrown path, she stopped short of the wood's edge. In the stark moonlight, she could see that someone now stood in wait beyond the arched ruin, a thin shadow cloaked in black.

Rianna slowly stepped toward the gate. "Is it you?" she whispered, her voice trembling.

The dark form moved to position the gate between them, then drew closer. Rianna stood motionless, her heart pounding, and watched as bony, white fingers with long, sharp nails slowly protruded through the gate's openings and clutched the wrought iron. A sense of dread befell her and urged her to flee once again, but then the shadow spoke.

"Rianna..." the voice whispered. "You should not have come. You are not safe here." The shadow lifted its head. Rianna gasped as she looked upon her beloved Brom, his face ghastly pale and gaunt.

"What has happened to you?" she asked. A look of dire concern, almost pity, swept across her face. "Come, return to the village with me."

"I cannot," he said, turning his gaze toward the tower. "I am bound here."

"Bound? By whom? The elders say the Baron's reign has ended."

"The Baron is dead," he said in a solemn tone. "Indeed, I have seen to that."

"If the devil be dead, I say fond riddance," Rianna stated coldly.

He turned back to her and said, "You do not understand nor could you fathom the burden he bore, the torment he endured in this forsaken place. No demon was he, nay, merely a man, cursed to suffer in eternal darkness. No longer master of his own will, he begged me to end his life."

She stared at him, trying to make sense of his words and his strikingly pallid appearance. "Then what duty binds you here? How do you fill your days?"

"My days are filled with dreams and nightmares."

"Nightmares? During the day?" she questioned.

"For periods of time, I am uncertain of their length, I find myself lost in strange reminiscence, though I know not where true memory ends and my dark musings begin." Brom paused as if burdened by his thoughts, then continued. "More than once I have dreamt of a woman, dark and beautiful. She tempts and entices me. She whispers my name, her siren's call beckoning me, luring me to where she dwells."

"It is Mara, the Dark Queen," Rianna whispered, as if wary of speaking the name aloud. "She comes to the men of my village in their dreams and beckons them to the tower. Those who cannot resist her call do not return. The elders warn young boys of this when they come of age and all are forbidden to venture near the tower. It is said she lies entombed within the keep, but her wicked spirit can find no rest."

Brom nodded slowly. "The Baron left behind volumes of journals. They contain translated texts of arcane scrolls as well as wisdom of his own which he wished to impart, perhaps as a warning. He wrote of that which waits below. It must be this Dark Queen, Mara, to whom he referred."

"Does she alone fill your dreams?"

Brom looked deep into her innocent eyes. She was truly the most lovely vision he had ever beheld. His eyes slowly dropped to her neck, soft and fair, and he held his gaze there, transfixed upon the slight pulse of her throat, then his eyes crept further down her well-blossomed form. The full curve of her bosom should have stirred passions within him, but instead his eyes were drawn again to her throat. He turned to tear his wanton gaze from her.

"You too, Rianna, are ever present in my mind's visions. When I close my eyes, I can see your fair visage with a haunting clarity, as if you stood before me. Never have I felt this deeply for another. It is this vision of you that renews my strength through each long night I spend in this place. Mere words cannot describe the loneliness of my solitude. I long for companionship, you, my sweet Rianna, most of all."

"Then I shall stay here with you... to comfort you and ease your loneliness." Rianna grasped Brom's hand, clenching his fingers through the gate. There was no warmth to his touch.

Brom quickly pulled his hand away. "Nay. The desires I

harbor are far beyond those of mortal men, the hungers dark, the thirst insatiable, but I dare not succumb. It is for this very reason that you, most of all, should not come here. Leave now and do not return," he said, then turned away.

Rianna watched his cloaked silhouette glide across the ground mist and disappear into the shadows of the keep. She stood, hesitantly shifting her gaze between the forest path which led back toward the safety of her village and the ominous castle in which her beloved Brom now dwelled.

After a moment of deliberation, Rianna followed him. She made her way to the base of the crumbling stone staircase that led to the tower's entrance. As she climbed the weathered steps, she tried to avert her gaze from the leering gargoyles perched high above. The moon shone down upon the fearsome creatures, casting long shadows upon the black stone of the tower. The misshapen silhouettes clung to the tower, their limbs elongated and distorted, reaching menacingly downward with taloned fingers. Rianna hurried up the last few steps, keeping her eyes fixed on the immense castle doors as they loomed tall before her.

One of the massive doors hung slightly ajar. Rianna drew a deep breath, then nimbly slipped through the narrow passage and into the keep. Finding herself in utter darkness, she stood still for a few moments, letting her eyes adjust until she eventually spied a dim patch of light in the distance. She began to walk slowly toward it, feeling her way along the damp, stone walls. After a few short steps, she felt the caress of something like strands of silk and, as she moved forward, they stretched taught against her face. Rianna clamped tight her eyes and mouth and jumped back. She dared not cry out, for fear of alerting all denizens of this cursed place to her presence. Reaching up, she pulled the spider's web from her face and shook it free of her hair. She continued now, holding one hand out before her.

The near-pitch foyer opened into a much larger chamber. Here, beams of moonlight shone in from tall window slits along the southern wall. Rianna strained to see the details of the surrounding architecture. Broad columns lined the walls and rose to disappear into the vastness above. Directly ahead, at the far end of the chamber, stood an archway flanked by two rising staircases.

Rianna stood for a while within a narrow beacon of moonlight that fell upon the marble floor, trying to choose which path to pursue. She then heard a sound, a whisper perhaps, which seemed to come from the archway before her. Slowly, she stepped closer and listened more intently. The whisper came once more. This time she heard it call her name. The voice was soft, and emanated from somewhere beyond the arch. She peered into the archway and saw a narrow staircase leading downward. A dim red glow illuminated the stairwell and guided her down the steps. She followed the crimson light through a narrow corridor of dank, stone walls. The air was stale and thick with dust. The faint light grew steadily stronger and eventually led her to an open doorway.

She rounded the corner to find herself inside a chapel. The walls were lined with tall windows of stained glass, and statues of angels and saints peered from darkened alcoves. Candelabras held red votives in which vigil lights burned. Mosaic tiles were set into a labyrinth motif that wove its way round the stone floor. The elaborate artistry of the chapel's design was breathtaking to behold.

A sudden chill fell over Rianna as if a cold draft swept past, though no candle flickered. Gooseflesh raised on her arms and shoulders. She sensed she was not alone. Rianna turned around and looked back the way she had come.

Beyond the doorway of the chapel and across the hall, there stood a shadowed archway which she had failed to notice before. Twin skeletons were carved into the stone of the arch pilasters. They each bore wings folded in at their sides and held their arms across their chests like the repose of an entombed corpse. Above the archway, an ancient inscription was chiseled into the black, veined marble, *Noctem Aeternus.*

From the darkness within the arch, Brom emerged.

Rianna started toward him, but he made no motion in return. He remained as rigid and still as the skeletal angels of stone that stood at his sides. When she was but a few steps away, Brom thrust out a hand in a gesture to halt her. His white palm appeared before her face so quickly that she did not see it rise. Long claws extended from his bony fingers, only inches from her eyes. He lowered his head into the shadows and his eyes gleamed savagely in the darkness. Neither spoke a word. Brom took a step back into the room. Reaching behind him, he grabbed the edge of a heavy, wooden door and began to swing it closed. Hinges squealed and the door grated as it slowly scraped along the stone floor.

"No!" Rianna cried, thrusting herself against the door. Her hands fell upon three words carved deep into the thick wood. She pushed against it with all her weight, but could not slow the door's steady progress. Desperately, she cried aloud the inscribed words... "Sanvi! Sansavi! Semangelaf!" They echoed through the corridors of the keep and reverberated long after in the vaulted ceiling of the chapel behind her.

The heavy, wooden slab ceased only inches from closing. A moment later, the door drew back once again. Brom stood beyond the threshold, his composure regained. He turned to face the door and ran his fingers across the letters inscribed there.

"These words, what do they mean?" Brom asked.

"I do not know their exact meaning, but they stand as a ward to protect from evil things. When I was born, my father carved the same glyph upon my chamber door. He spoke the words, as a blessing perhaps, each night as he closed the door."

Brom's gaze remained transfixed upon the chiseled words. Behind him, tall shelves filled with books lined the walls of the dim room.

"What is this place?" Rianna asked.

Brom looked back into the chamber. "It is the Baron's library, my inner sanctum. I have spent countless hours reading these tomes, for the Baron told me I would find answers within them, though at times the true meaning of this cryptic wisdom is difficult to discern." He glanced about the room until his eyes came to rest upon the Baron's relic sword which hung above the mantel. A grim realization overcame him once again. He turned to Rianna, his words now heartfelt and solemn, "Rianna, I beseech you. Heed my warning. Only darkness and sorrow await you here."

"I have known only darkness and sorrow without you. Do not send me away," Rianna pleaded. "Let me stay here with you." She moved in close and reached up to touch his face, but he caught her hand and gently moved it away.

"I cannot... you must not," Brom replied. "Once you cross this final threshold, the life you have come to know shall cease."

"I care not, I beg of you, let me stay. I desire only to be at the side of the man I love."

"I am lord of the keep now. The man I once is dead," he said coldly.

"Did you not swear to love me even beyond death?"

Brom's only response was a long, contemplative stare.

Rianna's hand dropped from his cold grasp. Tears welled in her eyes as she turned to leave.

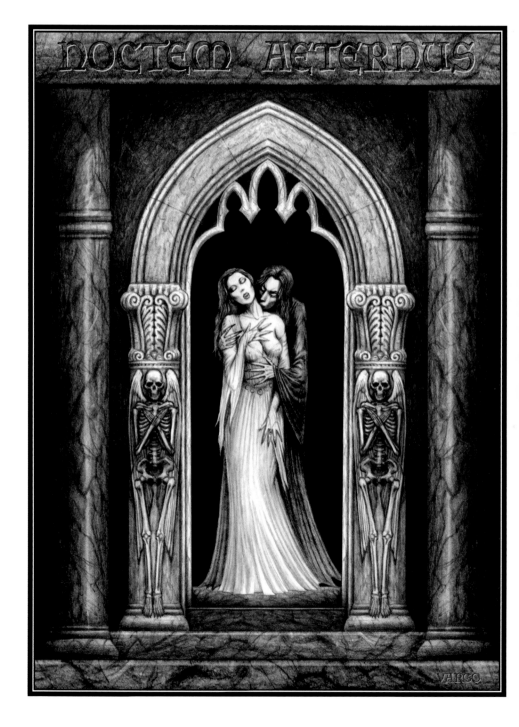

Brom stopped her from behind and held her within the archway of the inner sanctum, his arms encircling her, drawing her close. Rianna clutched the cross and tore the rosary from her neck, then leaned her head far back and closed her eyes, surrendering her throat to him. Brom's teeth pierced the soft flesh of her neck. Rianna shuddered, then writhed as he drank deeply. Her hand, which held the broken rosary, fell limp at her side. The crimson beads slipped through her fingers. They dropped down the stairs of the inner sanctum, falling from step to step like droplets of blood. At last, her grip relinquished the rosary cross and it fell from her hand, following the scarlet trail of beads, coming to rest upon the floor of the sanctum. She turned a pale hue as her life's blood slowly drained. He tried to stop himself, but could not, as each heartbeat pulsed more of the rich nectar into his mouth. She slumped, trembling against Brom. He held her upright until at last she expired.

Sweeping her lifeless body into his arms, he carried Rianna down the steps into the sanctum. Her arms hung limp and her head slumped heavily against his chest. He crossed the room and laid her body upon a couch of red velvet. Her skin was alabaster white. As she lay in surrendered repose, she looked like the statue of some Greek muse, perhaps the goddess of purity or innocence. Her beauty radiated, even beyond this deathly state in which she now lay. Brom knelt beside her, taking her small hand in his.

She stirred occasionally, making small sounds of pain. He knew too well the agony she was now feeling. Brom cringed, remembering his own dark passage. She squeezed his hand. He could not tell if it was a spasm of pain or if she knew he was with her, but he held her firmly, praying that somehow she would not feel as hopelessly alone as he had those long months ago.

At last, her hand fell limp again and she lay as if sleeping. An indigo cast spread over her pale features. Brom looked up and saw that a dim azure light filtered throughout the air in an even haze that, though not itself bright, subtly illuminated even the darkest shadows of the room. He rose to his feet and saw that the light emanated from somewhere beyond the open sanctum door. He felt something else as well, a kind of presence that flowed toward him into the room, like a wind filling a sail, though the flames of the candles burned steadily and his papers lay untroubled by any breeze.

Brom looked down at Rianna as she lay still and undisturbed. He stepped to the mantel and took down the Baron's sword. He climbed the steps to find the source of this unnatural azure glow. He followed it across the corridor and into the chapel.

He stared in wonder at the chapel's strange transformation. The blue light reflected off the windows as if daylight were pouring in from outside, their ghastly stained glass patterns invisible in its glow. The statues and reliefs along the walls took on a beneficent air as if they had long been misunderstood or had wandered astray but now basked in forgiveness. All the candles had been extinguished save the solitary vigil light that hung above the altar and now burned as high as a torch. Still, Brom felt none of the pain that even all but the dimmest candlelight inevitably brought to his eyes. He seemed to sense a voice, no, a chorus of voices echoing through the vaults of the ceiling, somehow distant, just beyond the range of his hearing.

The eerie light seemed to radiate from a figure standing before the obsidian altar, a darkly clad knight, tall and regal, his back to Brom. Long, black hair fell over the dark cape that hung from his shoulders into elegant folds upon the floor of the sanctuary. The blue light intensified along the edges of his figure to the argent blaze of the hottest flames of a forge.

Though awe-struck, Brom summoned his courage and called in a firm voice, "Who goes there?" His voice fell flat as if trapped by the blue glow that suffused the room.

Without turning to face him, the knight spoke, his voice

full and deep, yet quiet and intimate, speaking as if directly into Brom's ear. "I am a voice, a message to be delivered unto thee at an appointed time."

The knight turned. His black breastplate and bucklers gleamed darkly. As he moved, his mail shimmered in a limitless spectrum of somber purples and blues and blacks. He walked down the steps and onto the stone tile of the labyrinth, moving with the strength and ease of a great cat pacing its cage, its power held, for the moment at least, in graceful check.

"There is but one path to salvation," said the knight. His natural gait brought each footstep down on one of the suddenly vivid blue tiles of the maze's design, avoiding the clashing red stones that formed their own eccentric pattern on the floor. He stopped just short of the center, where the pattern curved outward.

Brom's gaze was drawn irresistibly upward to the knight's face. He was handsome, even strangely beautiful, yet masculine. His complexion was bone-white and pure, untouched even by the cerulean radiance that flowed from him. A crown of dark jewels glistened atop his long, black hair. His eyes were clear as glass and filled with light, but looking into them was to fall into vast depths of memory and knowledge. Brom could not look away.

The knight spoke again. "Brom of Falkirk, thou hast damned an innocent soul. Though thy will is strong, thy heart hast led thee to weakness. Unwittingly, thou hast granted Lilith a passage back into this realm."

Brom could not find the words to speak. He stared at the knight, trying to take in the full depth of all he said.

The dark knight continued, "Thy deed, unless amended, shall damn thee both. There is but one way to set things right, though it shall surely lengthen thy penance, perhaps beyond endure."

Though Brom could not grasp his meaning, he could feel the knight's words etch themselves into his memory, as if waiting

for later reflection. "What... what must I do?" Brom managed to stammer.

The knight's eyes darkened as they dropped to the sword in Brom's hand. Brom now saw that a darksome blade, that might have been the twin of the one he held, hung at the knight's side. A grim comprehension began to steal over him.

"This world with all its glories dost pale by compare to the realm I once knew," said the knight. "Serve well and thy true love shall await thee there."

Brom forced himself to speak. "How can I believe you?"

From beneath his cape, great dark wings arose, ebony-feathered and sleek as those of a raven. Their delicate tips met high above the knight's head, the outstretched wings encircling him like a shadowy aurora, a blue nimbus shining around him. "I am the avatar of truth," he said. "Have faith in my word."

Brom gazed in wonder upon the dark angel as it stood before him. "Forgive me," he whispered humbly, bowing his head before the strange, yet majestic being. He barely suppressed the urge to kneel.

The angel's words echoed through the chapel, "There is but one way to set things right."

A darkness fell over Brom and he raised his head. The chapel was cold and dim, the vigil light burning evenly in its sconce above the altar. He was alone.

Brom quickly returned to the library, but found the door closed. For a moment, the strange inscription seemed to hold the azure glow, then slowly faded to become part of the dark wood again. He threw open the door. The library was completely dark, the candles cold and dead.

Rianna no longer lay upon the couch. She was gone.

Brom leapt up the stairs and ran along the twisted corridors, desperately winding his way to the main hall. He found no trace of Rianna. He called out, and her name echoed up into the empty hollows of the ceiling, but there was no answer.

The tower was vast. He had been there more than a year and had not yet explored it in its entirety. The number of rooms seemed without limit and at times he even imagined they changed position within the structure. Halls wound away into strange annexes that seemed to fall between floors. Outside the keep but still within the grounds was the cemetery, of which he had only explored a fraction. Perhaps she gained access to the endless network of catacombs of which the Baron's writings hinted, but to which Brom had never found an entrance. She might be anywhere.

Just then, a sound from somewhere above caught Brom's attention, a whisper as faint as the slightest autumn breeze. As he ascended the tower stairs, the whisper grew louder and took on a haunting melody. He knew Rianna was now as he is, as he was when he was first transformed, born anew into death, into lifeless immortality. He had hidden himself in the sanctum from the harsh light of day, but when fresh night had settled, he went out to see it with new eyes. As he climbed higher through the castle, he felt drawn, as if lured by the siren's call.

Brom emerged atop the keep beneath the cool light of the full moon. He found Rianna amongst the gargoyles along the castle's eastern facade, leaning far out over the rampart's edge into the keening wind. A bare foot rested gingerly upon the ledge and one hand touched the granite wing of an immense gargoyle beast, but she seemed suspended, aloft. The wind had turned suddenly bitter, and her gown billowed out around her, her bodice loosened, her long hair free and flowing.

She spoke without turning, as if she had sensed his approach. "The night beckons. The cool touch of moonlight, the secret rustle of wind, the dark pleasures that await us. How have you resisted it so long? And why?" She glanced over her shoulder at Brom. Her face still held its ashen pallor,

but her eyes, now in stark contrast, were pools of black. "Were you waiting for me, my love?" She leaned her head back and laughed discordantly.

Rianna stepped down from the parapet, alighting gently on the walkway. She languished against the rampart, her long nails absently stroking the pointed chin of a stone devil. She grinned and slid her tongue slowly across her fangs, then turned back to look out over the village. "First, I shall quench my thirst upon this sorrowful lot. And then..." she said. "Ah, and then." She turned back to him. "And you, my love, shall be at my side."

Brom stepped toward her. She ran her hands slowly along her sleek form, caressing its curves and contours as if exploring them for the first time, her face caught in unearthly rapture. "This will be a good life," she said, more to herself than to him, "perhaps even a better life."

Brom lifted one arm from beneath his cloak and drew her toward him.

"Surrender," she whispered. Her black eyes stared coldly into his. She leaned in close and whispered again, more softly now, into his ear, "Surrender..."

Rianna let out a gasp as she felt the sharp blade enter below her ribcage. Brom held her neck and thrust the blade upward, through her heart. He leaned her back, against the wall between two stone demons. Her face spasmed with dread, her mouth struggling to form words, curses. He withdrew his sword and blood ran off it in sinuous streams, black and glistening in the moonlight as the demons looked mournfully on.

Rianna lifted her head. Her face now looked serene. Her eyes, returned to their normal hue, filled with tears. "Even beyond death... I shall love you," she whispered.

Brom leaned forward and tenderly pressed his lips to hers. Rianna's last breath subsided in one final kiss.

A simple headstone marks her grave. It bears only the name of my one true love.

— Rianna —

I can almost hear her voice calling my name on moonlit nights, a whisper as faint as the slightest autumn breeze.

Masque of Sorrow

CHRISTINE FILIPAK

No one is certain how long the Dark Tower has stood. It is said to have been built upon unholy ground and thus cursed before even the first stone was set. Though its true origin shall forever remain shrouded in mystery, what is known is chronicled herein. Only this legend remains.

Long ago, a great king ruled the lands. Though his name has since been forgotten, it is told that he was strong and just. The realm prospered beneath his reign. The castle was to be a palatial home for the king and his queen, a mountaintop citadel from which they could look out over their domain. However, before the tower was completed, the queen died, leaving the kingdom with no heir to the throne. In his grief, the king became susceptible to the enchantments of a beautiful witch and found solace in her bed.

The sorceress was soon with child. She bore him a daughter, but the woman died in the labors of childbirth. The infant, Mara, was brought before the king by three ancient women from Vasaria. The old crones presented the abandoned child to the king, as custom decreed, so that he might decide her fate. The king looked upon his bastard daughter and could not bear to leave her for the wolves.

And so, Mara was cared for, sheltered and raised in the castle, though not named as heir. She lived a secluded life, isolated from other children, and as she grew, she retreated deeper into her own world. The king's subjects spoke in hushed whispers of her suspected parentage.

Mara was seen nightly roaming throughout the castle and was often overheard speaking to the various stone figures that adorned the tower. Oftentimes, the servants or guards would come upon the girl, her attentions drawn to one of the menacing gargoyles, laughing and answering unspoken questions. Knowing her heritage and believing her to be in league with dark powers, they gave her a wide berth whenever possible.

In time, the Christian faith reached the realm, and the king adopted its beliefs. He turned to the local priest for guidance, and the holy man soon became his closest advisor. The king constructed a chapel within the castle to honor his newfound god.

Soon after the chapel was built, the ravens came. Each night, three ominous birds, their feathers sleek and black as jet, came to perch upon a stone ledge outside Mara's chamber window. Beneath the ledge, the countenance of a mournful harlequin was chiseled into the stone. It had become her favorite of the many gargoyles and grotesques that adorned the castle. Mara often spoke of her woe to the carved face while the ravens silently watched and listened from their perch above.

One night, a strange visitor in the guise of a jester came to Mara's chamber. He delighted and mystified her with feats of magic, and the two made fast friends. The jester visited often to guide and instruct Mara in her forbidden heritage. Though she spoke of him to others, no one ever saw him, but at times the girl was overheard conversing with someone late at night while alone in her chamber.

As the years passed, the jester's visits became less frequent until one day he came to call no more. The ravens still appeared from time to time, alighting upon Mara's window ledge, silent and ever vigilant. All the while, Mara withdrew further from those around her, honing her dark craft and growing more spiteful. She delighted in toying with the castle servants. As she blossomed into a dark beauty, she learned to use her feminine wiles, relishing in the seduction of the king's male subjects.

Mara's actions did not go unnoticed, and one day, when she was eight-and-ten years of age, the king visited the chapel to consult the priest about his problem child.

"The girl is well past the age when she should have been betrothed. I know not who might dare to marry one such as she. I fear..."

"Fear not, my king," said the priest. "I have thought long on this matter and I believe I have a solution."

The king listened attentively while the holy man offered his counsel.

Sometime later, the king proclaimed that a masked ball would be held in the castle to celebrate All Saint's Eve, and invitations were messengered to nobles of lands near and far.

Soon afterward, the queen's dressmaker came to call upon Mara. Rapping at her chamber door, the woman announced, "The king has sent me to fashion you a costume for the upcoming masque."

"Go away, old woman," Mara replied, speaking from the other side of the closed door. "I have no wish to join in any festivities."

"But the king has asked specifically that you attend as an honored guest and has put me at your disposal."

"Me? An honored guest?" Mara scoffed. "The king has scarcely acknowledged me these eighteen years. Why should he do so now?"

"I know not why the king does what he does, but he has instructed me to make a gown for you to wear to the ball. If you will permit me..."

"Leave me. Go away, I say."

"Will you not allow yourself some small pleasure? Surely, you deserve that much," the dressmaker persisted. "Come, simply open the door. See what fineries I have assembled. If all of this still displeases you so, then I shall depart and trouble you no more."

There was silence behind the heavy door, then the sound of a bolt being drawn. The door crept open an inch and Mara peered out.

Standing in the hall was a matronly woman, short of stature and gracefully aged in the face. She had obviously worked hard at her trade, though, for her fingers were curled and gnarled from years of pushing needle and thread. The old woman smiled coaxingly and Mara opened the door a bit further. The dressmaker clapped her hands, then stepped aside as an entourage of servants carried in bolts of fine fabrics.

Beautiful linens and richly colored brocades were strewn across Mara's bed. Wondrous patterns of lace and sumptuous lengths of silk were unfurled before her eyes. Mara ran her fingers lightly across the intricately woven threads.

"Indeed, they are lovely," she said, looking warily at the old woman. "But, this cannot be..."

"They are all for you, milady," assured the woman. "And I am at your disposal, here to create your heart's whim."

Mara turned again to the fabrics and caressed the shimmering silks, marveling at the motifs of exotic flowers that were embroidered into the soft linens.

"You are a beautiful young woman," said the dressmaker. She turned Mara to face the mirror, holding up one of the silks to the girl's cheek. "See how your eyes sparkle, and your skin, how smooth, and your hair..." She lifted Mara's long, dark tresses. "Soft and full, your mane shines like polished ebony." Holding Mara's hair atop her head, the dressmaker continued, "And you are blessed with an elegant neck, my dear, and your figure..." She unfolded one of the velvety fabrics and wrapped it tightly around Mara's waist. "You have the figure that every woman desires... every man as well." The woman smiled at Mara in the mirror, her old eyes wrinkling in jest.

Mara nodded her silent approval, overwhelmed by all she had seen.

The woman immediately set to work. She measured the girl and jotted down the dimensions for a pattern. After Mara had made her choices from the many bolts of fabric and trims, the seamstress gathered together the items that Mara preferred, then said, "I shall return in the morning. We shall begin with the sun's first light."

The dressmaker arrived each morning for fittings, adding delicate details to the garment. Mara stood upon a stool while the woman ran her needle back and forth, the stitches so tiny and set so closely together that the gown appeared seamless.

For three days the seamstress toiled, working her needle with the deftness of a true artist. The bodice and skirt were made from an azure blue brocade, gilded with a pattern of oak leaves. Fine lace decorated the neckline and poured over the shoulders to compliment the long train at the back of the gown.

The sleeves were of an ivory silk, the fabric sheer and weightless. They fit snugly along Mara's slender arms, coming to a point at the back of her hand and held securely in place by finely braided threads around her forefinger. Tiny golden rosebuds, each flower meticulously hand-crafted, adorned the neckline, spread across the shoulders, and cascaded down the sleeves. Braided silk cord crossed the bodice and bound it tightly, accentuating Mara's shapely bosom and cinching her slim waist.

Mara's headpiece was fashioned with a fine golden mesh,

criss-crossed with beaded lengths of tiny pearls. An ornately set sapphire hung from the center on a thin, gold chain and lay against Mara's forehead.

Mara stood in the archway of her balcony window and admired herself in a large mirror. For the first time the sun's warmth brought a smile to her face. The dressmaker helped Mara adjust the headpiece, then stood back to examine her work once more. When Mara held out her arms, billowy lengths of the ivory silk flowed from her sleeves to the back of her gown. As the sunlight shone through the sheer fabric, the effect was absolutely angelic.

The old woman was a true master of her craft. She smiled and handed Mara a mask which had been fashioned from soft, white owl feathers. It framed the girl's dark eyes as she held it before her face. Mara beamed with delight from behind the mask. She truly felt like a princess.

"There are still a few minor adjustments I would like to make, but they can wait until the morrow," the dressmaker said. Then gathering up her threads and needles, she smiled once more and took her leave.

That night Mara was happy, happier than she had ever been. She gazed from her window and spoke excitedly to the jester-faced gargoyle outside. "My entire life has been filled with loneliness and gloom, but that shall change on the morrow's eve. I shall be presented as the king's daughter, and all the realm shall bear witness. They shall know of my true lineage and revere me. No longer shall my heritage be denied, for indeed, my father truly loves me."

From behind her came a familiar voice, "No Mara, I alone care for you."

She turned to behold the jester standing in her chamber. Even she had begun to think that he had been simply the wild imaginings of a lonely young girl, yet here he stood, just as he had long ago.

His flesh was void of color, and the jagged strokes of black about his eyes and mouth exaggerated his features, appearing to be more a part of his true skin than paint. His stark costume was made of opposing patterns of black and white. His thin fingers ended in long, sharp nails.

"Good tidings, young queen."

"I am not a queen, old friend," Mara said, "though my father has finally accepted me and I shall soon be recognized as his heir."

"Recognized, perhaps, but accepted... never," the jester stated coldly.

"That is not true." Mara ran across the room and brought the dress before him. "You see? My father had his servants make this for me... I am to attend the masque as an honored guest."

The jester's eyes narrowed to blackened slits as he looked upon the dress with disdain. "Your father is shamed by your very existence. His subjects only serve you out of fear."

"Why do you speak such lies?"

"My words are the truth. You shall see for yourself. Come with me." He turned and walked toward the chamber door.

Mara trailed a few steps behind. Though his costume was adorned with bells, they made no sound as he moved through the corridor. The jester stopped before the likeness of a crown and scepter chiseled into a stone wall. He pushed on the scepter and the wall opened, revealing a narrow staircase leading downward. Mara followed the jester into the dark passage. He took her hand and led her down the stairs.

They emerged from behind a wooden panel concealed behind a large tapestry. Mara peeked around the tapestry to discover that they were in the grand hall. The king sat upon his tall throne, speaking to the priest who stood before him. Mara turned to speak to the jester, but he raised a finger to his lips, signaling her to remain silent.

The king rested his bearded chin on his hand as he spoke. "I have instructed the court's seamstress to fashion a costume for her, something demure, something befitting a princess."

"Yes," agreed the priest. "She must look pure to conceal her true nature, for the child is dark and untamed."

The king sighed and nodded.

"And what of our prospects?" asked the priest.

The king handed the priest a half-dozen scrolls, the seals already broken.

The priest's eyes darted over the scrolls as he briefly considered each one. "Perhaps Lord Denrin of Antioch or Duke Fayln of Tarsus."

"True. Both hail from distant lands and know nothing of her lineage," replied the king. "They are to arrive on the morrow."

"One is certain to take her far away with him," assured the priest. "Once they lay eyes upon her and behold her beauty, they will be clamoring for her hand."

The jester turned to Mara and whispered, "Even the priest is not above your notice. The hypocrite preaches forgiveness and prays for mercy while he and his fold spurn and shun you."

"It will not please her," the king replied flatly.

"The child will have no say in the matter, my king. It is time we be rid of her."

Mara turned and hurried back through the passage, tears streaming down her cheeks. She ran to her chamber and threw herself upon her bed.

Moments later, the jester stood beside her. "They all plot against you," he said sadly. "They will never permit you to sit upon the throne, though you be the rightful heir. They will never allow you to rule their kingdom, but I can see to it. I can assure it, this and much more. What do you truly desire? Vengeance? Upon those who despise you and conspire against you? I shall grant you revenge sweeter than any nectar you have tasted upon your lips. Power? I can grant you power far beyond any mortal's dream... as well as life eternal."

He stroked Mara's hair and gently lifted her chin, turning her face to the mirror. "The beauty that you see within your looking-glass shall never fade or wither. Your reign shall be measured not in years, but in aeons." Lowering his face next to hers, he looked at her in the mirror. "All this in return for one deed, one true test of your devotion."

As the jester spoke, the designs about his eyes and mouth seemed to move and change with each expression. "The masked ball is soon. The king's subjects and nobles from afar shall be in attendance, all together, in one place, on one night, your father, the priest, your would-be suitors, all those who have scorned you. You could wreak revenge upon the entire lot in one strategic action. This would ensure your place in this realm. You would serve no man from this day forth."

Mara gazed at herself in the mirror and wiped the hot tears from her cheeks. "Vengeance... yes," she whispered and smiled.

That night Mara quietly left the keep, letting no one see her. She ventured beyond the marble gateway that surrounded the castle grounds, her own grounds if things be set right. She walked deep into the forest, stepping over bramble and pushing aside tangled and twisted vine as she went. Finally, she came upon a blackened clearing.

There, in the dense hollow, strange things flourished where most plants would wither: innocent looking blossoms that carried beneath their soft petals a bite more venomous than a serpent, and tangled roots that when used properly as a poultice would provide relief from most ailments, but when eaten raw would ensure a slow and agonizing death. Even the bark of the surrounding trees, when boiled and prepared as a tea, was lethal in small doses.

Mara knelt before a patch of plants and herbs that she tended regularly. She picked the youngest leaves from the hemlock, taking care to avoid breathing in the noxious fumes that rose from the broken stems. Using her dagger, she topped the heads from a flowering plant of valerian, then worked diligently to unearth sinewy roots of mandrake. She bundled together her deadly harvest and put it all into a large satchel, then left the clearing.

On her way back to the castle, she stopped by a roost of doves that the gardener's wife raised and kept. As Mara opened the latch and took one of the birds, it cooed softly and fluttered in her hand. Its mate opened its eyes and pecked at one of her fingers. She put the female dove in the satchel with the herbs and quickly returned to her chamber.

She lit a fire in the hearth and filled a cauldron with water, then hung it over the flames to boil. She spread the leaves and flower petals on the warm stone of the hearth to dry while she crushed the roots with the flat of her dagger. With mortar and pestle, she ground the ingredients into a smooth paste. She added a few spoonfuls of honey and several drops of dove's blood to conceal the bitterness of the mixture, then thinned it to a liquid with the boiling water.

When the cooks and the remainder of the servants retired to their beds, she quietly made her way to the kitchen quarters. Plates and bowls were stacked and wine goblets were set in rows in preparation for the next evening's festivities. The food and flasks of wine were still locked away in the cellar stores. No matter, her plans were not foiled.

Mara began by pouring her mixture into a goblet, then swishing it round. The honey she had added helped the liquid adhere to the insides of the cup and would keep it from dissipating by the following day. She poured the liquid from the first cup into the next, then meticulously continued the process until each goblet was laced with the lethal concoction, all but one. When she had finished, she left, taking the virgin chalice with her. She then went to her father's library and searched amongst the quills and parchments used by the king's scribes, until she found a flask of black ink. Taking it with her, she returned to her chamber.

Mara went to the hearth, prodded the dying embers and rekindled the fire. Filling the cauldron once again with water, she left it to boil. She spread her new gown across the bed and, picking up her dagger, prepared to create something more befitting her true nature. She worked feverishly until morning.

The following day was filled with the excitement of the upcoming event. The grand hall was being prepared for the masque and banquet. Servants scurried back and forth, arranging benches beside long dining tables. Regal tapestries hung between the thin, slitted windows. Dried flowers and vines wrapped the marble columns. Wreaths were placed upon the heavy wooden doors. Candelabras were set in every corner of the massive room. Fresh candles, scented with fragrant oils, were placed in the sconces and in the chandeliers hanging overhead.

In the kitchen, cooks labored over boiling kettles while flames lapped around honey-glazed carcasses of lamb and boar which hung skewered above the fire pit. The delicious aromas wafted throughout the castle.

Rooms were made up in readiness for the overnight guests. Tall wooden posts, some bearing long banners, others supporting flaming torches, were staked along the path leading to the castle's main entrance.

The dressmaker came once more to Mara's chamber and knocked at her door.

Mara did not open the door, but answered, speaking through it, "Yes?"

"I have come for the final fitting of your gown, milady."

"It is a perfect fit, I love it just as it is," Mara assured the woman.

"Are you certain?" the woman inquired uneasily. "The alterations are few and will not take long."

"Do not be concerned," Mara answered, "I assure you, the gown is enchanting. All eyes will be upon me." Mara turned and looked at the gown draped across her bed.

"Very well, milady," the dressmaker said. "I shall look forward to seeing you this evening."

Mara waited a moment, listening as the woman walked away, then opened her door. Propped against it was a large bouquet of freshly cut yellow roses tied with a length of the same braided cord used on the bodice of the gown. As she picked them up, she pricked her finger upon a thorn. She smiled wryly and closed the door.

By the time the sun had set, the grand hall was filled with guests. The music had begun, and everywhere beasts of nature mingled with creatures of legend to dance and sway gracefully across the gleaming marble floor.

A tall woman, her headpiece crested with an array of brightly colored feathers, whirled round like some exotic bird as she danced with a man wearing the mask of a serpent. His eyes glistened with desire as they peered from beneath layers of green lacquered scales.

Several guests stepped aside as a huge man wearing the skinned furs of a bear lumbered by, growling fiercely at everyone in his path. A woman donning a pair of shimmering butterfly wings feigned alarm, then laughed as she leapt out of his way.

A waif walked through the crowd, effortlessly juggling pieces of fruit. A man in a boar-tusked mask snatched an apple from mid-air and took a bite from it, then tossed it back to the boy who resumed his act without flaw to the delight of the onlookers.

Another guest donned the horns of a goat upon his head and strode along on cloven hooves accompanied by a young maiden, her hair wreathed with fresh flowers. The satyr played a wooden flute as the fair lass sang ballads of love and good cheer. A man in a green velvet cloak, his mask bearded with autumn leaves, watched her longingly and listened in rapt attention.

To one side of the chamber stood the dressmaker, adorned in one of her own creations. Her flowing lavender skirts and silk veil were embellished with hand-painted grape leaves. She smiled as she spoke to an elderly gentleman dressed appropriately as Father Time, his long, white beard nearly reaching his belt, his dark-blue cloak covered with stars.

The king was attired in royal garb. A purple velvet cloak lined with fox fur draped his shoulders. His beard was neatly trimmed and he wore a crown bejeweled with rubies. He sat upon his tall throne and laughed heartily as he watched the revelry.

All rejoiced and joined in the celebration.

The priest stood upon the dais, to one side of the throne, slightly behind the king's shoulder. He wore scarlet robes beneath his vestments of gilded linen and held a tall golden staff. His pious demeanor slowly faded to a look of distress and he leaned over to whisper in the king's ear.

A hush fell over the revelers and the dancing came to an abrupt halt. There, in the midst of the sea of vividly colorful, flowing gowns and cloaks, stood Mara, draped entirely in black. The once angelic gown now clung to her immodestly, like the wrappings of a funerary shroud, shrunken and blackened by the boiling ink.

Mara began to walk slowly and deliberately through the hall toward the dais. Turning for all to see, she spread her arms wide. The tenebrous silk, streaked where the dye had settled, hung in tatters and resembled the veined wings of a bat.

Long, black thorns flanked her headpiece, and more sharp spikes protruded from her shoulders and back.

As Mara strode through the crowd, she passed the dressmaker who stared at the gown in obvious horror.

"As I promised, all eyes are upon me," Mara whispered to the old woman, then ascended the steps to the dais. The gown's long train flowed behind her like a shadow.

The king and priest stood speechless.

The Duke of Tarsus stepped forward to make his formal introduction, his dull brown eyes brimming with wonderment. He was adorned in the plated armor of a warrior, though his delicate features betrayed that he had never seen battle. Bowing deeply, he nearly fell forward under the weight of the sword that hung from his hip. He took Mara's proffered hand, but then hesitated before kissing it.

Mara had replaced the tiny silk blossoms along her sleeves with rose thorns. "Will you not kiss the hand of the lady that you have come so far to meet?" she coaxed.

Shamed, the young man lowered his head. Carefully and lightly, he kissed her hand. No sooner did his lips touch her skin than Mara quickly yanked her hand away. Standing back, he brought his fingers to his mouth. A droplet of blood trickled from his lips.

The king was aghast.

Turning to the priest, she stroked his face seductively and asked, "How many more do you think will be clamoring for this hand?" Mara smiled as she watched the priest's eyes travel to her bosom. The fine lace covering the front of the bodice had been torn away, revealing much of her young flesh.

The servants carried out the wine, placing a cask on each table. Guests began to gather round and soon every goblet was filled.

Mara took a goblet from a serving girl and placed it in the priest's hand. Closing her fingers around his, she brought the

cup to his lips, enticing him to drink. The priest blushed a deep scarlet from his neck to his deeply creased forehead. The king needed no prodding. He merely shook his head and took a large gulp from his jeweled, silver chalice. Turning to face the crowd, Mara proclaimed a toast to the king. With a hearty cheer, all raised their goblets and drank.

Mara descended the steps and proceeded through the crowd. Stopping before two guards, she charmed and cajoled them into drinking, tipping their cups and laughing merrily with them. Across the room, she watched her father as he conferred with the priest, his brow drawn in concern. Both drank as they spoke. Mara smiled secretly and took a sip from her untainted chalice. As she watched over the rim of her cup, she began to notice a gradual change in the guests' demeanor, a strange delirium, caused not by mere drink, but instead born of her own conjuring.

A man pushed up his mask, the long snout of a wolf rising above the crowd, its mouth open wide, its sharp, white fangs dipped in red. He took a gulp of wine, then let out a forlorn howl.

The songstress began to sing of sorrow and misery as tears streamed her face.

As a buxom wench bounced past, the goat-horned man swept her into his arms. He drew her toward him, fondling and groping her. The wench kissed him lustfully, then bit into his cheek and squirmed free. The satyr lowered his horned head and ran after her.

Mara started toward the main doorway to exit the hall, but a clash erupted before her. The two guards had begun dueling, brandishing their swords wildly and stabbing any who were unfortunate enough to wander near. She spun around and began to weave her way back through the rapidly degenerating celebration, heading for the secret passage.

The satyr let loose a devilish laugh, his horns now dripping with gore as he stood over the wench who lay dead at his feet. The young juggler, his vest spattered with blood and wine, gaped in shock at the vicious drama that had just played out before him.

The hulking man dressed as a bear growled and pawed ferociously at the guests around him. A servant wielding a kitchen knife leapt onto his back and stabbed him over and over, until they both went down in the slippery pool of blood that had formed on the floor.

A candelabra toppled against the priest, setting the back of his robe aflame. He wandered aimlessly, gibbering and uttering rhetoric, unaware that he was afire.

The Duke of Tarsus sat slumped against a wall. Blood no longer trickled from his lips, but gushed forth from his mouth in a deep red stream.

As Mara continued through the grotesque revelry, she was startled by the boar-tusked man who leapt in front of her, blocking her path. The beast grabbed her and pulled her close, laughing. He picked her up to carry her off, then squealed and dropped her when the thorns of her dress punctured his arms and chest.

Almost frantic now, Mara turned to flee.

The crowd parted as the priest preached and loudly recited scripture, still oblivious to the flames which had engulfed his robes and now lapped at his flesh.

Mara ran and finally reached the tapestry, then turned to look one last time upon the nightmarish scene.

The king slumped back into his throne, his face frozen in a horrified stare as he looked out over the writhing mass.

Mara slipped behind the tapestry and into the concealed passageway. The howls and shrieks of the guests followed close behind as she fled down the corridors and back to her chambers. She burst into her room, then slammed and bolted the chamber door.

As Mara leaned against the door, breathing heavily, she was startled by a sudden pounding behind her.

"What have you done, child?" the dressmaker shrieked from beyond the door as she beat her fists desperately against the wood. The voices of an angry hoard bellowed through the hall. The old woman screamed again and again, scratching and clawing against the door.

Mara covered her ears, but it only muffled the sounds. "Die... Die... Die!" she screamed. She looked to the stone relief of the jester outside her window. The harlequin grotesque laughed maniacally.

All through the night, Mara was kept awake by maddening shrieks which pierced the thick stone of her chamber walls. The tortured wails did not subside until after the sun had risen. At last, weariness overcame her and she slept through the daylight hours.

She awoke at dusk and cautiously descended into the main castle. Though the infernal clamor had subsided, the castle was not altogether silent. The screams of the guests were now replaced by the hoarse cawing of ravens.

Mara crept to the grand hall and threw open the doors to behold a horrific sight. Hundreds of ravens filled the hall. Enormous birds, black as night, greedily fought for rank amongst the feast. The guests lay where they fell. Some still bore their hideous masks while the faces of others had been picked clean to the bone by the ravenous birds, leaving them eyeless and leering with cadaverous grins.

Low laughter carried across the grand hall. Mara slowly advanced toward the dais. There, in the king's throne, sat the jester. He leaned forward holding the priest's staff, the king's head impaled upon the pike. He looked over the carnage with evil delight. "Your deeds have surpassed even the treachery and venomous cruelty of Jezebel." He stood, then turned the staff so that the king's severed head faced him.

"Yes, I think your father would agree."

The hollow jingle of bells accompanied each step as the jester descended the dais. He stopped before Mara and held forth the pike. Mara's gaze shifted between the morbid frown of the disembodied head and the maniacal, fanged grin of the jester's face. He removed the crown from the king's severed head and bestowed it upon Mara.

The ravens croaked a blasphemous chorus to announce the Dark Queen's coronation.

The jester let the staff drop, then put his hands to Mara's face and drew her near. He placed a soft kiss upon her trembling lips, then tenderly stroked her hair aside to reveal the flesh of her neck. He whispered into her ear, "My child," then lowered his cold lips to her throat.

She gasped for breath as sharp tendrils of burning pain suddenly shot through her, racing across her shoulders and down her spine. It felt as though the blood in her veins had turned to ice, frozen, yet ablaze. Slowly, her agony twisted to rapture. She fell into the jester's arms. Her vision dimmed to shadows, then darkness swarmed over her.

Mara awakened to find herself seated in the throne. The hall now held an azure tint, though the candles were long cold. The king's blood had since dried to a black stain which ran along the stone armrest and down to the floor. A sweet scent now hung heavy in the air. The ravens still gleefully feasted among the carrion.

Amidst the carnage, a tall shadow stood. Leathery wings rose from its back and, though the form was that of a beast, the thing stood upright like a man. Its ears were pointed like those of a wolf or a bat. It turned to face Mara, its eyes aglow like seething embers. Its claws scraped across the floor as it stepped toward the throne.

"Hail, the Dark Queen." The creature's voice bellowed through the hall, stilling the raven's caws.

"Who are you?" Mara asked, her voice straining to hide her fear.

"I am known by many names. I exist in many forms. I am one of the Fallen. We are kindred spirits, now bound by blood."

"What have you done to me?" Mara asked.

"You shall never again suffer the pains of human frailty." The thing gestured a clawed hand toward one of the many corpses at its feet. The stiffened body lay frozen in the throes of death. The demon's long tail swept across the carcass, lightly caressing its withered flesh. "These weak creatures shall grovel beneath your feet. You shall feed upon them, their fears... and their blood. All I have promised you shall be fulfilled. Your kingdom shall have no bounds on this earth."

"How can this be?"

The black beast spread its great wings, rising before her. "You are a creature of darkness," it said, its deep voice sending a resounding rumble throughout the vaulted chamber, "and in the night you shall reign immortal." With that, the demon's form shifted, becoming a writhing mass of blackness, until at last it vanished in a chaos of swirling shadows.

Mara looked out over her ghastly inheritance. The ravens now stood motionless, perched upon the sea of corpses. They glared at her with eyes as black as sin. Mara sat still, locked in a cold stare with the silent birds. Slowly, the Dark Queen bore a fanged smile, then threw her head back in a wicked laugh. The ravens erupted. Their shrieks, echoing amidst cruel laughter, filled the halls of the Dark Tower.

I reflect upon the tragedies I have borne witness to throughout the bleak and trying years. Beneath the cruel shadow of the tower, mortal lives wither and fall to ruin, their souls lost to temptation and dark desire. For the tower doth beckon all who would listen, luring them closer, deeper, until at last they are consumed by the Abyss.

Shadows

JOSEPH IORILLO AND JAMES PIPIK

Nicolai guided his massive brown steed along familiar paths until he came into an abrupt highland clearing, where he paused. Below him the village of Vasaria was laid out in the same sparse pattern of humble huts and cottages he remembered all too well. The westering sun threw a long shadow across the village like a blade into its heart, the shadow of the tower, rising west of the village, stark and blank like an indifferent deity. The western face of the fortress glowed scarlet-orange with the ominous life of the setting sun, while the side facing the village remained shrouded in darkness.

At the sight of the foreboding keep Nicolai felt a solemn, childlike dread welling up within him, so familiar from long years of gazing up at it in fear and wonder, though now the emotion was tinged with the bitterness and rage that had come with maturity. He urged his stallion onward into the village.

As he rode down the main road, boyhood memories flooded back in a torrent. He knew every house, every field and shop, every side path. Here at the well he had filled buckets for his grandfather's horses, there at the tavern he had fought with the smith's son over a gambling debt, and on a bright summer's morning in his youth he had seen Katrina step out of her father's shop, her dress billowing in the breeze...

Nicolai turned his thoughts fiercely away from such

memories. After his many years in prosperous Cherenka, the narrow dirt roads and dilapidated homes of Vasaria seemed stunted and mundane. He brought his horse to the communal stable near the village square and dismounted. A wide-eyed stable boy took the reins, gaping at Nicolai's fine black boots, thick woolen cloak and soft leather gloves.

Nicolai held a glittering silver piece up before the boy's eyes. "What is your name?"

"Willem," the boy said numbly, as if enchanted by the coin.

He pressed the coin into the boy's palm and held his wrist. "Willem, you will instruct the Elders that Nicolai has returned and demands an immediate audience. You will do so without delay and bring their answer to me here."

He released Willem's hand and the boy shot away like an arrow. Nicolai lingered near the well. The sun had dropped below the surrounding mountains and the village was in shadow. People hurried home before nightfall. Among the scarce passersby he saw familiar faces, wrinkled now and sallow with age. Some eyed him with suspicion, as the villagers of Vasaria did any stranger. Others looked at him curiously, perhaps struggling to remember how they might know him.

A few recognized him and gathered around him. They greeted him warmly, calling out to the others, "Look, here is our Nicolai, home from the outlands." They expressed sympathy for the death of his grandfather several weeks before and inquired as to the occasion for his return.

"I have come to settle my grandfather's affairs," he told them, "among other things."

Then their eyes filled with pity. No doubt they would return to their homes, whispering the old, sad tale of poor Nicolai's true love, Katrina, lost all those years ago, and of Nicolai's brokenhearted flight from the village. To them his life was but another tragic chapter in the dark history of Vasaria.

Let them whisper, Nicolai thought. I am no longer the peasant boy they knew. I am no longer like them, slaves in thrall to the demonic force that dwells within the tower, holding them in its twisted grasp.

As the square cleared, Nicolai noticed a man across the road, silhouetted in the narrow alley between two huts. Though he could not discern the man's face in the dying light, he had the unsettling feeling that he was staring at him, studying him.

Nicolai stepped forward and the dark figure stepped backward into the gloom. Just then Willem returned, stopping him. "Three members of the council will see you now," he said breathlessly. "They are gathered in old Masaryk's homestead."

Nicolai looked down at the boy, then back at the figure, but it was gone. He took a step toward the alley again.

"I can lead you there," Willem said, eager for a second coin, no doubt.

"I know the way," Nicolai said and strode off down the road without a backward glance.

Masaryk's daughter, now an old woman caring for her even older widower father, showed Nicolai into the rear chamber of his house where the Elders still met. He had been in this room once as a child and had thought it fabulously luxurious, with its large chairs and oil lamps and the great council table. He had believed Masaryk to be the most prosperous man in the world. Now he realized the home was little more than a hovel, less comfortable than even the poorest dwelling in Cherenka.

Alexi and Valis rose shakily to their feet as he entered and shook his hand, polite but guarded. Masaryk, massive and venerable, remained all but motionless in his heavy armchair. He nodded his greeting, his eyes bright and alert beneath his heavy brow. Nicolai noted sadly that the two decades since he had seen these men last weighed heavily on them. Alexi's beard had lost its pepper and his pale scalp now shone through his wispy hair. Valis, the youngest of the three, had not been an Elder in Nicolai's youth, but his face was now lined with years of concentration that had worn his head bald. In contrast to other men of his advanced age, Masaryk had grown even larger. At over eighty years he retained his gray, lush mane, tied back in a long braid.

Alexi offered Nicolai a chair, but he refused. He had little time to waste on pleasantries. "Years ago I left Vasaria, my lifelong home," he said. "I entered the world of sunlight and its warmth melted the memories and ghosts of this village away like mist on a summer morning. I made a new life for myself and thought of Vasaria no more. That is, until word came to me of my grandfather's passing."

"We thought you should know," Alexi said, stroking his beard like a cherished pet.

"As you know, my grandfather and I were not close," Nicolai said, pacing the length of the table. "He disapproved of my leaving and in any case owned nothing that I wanted. I might well have let his passing go quietly by, perhaps having a Mass offered for his poor, lost soul, but when I thought of my last living relative dead, having wasted his life toiling and struggling beneath the curse of this blighted village, I could bear it no longer. I shall remain silent no longer. I have come to speak of the thing known as the Baron."

Alexi and Valis were visibly stunned, only Masaryk remaining unmoved. Before they could utter a word, Nicolai began again, pointing an accusing finger at them.

"You are all accomplices to a ravenous evil," he declared, "an evil that lurks within the tower and uses Vasaria as its unholy feeding ground. Throughout the years it has claimed the souls of the unwary innocents of this village. It cannot continue."

"Nicolai, you do not understand," Alexi stammered, his image of himself as a benevolent patriarch obviously shaken.

"You were so young when you left. You have never received the wisdom of the Elders."

"Wisdom? Do not preach to me of your wisdom." Nicolai's tone became more heated and increasingly bitter. "You meet in clandestine congregations and decide the fate of your fold, who shall live... and who shall be sacrificed to the tower. What dark pact did you strike with the Devil? What does he give you that is worth the lives of your fellow men?"

"Our only allegiance is to the greater good," Valis said calmly, his ancient eyes narrowing. "We struck no deals with the Devil, nor are we in league with him."

Alexi added, "My child, you understand neither the true nature of the lord of the keep nor the secrets of the tower itself."

"It is as I suspected," Nicolai said. "The Dark One bends your wills to serve his own blasphemous needs. Blood has been spilled. Lives are being wasted, even your own, and yet you do nothing. You are madmen, no longer in your right minds."

Valis grimaced angrily, but Masaryk laid a heavy hand on his arm and spoke in a soft, low rumble. "We know of your pain, Nicolai. We know the depths of your loss. You must not allow your sorrow to turn to a hatred which blinds you."

"It is you who are blinded," Nicolai retorted, "blinded by the Baron's black will. You have fallen prey to that demon, and unless you awaken and reclaim your own wills, you are lost and all Vasaria is lost with you."

"Enough," Valis said with weary finality. "You are not an Elder. You do not know the truth."

"I speak the truth," Nicolai said, "but it falls upon deaf ears." He stomped to the door and slammed it shut behind him.

Though it was now fully night, Willem met Nicolai as he left Masaryk's homestead. Still hoping for further payment, Nicolai supposed, he had brought along Nicolai's bags from the stable and a pair of torches. Nicolai took one of the torches and stalked into the moonless night. The boy had to hurry to keep pace with Nicolai's angry strides.

The wind-blown torch cast uneven, pulsing shadows on the buildings along the road. Growing uneasy as he made his way through the deserted village, Nicolai slackened his pace. He had the growing impression that he was being watched, followed. Curtains in windows closed just as he turned toward them. Doors to houses swung shut just as he approached. He thought of the silhouette he had seen earlier that evening and peered carefully into the jet shadows between the houses as he passed.

With nowhere else to stay the night, Nicolai went to the modest, stone home that had belonged to his grandfather. It stood somewhat apart from its neighbors on the edge of the village. The casements of the empty house still bore the black draperies of mourning and withered sheaves of lilies still lay heaped at the entryway. Nicolai had almost forgotten this pathetic village custom.

As Willem unlatched the door for him, Nicolai stared at the house across the avenue, its windows aglow from the hearthfire within. A dark form crossed in front of the outside of the window and slipped into the shadows between the houses.

"Who is there?" Nicolai called out, his heart suddenly pounding fiercely against the walls of his chest. Holding his torch high, he stepped boldly across the street, but by the time he drew near the house, the figure had receded into the shadows and disappeared. He began to search around the house then glanced back at Willem. The boy was still standing across the road, before the now open doorway, staring at Nicolai, his head cocked slightly. Suddenly, the shadowy figure emerged from the doorway behind him, rising up like an animal rearing on its hind legs in a ghastly parody of a man.

"Willem!" Nicolai shouted, gesturing to the thing behind the boy, but when Willem turned and held out his torch, there was nothing there. The boy looked back at Nicolai, his eyes wide and wary.

Nicolai recrossed the road. Willem lifted the saddle bag into Nicolai's hand, then turned and raced off, not waiting for thanks or payment. Nicolai stood in the open doorway, watching the light of the boy's torch weave its way through the town and finally vanish in the gloom.

The boy had seen no specters, no demons. They had been nothing more than tricks of the eye, Nicolai thought, brought on by the weariness of the long days of traveling, the frustration of the confrontation with the Elders. He turned back to the abandoned house, shaken and confused.

Nicolai would not sleep in the bed where his grandfather had died, so he curled himself once more into the familiar cot in the front room in which he had slept as a boy, still nestled in a low corner. The straw mattress was stale and brittle. Weary though he was, he slept uneasily. He started at every sound, the distant cry of an owl or a neighbor's shutter banging in the wind. When he at last managed to slip into sleep, he fell into a nightmare of drowning and awoke gasping for air.

The room was still and dark. Though he had not had that dream in years, he knew he would not sleep again before dawn. He sat up and lit a candle. He took up his cloak and with the candle held before him made his way into the bedchamber.

He wedged the candle into the candlestick upon the nightstand. An occasional breeze swept through the open window and shook the slender flame, its fluttering light thrown across a heavy tome that lay closed upon the night stand. Nicolai recognized the book of psalms his grandfather had found decades ago in the ruins of a deserted monastery. The old man had read to him from it through many a long evening in his youth. Nicolai knew he would find no comfort there and turned away.

He drew his cloak around him and slumped heavily into his grandfather's tall, stiff chair. He leaned forward, his head in hands. The memory of the dream lingered. In it, he held his breath, water pressing in on every side, the light from above receding as he was pulled deeper and deeper. He shook the dream from his mind and looked up and his heart froze within him.

Upon the wall, towering above the meager silhouette of his chair, a shadow stood. Whatever was casting the shadow, whatever he had seen in the street earlier, was standing directly behind him.

Nicolai felt as if a frigid winter gale had enveloped him. His heart pounded at a dangerous pace and he had to struggle to retain his composure. He sat bolt upright in the chair, holding rigidly to its arms, his eyes riveted to the narrow shadow before him.

Slowly, he unclenched his right hand from the arm of the chair, one flexed finger at a time. He lifted his hand so carefully that one could scarcely say it moved, then let it drift inch by agonizing inch to the pocket of his cloak. He found the reassuring weight of his dagger among its folds. His fingers deftly unclasped the sheath and drew the blade forth. He clenched the hilt in a fist damp with perspiration.

His eyes were still transfixed upon the motionless shade. How long had they been locked thus? Minutes? Hours? Perhaps, Nicolai thought suddenly, it was merely an illusion of candlelight, a shadow cast by something he had not noticed upon entering the room, his grandfather's greatcoat or a tall bureau. Why else would the specter remain so still when it must know he was aware of its presence?

As if reading Nicolai's thought, the shadow stirred, lifting morbid, skeletal arms up and outward. Nicolai sat for an instant that seemed an eternity, unable to move, enthralled by the long, twisted shadows wavering in the flickering candlelight like writhing serpents.

Snarling, Nicolai whirled and with all his strength he thrust his blade forward at the specter, meeting nothing but empty air before the dagger slipped from his grasp and lodged in the windowsill, splintering the wood with the force of the blow.

He stared out the window and looked off toward the mountain and the baleful tower that was virtually invisible in the moonless night. It betrayed its presence by blotting out the stars in that region of the sky, just as it had eclipsed the souls of the villagers throughout the generations. He took the dagger in his fist and wrenched it from the windowsill. The hand that held it shook, though whether from anger or fear even Nicolai could not say. He screamed out into the night, then closed and bolted the window shutter.

After only a few fitful hours of sleep, Nicolai's nerves were ragged and raw. He went out into the dawning day, leaden clouds hanging low upon the mountains. The tepid drizzle never quite thickened into rain, never quite stopped completely. He called on old friends, but after accepting their condolences, he cut the visits short. He could not bear to spend time with them. They had become pitifully shrunken and withered in the years since he had seen them last, their growth stunted in the shadow of the tower.

As afternoon drew on, he paid his respects at his grandfather's grave in the overgrown cemetery that rose along the hillsides east of the village. He could not bring himself to feel sorrow for the old man. They had not spoken or exchanged letters in all the years he had been away. Even before he left Vasaria, Nicolai had hated the old man for the endless, thankless hours of labor he had heaped upon his young back, all the while hypocritically moralizing like the other Elders, preaching duty and fidelity to God while colluding with the

Devil. Farewell, old man, Nicolai thought, I will pray for your poor, damned soul.

As he stood before the simple stone, from the corner of his eye he saw someone watching from a nearby thicket of trees. All day he had caught glimpses of this figure following him throughout the village, always on the periphery of his vision. When he tried to focus his attention squarely on it, it slipped away between the cottages or into a group of villagers. If they had noticed, and Nicolai thought they must have, they said nothing. All of them were in the Devil's thrall.

The sensation of being watched was not entirely new to Nicolai. He had occasionally felt the unwanted presence of some nameless, vaguely threatening force following him throughout his life, even far away in the bustling marketplace of Cherenka. He began to realize that the Dark One's influence had reached him even there. In Vasaria, though, the power of the fiend was at its strongest. Nicolai turned away then, feeling the eyes of the tower upon him as he walked back to the village.

After eating alone at the tavern, Nicolai returned to his grandfather's house and lit candles in every room. He waited, dagger at hand, for the dark apparition to return, to try to finish the work he had spoiled the night before. But the candles burned low, without so much as a dog barking outside, and at length Nicolai drifted into sleep.

He dreamed that a gaunt figure stood in the doorway to the bedchamber, lit from behind by a pale red glow. The skeletal silhouette moved slowly, as if burdened by great weight. It came toward him, each step heavy and wet, and Nicolai started back to consciousness.

The candles had burned out as he slept, save one in the bedchamber. The doorway glowed a dim ember red, just as in the dream. He could hear something moving there, trudging back and forth across the room with thick, ponderous steps. A shadow passed before the doorway, breaking the bloody glow, then moved away again.

Nicolai prepared himself for the thing to come into the front room as in his dream. As he reached for his dagger, he heard a new sound that turned his blood to ice. Whatever the thing in the next room was, it was trying to form words, its voice a wrenching, choking gasp. Unnerved by the terrible screeching rasp, Nicolai closed his eyes and clamped his hands over his ears.

Suddenly all was quiet. Nicolai opened his eyes. The room was dark, the bedchamber now unlit. Nicolai struck a flame to a fresh candle and took up his dagger. He edged his way carefully into the next room.

There was no one to be found in the room. All was just as he had left it earlier that evening. Had it all been a dream? Then he noticed that the book of psalms on the night stand stood open.

He was certain it had been closed when he was here earlier. The window was still secured, not that any breeze could lift the heavy leather cover.

Nicolai stared at the open leaf, the archaic script delineating a passage long familiar from his grandfather's recitals:

> I am afflicted and in agony from my youth;
> I am dazed with the burden of thy dread.
> Thy wrath hath swept over me;
> thy terrors hath cut me off.
> They encompass me like water all the day;
> they close in upon me on all sides.
> Lover and friend hast thou taken from me;
> my only companion is darkness.

As he read the words, the horrible voice came back to him, straining to form these words. Upon the page Nicolai detected a damp handprint. He slept no more that night.

The following morning, Nicolai went early to the stable and instructed Willem to prepare his horse. The boy avoided his gaze and quickly carried out his orders without speaking, then departed as if fleeing a ghost.

Nicolai mounted his steed and rode west out of the village. As he reached the moss-covered stone that stood upright at the edge of the woods, he came upon Masaryk. The old man stood as massive and unmovable as the stone itself. He raised a hand and almost against his will Nicolai drew to a halt.

"I know where you are going," Masaryk said, his voice heavy and resonant. "Do not allow your hatred to lead you down this path. All who venture..."

"Yes, I remember the tales, old man," Nicolai interrupted. "All who venture too near the Dark Tower are never seen again."

"It is not mere rumor," Masaryk answered. He looked long at Nicolai before asking, "What do you hope to accomplish?"

"Something that should have been done long ago, were the Elders not too timid. I shall confront the Demon, this thing that corrupts the wills of good men."

"I suppose I should be grateful that you think us good men, at least," Masaryk said without mirth. "But whether we are good or not, we are not slaves who follow the Baron's evil whims in humble servitude. We owe the Lord of the Dark Tower a debt of which you know nothing."

"The tower is an unclean fountain, flooding down this valley and washing away all our lives. It breeds demons and abominations, just as a river in flood brings with it hardship and disease. And you speak to me of being indebted to it? I spoke truly when I saw you last. You are mad."

"The tower is indeed the source of great darkness, my child," Masaryk said, "but not all the evil in this land is its work. The world is not so simple. Nor is the human soul."

Nicolai looked down at the old man with disgust, then impatiently spurred his stallion up the trail into the wood. When he glanced back over his shoulder he saw him still at the boundary of the village, like the standing stone beside him, permanent and indomitable.

Soon Nicolai was ascending the twisting path through the dense mountain forest. The withered trees and vines formed a tattered canopy which filtered the sunlight and shrouded the path in an oppressive gloom. As the trail grew steeper, the trees underwent an ominous transformation, becoming more angular and twisted, and their spindly, low-hanging branches scraped against his flesh like skeletal fingers. His horse stumbled over the roots that snaked the path. Nicolai continued his trek at a slower pace, his throat tight with trepidation.

The trees grew closer together, like ranks of soldiers surrounding an outnumbered adversary. Large ravens, their feathers as sleek and shiny as leaves of polished ebony, perched silently on the gnarled branches of the dead and dying trees, watching him with soulless, glittering eyes. There were scores of them, and they grew in number as he neared the tower. A whispery, gray mist clung to the hillside, twisting and rising in chaotic tendrils around his horse's legs.

Nicolai had hoped that daring the forest by daylight would offer him relief from the dreaded, dark shapes that had plagued his nights, but now the loathsome, shifting shadows cast by the trees and the flitting shapes of the ravens encircled him like writhing plumes of smoke. In the distance between the dark trees he thought he discerned shadows of vaguely human form, drifting like a coven of cloaked monks, following and closing in on him.

Suddenly, a single tall shadow arose before him. It stood as a man, wrapped in a cloak of solid black, its face shrouded beneath the tattered fringes of its hood. Nicolai pulled hard on the reins and his frightened steed reared and bolted, throwing Nicolai from the saddle.

Lying stunned on the dirt path, he shut his eyes, praying silently. When he opened them, the shadowy form had vanished, though the mist along the path before him whirled madly. Behind him, his horse was in full gallop, heading downhill toward the village. The flocks of ravens watched over all, silent and impassive.

Now on foot, Nicolai hurried uphill along the path until at last he reached the dark wood's edge. He found himself staring in awe at the massive tower that now loomed before him, a pile of indistinct black slabs and spires against tumbling gray clouds. He proceeded slowly, passing the stone ruins of an ancient arched gateway.

He felt curiously empty of emotion. Even the fear he had felt in the woods had dissipated now that he drew near his grim destination. Perhaps, he mused, it was another insidious spell worked by the Baron to draw the unwary further into his violent abyss.

Behind him in the dead trees, the flocks of ravens rustled through the branches, finding perches and studying him with their cold, distant eyes. He tried to ignore them, but when he set foot upon the first step of the stone staircase leading to the keep's massive, arched doors, his ears were assaulted with the raucous, agonizing shriek of the birds. The sky above him darkened as the ravens took flight from the trees, their wings beating thunderously as they scattered to the many niches and cornices, to alight among the sentinel gargoyles of the tower's facade.

The demon birds would not deter him. Nicolai quickly ascended the steps to the tower's entrance. Facing the strange,

twisted design set in metal into the heavy, wooden doors, Nicolai's uneasiness returned. He let his fingers touch the rune, but he immediately withdrew them in surprise. Rather than being cold and hard, it was warm and supple, like blood from a fresh wound.

He took a deep, steadying breath and pushed against one of the doors. He expected to find it utterly unyielding, but with a piercing cry of the ancient hinges, it swung open halfway before grinding to halt against the uneven stone floor. Nicolai stepped cautiously through the doorway.

The thick fog-like gloom and the stench of stale neglect disoriented him and he struggled to maintain his balance. He peered from the entryway into the interior of the unhallowed fortress. Night permanently held the tower in its brutal grip. Even the pallid light from the open door and the high casements did little more than suggest a distant twilight. Shadows reigned like an occupying army and a finger of cold fear touched Nicolai's heart.

The fear somehow stirred an anger inside him and he called out into the dark, "You should welcome me with something more than silence," his voice tremulous despite himself. "Now you can make an end of me. Come forth from the shadows. I am willing to face my death." His voice rang out in the enormous heights of the hall and faint, distorted echoes whispered back at him from the darkness.

A low reply came down from above. "Such an admission is no sign of courage, child. Were thou brave, thou wouldst be willing to face thy life."

Nicolai stepped forward into the hall and stared hard into the shadows. A great balcony spanned the other side of the room. As Nicolai's eyes adjusted to the dimness, he could make out a pale, gaunt man standing there, his severe, almost skeletal face and shaven head emerging like a ghost from the darkness. The man bent forward slightly, resting wan, claw-like hands upon the marble railing and gazed down at Nicolai.

Nicolai halted in mid-stride, his eyes locked on the Baron towering over him. "Cease your taunts," Nicolai said. "Haunt me no longer."

The Baron stood motionless for long moments. At last he leaned forward over the railing and spoke, "Who art thou?"

Nicolai came forward, standing between the arms of the twin stairways that led up the walls on either side to the balcony. "Do you not recognize me? You have followed me in the village. I have seen your black shadow there. You have stalked me even in the house of my family, plaguing my nights with your Hell-born apparitions."

"I tell thee, young one, I hath not wronged thee, nor do I know thee."

"You lie! You are the Lord of Deceptions, bending men's wills with your own, leading them down a dark path. The village has become but a collection of slaves in thrall to your unholy magic."

"I possess no such power," the Baron said. "Since the Fall of Adam, Man hath needed no magic to compel him toward darkness. He doth seek it willingly enough on his own."

"You lie, I say! I have borne witness to your dark powers. I have..." Nicolai stopped, tears welling in his eyes.

"Thou art in pain," the Baron said, his voice calm and close. "Unlock thy heart. Unlock thy soul. Tell me of thy suffering."

Nicolai opened his mouth, but found himself unable to speak. The image of his beloved Katrina hung before his mind's eye just as he remembered her, flushed with the full bloom of youth.

Suddenly, as if a dam burst within him, all that had been held back behind the walls of silence spilled forth into words. "I... I met Katrina at the river's edge as I had many times before. She came there to watch the forest animals. She enjoyed watching them... I enjoyed watching her."

Nicolai stared blankly downward as he continued in a low voice. "She was so beautiful as she stood on the bank, her delicate features radiant in the sunlight, her white gown flowing in the soft breeze. Many nights I had lain awake, dreaming of making her my betrothed. That afternoon, alone by the river, I could wait no longer. I fell to my knees before her and professed my love, asking for her hand in marriage. She scoffed, thinking my proposal a jest, but when I protested that I was in earnest, she began to laugh aloud.

"I got to my feet, my face burning. She looked at me, my knees muddy, my face red, and laughed all the more. I warned her to be silent, but she would not cease.

"And then I heard a voice within me, telling me to stop her, to make her be quiet." Nicolai looked up at the Baron's calm, white face, now quite clear in the gray light. "It was your voice, the voice of the Dark Tower, looming above us. You forced me to..."

His voice trailed off and his head bowed again. The Baron said nothing. The tower hung silent around them, its terrible weight crushing down on Nicolai. At last, he went on.

"I covered Katrina's mouth with my hands. Her shrill laughter was muffled, yet it continued. The cruel pity and scorn in her eyes pierced my heart, more painful than any dagger. A darkness took hold of me, a will that was not my own. My hands slipped to her throat... and I tightened my grip, choking her laughter... and her breath.

"I plunged her head into the river and held it below the cold water. As she struggled, her frail hands grappling in vain with my arms, I watched her face change from an expression of fear, to helplessness, to an icy stare. As the frigid water numbed my hands, I feared that I might lose my grip on her throat. At last she stopped thrashing and lay still in the water. She was... no longer alive.

"I weighted her body with heavy stones and left her in deep waters. I gave no explanation when the village learned she was missing. I had no need. No one had known we were together. When she did not return, the villagers turned their suspicions toward the tower... and I remained silent. They spoke in hushed whispers that Katrina had fallen victim to the Baron.

"And they were right, I thought. I had not harmed Katrina. My hands had been the tool of your dark will, your magic..."

Tears streaked Nicolai's face as he finished his tale. He looked up at the ashen-hued countenance of the Baron, but found there neither condolence nor judgment.

"I cannot absolve thy sins," the Baron said softly, "nor will I end thy pain. It is not I who hath plagued thee. The shadows which haunt thee art of thine own conjuring, born of guilt."

Nicolai fell to his knees, his hands clenching into fists at his sides. "Am I ever to know release from this torment?"

"Thy pain is as much a part of thee as thine own heart. Every man doth carry within himself the power to conquer the darkness in his soul... or to surrender to it. This battle must be fought by thee and thee alone." The Baron's face became even more indistinct, receding into the darkness. The shadows all around Nicolai grew longer and more threatening.

Nicolai leapt up one of the winding stone staircases after the Baron, screaming furiously for him to stop. He halted midway up the stair, though, as one of the shadows detached itself from the prevailing murk of the balcony. It stood, with all the solidity of a human form, at the top of the stairs.

Nicolai stared in breathless fear at the slight silhouette before him. He watched as a foot, as pale as ancient marble, emerged from the shadows. As the apparition stepped forward into the gray light of the hall, Nicolai beheld it with awe and horror. It was Katrina, risen from her watery grave. Her hair was drenched and dripping, and her torn, waterlogged dress clung to her cadaverous form like a shroud. Rivulets of water ran silently down the marble steps toward him. With an unsteady gait, she began to descend the stairs.

"No," Nicolai rasped. He stood petrified as Katrina slowly advanced toward him, stopping one step above him. She stood silently before him, the same icy stare in her eyes as when she died. Her flesh was white and drawn tight over her bones, her lips a deep scarlet, nearly black. Her cold, penetrating eyes glistened like wet jewels. She opened her mouth and water ran like clear blood down her chin. The gurgling, gasping voice he had heard once before in his grandfather's house spoke his name.

Nicolai began to utter shrieking sobs as he retreated, nearly stumbling on the steps below him. He turned to flee the tower, but the shadows that had lain in wait all around him had now come forward from their hiding places. He could no longer see the doorway. Tall, cloaked figures had surrounded the bottom of the staircase. Nicolai screamed madly and fell back against the stairs as the avenging wraiths swarmed over him.

Nicolai was found alone along the riverbank. No one doubted that he, like his beloved Katrina, was a victim of the Dark Tower. As he knelt on the shore, gazing into the slow moving, black waters, he repeated the same verse over and over in a hoarse voice, tinged with manic laughter.

> "I am afflicted and in agony from my youth;
> I am dazed with the burden of thy dread.
> Thy wrath hath swept over me;
> thy terrors hath cut me off.
> They encompass me like water all the day;
> they close in upon me on all sides.
> Lover and friend hast thou taken from me;
> my only companion is darkness..."

In the unhallowed dead of night,

Voices echo through the empty corridors.

"Beware..."

Is it merely the murmur of the wind,

Or do the stones of this ancient keep whisper to me?

There are forces that would conspire against me,

To challenge and destroy me,

So their queen may rise again.

For she who waits below is darkness immortal.

"Beware..."

Is it merely the murmur of the wind,

Or an omen of grim things to come?

Sentinels

James Pipik and Joseph Vargo

A thin ray of daylight pierced the twilit entrance hall. The massive oak door inched slowly, soundlessly open and the hoarse croaking of ravens could be heard from outside. Torin squeezed through the narrow opening and paused, squinting in the gloom, to verify that the dim foyer was empty, then heaved back against the door. At last it closed with a dull thud and the clamor of the ravens became a muffled drone.

Torin was inside the Dark Tower.

In the sudden quiet he could hear his labored breath, the blood rushing in his ears. Remembering his long years of preparation for this day, he willed his pounding heart to calm. Ahead of him the foyer opened into a much larger chamber. He stole silently to the end of the hall and peered into the vast circular room beyond.

Hazy, mote-dappled beams of faltering light dropped from narrow windows high up along the southern wall and came to rest upon a strange twisted symbol laid into the dusty marble floor, blood-red upon black. The same indecipherable icon was wrought upon the outer doors of the keep. Torin thought it must be the perverse coat of arms of this realm.

Great columns rose along the walls up into the shadows above the window slits. On either side of him a staircase curled away and up into the darkness, but Torin turned his attention to the archway directly before him that framed the passage into the castle's depths.

Though he had journeyed far through hostile lands and treacherous terrain to reach this forsaken place, he had known no fear. But now a sense of dread took hold of him, for he knew the darkest and most perilous part of his mission lay beyond the archway he now faced.

He drew a thick candle from one of the many pockets of his cloak and lit it. He crossed the room silently, extending the candle before him, but the light seemed unable to penetrate the thick darkness that hung beneath the web-strewn archway. Down, they had told him, and so he probed forward with his foot for the first step.

A noise from above, the sound of a stone grinding heavily against another, caused Torin to hesitate. The harsh groan reverberated through the keep, sending a chill across his flesh. He leapt to the side of the arch, extinguishing the candle with a quick flick of the wrist. He stood with his back pressed against the wall, every sense alert and on edge. He gazed up into the darkness. For a long moment he heard nothing and began to wonder if the sound had been nothing more than a loose stone of this ancient structure shifting with the passing years.

And then another sound drifted down from the recesses of the shadows, echoing through the hall. It was laughter, cold and whispery.

Torin stealthily crept from shadow to shadow, skirting the pools of dim light, to the foot of one of the rising staircases. He peered up the long curve of the stair to the balcony above but saw no one.

He put his hand to his belt and slid the sleek stiletto from its sheath. Its hilt felt sure and light in his hand and the long, thin silver blade gleamed even in the tower's murky light. Torin warily made his way up the marble stairs.

Again, the laughter echoed around him. He whirled about, his dagger before him, expecting to face some fiend which had somehow crept up behind him, but found only empty shadow. The laughter died away into an unnerving silence.

Realizing that darkness held no advantage for him, Torin lit his candle once more. As he ascended to the balcony, he held it high, illuminating the upper reaches of the hall. From this vantage he could now see the sole indigenous inhabitants of the tower.

A host of grotesque stone figures peered down out of the darkness from the ledge that supported the vaulted ceiling and various niches set high in the walls. They took on many shapes and forms, some recognizable as men or beasts, some a combination of both or a strange distortion of natural forms, the invention of some mad artist's sacrilegious imagination. Men with the wings of eagles or bats mounted the ledges as if preparing to spring. In the flickering candlelight the lifeless beasts seemed to stir and writhe. Their lidless eyes, chipped and cracked, lined with dust, followed him as he stepped onto the balcony.

A voice deep and hushed, sepulchral and cruel, now spoke to him from among the gargoyles. "Abandon hope all ye who enter here."

Torin willed his trembling hand to still. No one was to be seen but the grotesques. "Who speaks?" he cried, his quivering voice betraying his fear.

"We are the sentinels, the guardians of this place. All who trespass here put their lives in our hands."

"Where are you?"

"We surround you," the voice said.

Torin looked around at the stone faces, their grins and grimaces alive in the candle light. They seemed to bend down closer to him.

"Why have you come here?" the solemn voice demanded.

Torin squared his shoulders and replied, "I seek the master of the tower, the one known as the Baron."

"What dealings would you have with him?"

Torin thought he had placed the origin of the sentinel's voice, a great winged gargoyle in the form of a man crowned by a pair of horns sweeping up from its forehead into jagged points. In the uncertain light its head seemed to incline toward him. If it were somehow imbued with life, of what use would his dagger be against stone? Yet his mission must be fulfilled.

"It is an affair of honor," Torin said.

Laughter rolled around the vaults of the ceiling as if all the stone horde found him amusing. The sentinel spoke, lightly but without mirth. "What claim have you in the name of honor?"

"The lord of this place murdered my father," Torin said, regretting his words even as they left his lips. He had been told to tell those who dwell in the tower nothing, lest they use it against him and all his order.

"You confuse honor with vengeance," the sentinel said, "for your intent is murder as well. Is that not so?"

Torin gave no reply.

"There is no honor in the taking of a man's life, only sorrow," the voice admonished.

"This thing is not a man but a fiend, a demon," Torin said, "and it must pay for its evil deeds."

"The one who slew your father, the Baron, as he was called, has answered for his sins and is no more."

Torin hesitated a moment, remembering what he had been told... *they will lie to you, tell you what you want to hear, hoping that you will drop your guard, waiting for their chance to strike.* "The Baron is dead?"

"Yes, slain by the hand of our master, Lord Brom," the sentinel said. "It is he who now holds dominion over the tower. He owes you no debt."

"It is said that the legacy of darkness is passed on to each new lord of the keep," Torin said. "Call forth your master or I shall seek him out."

"No!" The voice resounded throughout the hall, reverberating deafeningly off the hard stone. "Though Lord Brom has not fallen to the depths of the Baron, he has within him the promise to be just as deadly."

"We shall see," Torin said as he moved back toward the staircase.

Stone ground upon stone again, the grating sound seeming to come from everywhere at once, bringing Torin to a halt on the top stair. He looked up at the horned gargoyle. It seemed nearer now, leaning out toward him.

"Heed my warning," the sentinel said. "This course you pursue leads only to death... or worse."

"Worse?" Torin said. "I can imagine nothing worse than meeting my end in this grim place."

"Ah, are you truly so ignorant of the unseen world which surrounds you? Look about you. Do you not see me... and my brethren? Know this, young one, we were once mortal such as you. Like you, we were foolhardy and vain. Like you, we dared to venture uninvited into this cursed place. And when the demon drained our blood and the carrion birds picked clean our bones, our spirits were caught forever in these macabre sculptures, an endless testimony to our foolish vanity. Never again do we know rest or sleep, love or warmth. We are sentinels only, standing eternal watch over the tower."

Torin surveyed the stone guardians, their hideous guises leering out at him from every ledge and cornice and alcove. A cold sweat ran down into his eyes.

"Yes, look carefully," the sentinel continued. "Choose a form to your liking, one that portrays your nature. There are yet those among us who are mere hollow stone. Ignore my warning, and one shall doubtless house your hopeless soul for eternity."

Torin searched the vile and loathsome faces, twisted into a mockery of smiles or frozen in anguished howls or collapsing into grief, their eyes blank and unblinking, staring out forever into the void.

The sentinel went on, "If indeed your father met his end in this place, then surely his spirit is here among us. Shall we seek him out? Shall this be his legacy to you, that you would meet your fate here, as did he? Shall you stand along with him to guard this keep, side by side as stone monstrosities, till the end of time?"

Torin looked down at the dagger in his hand.

"Nay," the sentinel said quietly. "Go back out into the world of light. Leave your vengeance and hatred here within these walls where they can do you no more harm."

"You lie," Torin said simply. "Just as those who taught me warned you would."

"Those who taught you?" the stone guardian whispered, then said no more for a long moment. "Who has sent you here?"

"Those who told me of my father's fate. Those who have protected and guided me. They are powerful and wise, and their numbers grow each day. I have sworn my allegiance to them. They, too, long for vengeance."

"Who?" the sentinel demanded, the anger in its tone raising the hair on Torin's arms and neck.

"They are called the Brotherhood of the Black Dawn," Torin said, trying not to sound meek and obedient. "The Baron vanquished their queen and keeps her entombed below. I shall win justice for them, as well."

The sentinel spoke, its voice suddenly calm and somehow more chilling. "If you would conspire with this brotherhood to restore this queen of theirs, it shall be your undoing. Those who battle against the lord of the tower have all met their end."

"I shall prevail. The seer has foretold it." Torin backed slowly down the stairs.

"Armies have fallen in the same attempt, legions of mighty warriors. What hope have you?"

Halfway down the stair, Torin spun around, brandishing his dagger. "This blade was tempered at the forge of the Grande Alchemist. It is a talisman, enchanted and blessed, bestowed upon me so that I might slay the evil that dwells here."

"They have lied to you. Your blade holds no magic. Cast it down along with your hatred. Renounce this brotherhood now," the sentinel said, "or never leave this tower alive."

"I shall relinquish nothing." Torin held the dagger high in defiance of the sentinel's warning. "This blade shall spill blood."

The silence hung as if suspended in the golden globe of candlelight that surrounded him. The gargoyles stood motionless in the terrible hush.

And then a single voice spoke, not unlike that of the sentinel and yet not the same. "So be it."

From beyond the sentinel gargoyle a shadow moved. Almost too fast for Torin's eye to follow, it leapt onto the stair beside him. Though Torin tried to lash out, the thing grabbed his hand, still holding the dagger, and brought it up to his throat. Torin could not fight its strength. The blade plunged into his neck. He looked into the face of the thing before him and saw not a fearsome creature of stone but a thin, pale man. His dark eyes pierced Torin's soul, gazing down at him in sorrow. And then Torin knew no more.

The intruder's body slumped upon the stairs. His life's blood spilled from him in a crimson stream, flowing down the marble staircase. Something dropped from the intruder's cloak and fell noisily down the stairs.

Brom followed the flow of blood down the steps to the bottom, where it pooled, thick and black. A large key of brass had come to rest upon the last step. Brom picked it up and examined it. Its design was unlike any he had ever seen.

He turned his gaze upward to the gargoyles that lined the walls. They sat cold and still, and as lifeless as any other stone in this giant tomb.

Brom turned his attention back to the key. It felt strangely heavy in his hand. Whatever door it was meant to unlock, whatever purpose the intruder had intended, he knew he had thwarted the attempt. He also knew well the danger was not ended, but only averted.

Far away in a darkened room, two hooded figures sat before the dying embers of a fire.

"What do you see?" asked one, leaning forward, his eyes shining scarlet in the molten glow. "Does he possess the key?"

"Yes, my lord," the seer said.

"Now he need only use it," said the first. His lip curled in a contented sneer. "And what of Brother Torin?"

"He is lost, my lord," replied the seer.

The other figure slipped back into the comfort of cool darkness. His whispered voice spoke from the shadows, "He has served his purpose."

Death is my solitary companion.
Lost souls suffer the nights with me.
They wander and roam
the corridors and castle grounds.
Their earthly remains lie buried
beneath gravestones,
Yet their spirits know no rest.

Sorrow's End

Jalone J. Haessig

A cold, dank wind blew as Brom made his way slowly from the tower to the forbidding cemetery behind the keep. The darkness which prevailed to surround the tower in an eternal gloom would have stricken him with mortal fear, he thought ruefully, if indeed he were mortal. His life, if one could call it that, had become a constant war: a war between his own base hungers and his concept of the higher purpose of life, and a war with the perverse forces which infested this realm.

His slow steps created swirls and eddies in the ground mist which was rising among the markers of long forgotten graves. The waning moon reflected from the top of the mist, softening the outlines of the standing stones and brambles, and giving a more peaceful aspect than the dreary place had in the daylight.

The vile obscenity which lay entombed at the base of the tower had, over time, tainted the whole area. It spread in the manner of a spiritual leprosy corrupting both the body and the soul of the people and the very land itself. Yet, he wondered, was he in truth any better?

To his left rose the walls of the black chapel. The outside gave scant testimony to the strange glory that the place claimed as its own. All around the cemetery, confined within the surrounding parapet wall, were the bent and barren and desiccated trees. Trees that neither bore leaf nor fell in death, but were trapped in some eternal limbo. They offered neither

133

grace nor beauty, such as the trees of his beloved homeland, but only contributed more to the overhanging pall of this place.

Lost was he in his ruminations, when from the corner of his eye he saw, where no one should have been, a young girl, perhaps of sixteen years, dressed in a sheer, silken gown. He was stunned by the child's beauty. Her light hair, which he supposed in daylight would have been butter gold, flowed softly in the breeze. Her skin was as smooth and pale as alabaster, her form sweet to behold.

The girl stood silently gazing in rapt attention at a statue of an angel holding a large, open book. The statue itself overtowered the girl so that she had need to crane her neck to look into its face, a face both intense and stern. The statue's draped robes and folded wings held intricate detail, though verdigris covered, a testament to the sculptor's skill. The angel stood as a lector reciting from his tome of chiseled scripture, forever fated to preach his silent sermon to his congregation of lost souls. The expression on the girl's face was one of hopelessness and remorse. Her body's attitude was that of absolute surrender.

He watched her in silence, not wishing to disturb her, as the mist around his feet deepened. The girl began to move, wandering aimlessly. She seemed to be speaking, perhaps praying, yet no sounds reached him. Her distress was obvious and her torment too great for one so young. She glanced in fear over her shoulder. She gazed right at him and Brom thought perhaps it was his own grim visage that had startled her. At the next instant, however, she resumed her pacing and he realized that she saw him not at all. When he at last noted that the mist remained undisturbed at her passing, he understood that this was no live girl but some sad spectre, no matter how real she at first seemed.

Her wandering steps at last brought her to the base of

another statue, an angel with outstretched arms. With one last plaintive and pleading look, the girl made a quick motion toward her breast, then collapsed, her arms about the base of the statue.

Brom moved toward the girl and, though he knew she was without substance, made to touch her shoulder. His hand passed through the girl with less resistance than passing through smoke. As he watched, she faded from his sight.

One heartbeat later, she reappeared at the statue of the tome-holding angel and began again her tortuous rounds of the graveyard. Brom's curiosity was engaged and he wondered what turn of events had caused the girl to be eternally denied the peace of those who had been buried in the once consecrated ground. It might be too late for her poor revenant spirit, but perhaps her tale might provide some insight to the mysteries of the tower, perhaps even some clue to his own salvation. Someone, he was certain, knew the tale, for such things never truly passed from human knowledge. He determined that he should know it as well.

The night grew darker still as clouds began to obscure what little moonlight there was. The ground mist began to sink and the wind picked up, whistling through the bony fingers of the barren trees. From above him came the muted cry of some night predator. Brom turned and made his way slowly back toward the Dark Tower.

Rain lashed the walls of the keep. The skies were illuminated by the lightning slashes as Brom leaned against the bookcase watching the old woman seated at the long table. She twisted and untwisted the scarf around her shoulders, glancing at him. It seemed that her curiosity about the Lord of the Dark Tower had not entirely overcome her fear and trepidation at having been summoned here. The candle on the table guttered in the drafty room, threatening to extinguish itself at any moment.

The woman fingered the goblet of wine at her hand. Brom

nearly smiled as he watched, thinking that she was surely afraid to eat or drink of anything in this place. He could tell that she wished she had run as far as possible before even accepting the thought of his summons. Yet here she was, sitting at Lord Brom's table, while the storm tore and raged outside. She was the oldest of her clan, so old that even she at times forgot how many years she bore. Her skin so deeply creased by time and her face so thin that she had the look of an aged reptile. He wondered if the children shied away from her and adults only came near when they had no other choice. He knew, for he had been told, that she lived for the most part undisturbed in her small hovel, giving fortunes out to good wives wanting to know the nature of their unborn children.

Now this. What must she be thinking? The woman stared at the candle as if gathering her memories. Brom quietly cleared his throat wishing that she would get on with the tale. Night was passing by swiftly.

The woman looked up fearfully. "Her name..." and she faltered. Her voice was rusty and harsh from long periods of disuse. She dared to take a small sip of the wine, then began again.

"Her name was Maeve and she was said to be the most beautiful girl ever to have been born in Vasaria. She was the jewel of her parent's eyes and the pet of all the people in the village. They would touch her golden hair and she would smile. She was beautiful and, by no choosing of her own, the villagers spoiled her terribly. Maeve had only to want a thing and it was given to her, just to see her smile. She was not a bad girl. In fact, she was quite a simple soul. She was happy and cheerful. The problem was that she grew believing that whatever she wanted she should have. That, of course, was the cause of her undoing. Better she should have been homely and wise to the ways of wickedness.

"In truth, the villagers were as much at fault in her fate as

Maeve herself. She is the one, however, who now pays the price for her mistakes. I believe that the villagers in their own guilt and shame have banished her from their memories so they will not have to shoulder their share of it.

"It was many years ago, a time when the darkness that eventually took hold of this realm began to stir and venture from the confines of the tower. Maeve had begun to blossom into a woman and her parents discussed the possibilities of matrimony for their beautiful, young daughter..."

"Our child has come of age," Maeve's mother spoke from the hearth of their small home. Her husband sat at the table finishing the last of his stew.

"Yes, wife, and what of it?" The man smiled softly at his wife of many years, already knowing what it was she had hemmed and hawed about all through the meal.

She smoothed her skirts, then ran a hand through her hair. "It is time that we begin to consider prospective husbands for our little girl, dear one."

"What say you, Ester, she is but a girl!" The man pretended to rage, then smiled once more. "Who would you have cast your eyes on for our daughter, then?" He rested his elbows on the table and tented his hands, regarding his wife over the tops of his fingertips. "That is, if you have had time to think on this matter."

"Well," Ester began slowly, "we have little to offer as dowry for her, Joseff. That does limit her somewhat."

Joseff rested his cheek on one palm. "I have done the best I could, wife."

Ester crossed the room to place a hand on his arm. "Of course you have, dear heart, but it is a fact of life."

"Well then, on with it. Who would you have take our sweet, beautiful girl?" Ester sat beside her husband and took his hand.

Outside, waiting by the window, having just returned with water from the village well, stood Maeve herself. She knew that she should not be eavesdropping on this conversation between her parents, but then, since it did concern her, perhaps it would be forgiven. She fantasized about who it could be that had caught her mother's eye. Her mind wandered through the possibilities. A count, perhaps? An earl? She mused for several moments, then was brought back to reality as if with a slap. What had she just heard?

"Wilhelm, the son of Franz? Well, he is a good man, I am told; more gentle than his father, they say, very caring and he is only a few years older than our little Maeve. I think you have chosen wisely, my good wife. Also, she will be farther away from the accursed castle. I will go to see Franz on the morrow and see what he would have to say on this matter." Joseff placed a burly arm about his wife's shoulders. "Fear not, loved one, I am sure this will please him. Even though our prize cannot bake a decent loaf."

Ester gasped at her husband's remark. "Joseff, that is not so!"

The man laughed. "Nonsense, wife, it is! Why the last one, I use to hold the door open."

Ester shook her head, laughing quietly. "For shame, husband."

Outside, Maeve was dumbstruck. Wilhelm! In truth he was a fine youth, fair to look on. She had seen him many a time. He always seemed to be where she was and smiled shyly at her. Still, a farmer's wife! The mere thought of a life filled with hard labor and toil made her cringe, for Maeve was vain about her looks. And why not? Since her birth, it seemed, they had been remarked upon. The voices came to her: *"Maeve is such a beautiful child." "Maeve has such fair and silky hair." "Maeve is so dainty and delicate." "Why, her skin is as smooth as cream."*

She could imagine it all now, in the future it would be: *"Poor Maeve, do you not remember her in her youth, such a lovely girl she was."* *"Poor Maeve, she had such fine skin, now the harsh field work has all but robbed her of her beauty."*

Maeve dashed a tear away. This could not be! Dropping the water bucket, the water puddling at her feet, she ran from the house and back into the village. She needed to find her friend Heather and tell her of all this.

Maeve found Heather sitting by the village well tending her youngest brother. There were numerous folk wandering about, including a fellow from the tower, whom Maeve steered clear of, giving him a suspicious glance in her passing. She sat beside her friend and began telling her of the decision that her parents had made, never noticing that the man had moved close enough to overhear their conversation.

At first, Heather lent a compassionate ear to her friend's predicament, but soon grew angry that Maeve seemed to consider herself too good for the son of a farmer.

"Honestly, Maeve, I do not see your problem. What could be wrong in having a good man and raising his children? It seems to me that you place yourself a little too high." She rose and looked at the girl. The lowering sun made her golden indeed. She shook her head and called to her brother, then she turned to Maeve once more. "Perhaps, if you are too mighty for the young Wilhelm, I will ask my parents if he would be interested in me." She cocked her head. "Though of course, being offered you, I will all but disappear in his eyes." Taking the little boy by the hand, she walked toward her home.

Maeve sat in dejected silence. It would seem that not only did Heather not understand, but now she even resented Maeve for feeling as she did. There was nothing for her to do, it seemed, but to return home to face her fate.

The man waited until the girl left to make her way home, then rushed as fast as possible toward the tower and his dark obsession, the queen.

Mara sat and listened to the man as he relayed, in great

detail, all he had overheard. She reclined in the high-backed throne, her chin resting on her hand as she lazily watched him tell his tale. One long fingernail gently stroked the soft skin beneath her chin as he spoke and she considered how best to use this information.

Since Maeve's birth, the Dark Queen had been somewhat jealous of her. There was no reason, save the fact that the child was beautiful and the village pet. The child was a woman now and as simple and innocent as she was, it would seem that her own vanity was beginning to surface. How delicious, she thought, to take that innocence and corrupt it completely. She laughed deep in her throat, her mouth opening to show long incisors.

"You have done well, Dravek. Come closer." Her voice was pure seduction to him. She beckoned him forth and he came with the obedience of a whipped pup.

Dravek knelt before her, his eyes alight with desire. With one hand she lightly stroked his face and felt his quivering need, her eyes gleamed ferally. With the other hand she extended one long fingernail and opened a vein at the wrist of the hand caressing his face. He turned his mouth to it and began to drink, making small groans of ecstasy as he gave himself over to the dark. The queen smiled slyly and began to conjure grim notions.

The next day, Maeve was to meet Wilhelm for the first time, that is to say, to be formally introduced to him and his family that they might begin courting. She sighed as she walked to the well, casting about for any way to avoid this. It was not that he was not nice enough, nor handsome enough, he was all of that. He would have lands of his own, that was true. Still, there had to be someone who would not only appreciate her, but try to keep her from fading like the last flowers of summer. For, she admitted deep down, aside from her looks, there was little of substance to the girl named

Maeve. Her father's jests about her cooking were not far from the truth. The things that she made were only half-edible, at best. Her needlecraft was just passable. Her mother said that she would learn these things in time, but Maeve was uncertain that was true. It was true that she was as kind as she knew how to be and that she always tried to be gentle and as helpful as she could. It was simply that she would begin to daydream about being carried off by some handsome knight or prince and the bread would burn or the needle slip. She shook her head; there would be no further need of daydreams from now on.

Evening had fallen by the time Maeve had finished her chores. Her final task brought her again to the well. Sitting at the well's lip was a girl whom Maeve had never before seen. The girl's face was shrouded beneath the hood of a scarlet cloak. She drew back the hood to reveal dark hair and bright eyes. She was not unpleasant looking, though a bit pale. She offered a slight smile and Maeve returned it. "Hello," Maeve said to the girl. "I have not seen you here before."

"Because, no doubt," the girl answered, "I have just come to the village. I know no one here. Who are you?"

She smiled warmly at the girl who seemed to be her own age. "I am called Maeve, so now you do know someone."

The girl laughed. "So it would seem I do. My name is Angelica. Tell me, if I am not prying, why it was that you seemed so sad as you were walking."

Maeve had no reason for confiding in this girl whom she had only just met, yet it seemed that she felt compelled to do so. It felt good to tell another person, one who did not judge her and seemed to understand her deepest feelings.

"But that is terrible," Angelica said after hearing the tale. Her voice was soft and gentle and Maeve felt better by simply listening to her. "Forgive me for seeming forward, but to think of you as a farmer's wife is inconceivable. Although, he perhaps has..." and the girl winked at Maeve, "...some other 'saving' graces."

"I am not certain that I understand your meaning," Maeve said in puzzlement. She looked at the girl curiously.

"Oh," Angelica laughed, "I meant nothing at all. So tell me, what other man would you have then, young Maeve?"

"Oh, someone who would treat me like a lady, who would not expect me to toil in fields beside him, perhaps someone who would have servants to wait upon him and me, of course." Maeve blushed. "Daydreams."

Angelica looked at her. "Perhaps, perhaps not. Oh, you probably would never be a queen, but there are others who might do. What of, oh, let us say, the innkeeper? I have seen him here and there. He isn't unpleasant to look upon. He seems quite capable to satisfy."

As Angelica continued speaking, Maeve sank further and further into the rhythm of her speech and her soft, seductive voice.

Maeve seemed to come to herself again as she listened to Angelica go on about the innkeeper's potential prowess. She blushed deep red. It was all too true. The innkeeper, Eban, was quite pleasant to look upon. He was tall with hair the color of wheat and eyes deep green. He was muscular and had ofttimes played the prince in some of her fantasies. Sometimes, when she went to the inn to collect her father, she saw Eban watching her. As she grew older and her body had filled out, his attentions became more evident. Sometimes he would hold her gaze too long to be comfortable and she had to look away as a strange heat enveloped her.

She shook herself. "But this is foolishness. Besides, he is married to Ilsbeth."

"Wives can be put aside, for one reason or another. Things can happen. I doubt that he would reject you. Perhaps he hungers for you as well."

Maeve looked at the girl, aghast. "I... I could never... why that would be..." she stopped, at a loss for words. "This is a terrible thing which you suggest."

Angelica laughed. "My dear Maeve, you and I are very different. I would go after what I want. If I did not want to be a farmer's wife, I would surely do something to change that." She touched Maeve's arm, sending a chill through her. "Were I you, I would get those dainty hands strengthened up. You will be doing a lot of milking with them. Not to mention threshing wheat and wielding a hoe and..."

Maeve stood up, suddenly aware that the sun had long since gone down. "I must go, the sun has set. You should go as well. It is not... safe... here after dark."

Angelica laughed lightly. "Oh, do not be such a goose, Maeve. I do not fear the dark, nor anything that goes about in it."

"You would be wise to start, Angelica. I must go."

"Wait," Angelica called to the departing of her new friend. "Think on what I have said, Maeve, before it is too late."

Maeve did not answer, but hurried on toward the light of her home.

Later that night, Maeve tossed in restlessness, drifting in and out of sleep. She lay in a bed not her own, her nightclothes in a state of disarray, and leaning over her was the face and figure of Eban. He smiled and touched her in a way that set her body on fire. He whispered endearments to her as he caressed her body, and her body responded to him. It arched toward him of its own accord as he lowered his head to her...

Maeve awoke with a start. Never had she experienced such a dream as this.

Shame filled her. She felt her face flush with embarrassment and quickly crossed herself, saying a brief prayer for forgiveness. What is happening to me, she thought in terror. Have I lost my mind? Not only to have these thoughts when I am unmarried woman, but to have these thoughts about a married man! Surely her very soul was in peril, and yet she thought about the touch of those imaginary hands and the way they had made her feel. She yearned for that feeling again. Why had she never thought of Eban before in this way? Was it a real feeling, she wondered, or was she simply trying to find a way out the courtship her parents planned for her? Thus she spent the remainder of the night, caught between a burning desire that she had never known and the shame that she should feel it at all.

The meeting with Wilhelm's family had gone quite well, though they had remarked upon the dark circles under the girl's eyes on the way to their home. They thought that perhaps it was merely because Maeve had found herself sleepless with the excitement of this new time in her life.

For the next few days, Maeve continued to see Angelica in the evening by the well. They sat and spoke for long hours. Though Maeve listened intently, she could never seem to fully recall their conversations afterward.

Every night, her sleep continued to be tormented by feelings that both repulsed and enticed her. She awoke from these dreams, sweat-covered and shaking, both from fear and desire. During the days, she began to position herself, however subtly, so that she was bound to encounter Eban, or even brush up against him accidentally as he went about his business.

Unconsciously, she found herself flirting with the man and was aware that he returned her attentions, though perhaps not to the extent that she needed and wanted. Her frustration revealed itself to those who would look closely. Her skin lost its glow and her eyes their shine. They may have wondered about this strange transformation, and yet none thought to speak of it, either to the girl or her parents.

Young Wilhelm came to see Maeve as often as he could in the afternoons after his own work was done. Always he would bring some small token to her, little wildflowers that he had picked on the way, or once, a nest of stones shaped like bird's eggs. For her part, Maeve accepted these things graciously and attempted to listen as Wilhelm told her amusing tales of things that had happened to him during the day, but even as she sat with him, she found herself sinking further and further into an obsession that she could not explain.

It was only a matter of time, she knew, before Wilhelm would ask her parents for permission to wed, and Maeve was now nearly mad with frustration and fear, as well as a longing for Eban. She sought Angelica out one last evening.

"I know not what I must do!" she wailed. "I have barely control of myself during the day and I have none at all during the night."

Angelica patted the girl's shoulder sympathetically. "Ah, poor Maeve, at last you have come upon a thing which even you may not have." There was an undertone of amusement in the other girl's voice and Maeve turned to her angrily.

"I thought that you were my friend," she said bitterly. "Was it not you who suggested that perhaps Eban might be the perfect match for me? I see him. I all but throw myself at him, and while he is kind and returns some interest, he still goes to Ilsbeth at night and shares her bed. What must I do? I fear for my very sanity."

Angelica was silent for a space of time, then turned to the hapless girl. Maeve saw not the hungry look in the other girl's face, for if she had, she might have run away in fright. "There may still be a way, but you must take the next steps on your own."

"What do you mean, Angelica?" Maeve turned her face to her at last.

"There is a wise old woman who lives back in the woods. An old hovel she has and a raven sits upon the roof always. She can help you in your plight. She knows many an arcane thing. She could make a potion for you that would make you irresistible to any man, even our good innkeeper. Also, you must take one gold coin, since that is the price of the old woman's knowledge."

Maeve was speechless in her horror; this was too much. "A witch, you mean? How could you suggest such a thing to me? What manner of person are you, Angelica?"

Angelica laughed, "Oh Maeve, you are a priceless gem. You know in your heart what I am." She then began to speak to the girl softly, so softly that Maeve could scarcely understand the words, they buzzed about her head like flies and she felt herself growing drowsy with the effort. Finally, she focused again on Angelica's words, hearing her say, "After all, it is what you want, is it not?" Maeve nodded sleepily at her.

"So, you understand the directions to the old woman's house?"

"Yes, but I wish you would come with me," Maeve sulked. "It is not safe to be out late beyond dusk, nor to venture into the dark woods."

"Is not a thing worth having also worth great risk?" Angelica answered testily. "Now hurry, you must go tonight... and do not forget the coin."

Maeve nodded, and with that Angelica said no more.

Maeve hurried home. She waited until her parents had fallen asleep, then during the darkest hour of the night, with only a candle to light her actions, Maeve crept to her dowry chest. She ran a hand lovingly across the top, thinking of how her father had hand-carved the chest for her when she was born. She opened the lid and hesitantly withdrew one gold piece. The box contained such a meager amount that it saddened her to take even one coin, for what little there was had been painstakingly gathered by her parents. With coin and candle, she snuck out into the night and made her way to the forest path, then ventured into the ominous and forbidden woods.

The farther Maeve wandered into the woods, the more oppressive they became. The very air seemed to press against her on all sides, making it difficult to breathe. Soon the forest canopy all but blotted out the stars in the sky above. Maeve stopped for a moment to get her bearings, unable to shake the feeling that something dogged her steps. She noticed the absolute silence, not a nightbird's call, not a cricket's chirp. There was no sound but the hammering of her own heart. The trees here grew close to the path and appeared to lean in toward the girl, as if to grasp her. They looked unhealthy and frightening. Suddenly, there came the caw of a raven and Maeve jumped, the hair on the nape of her neck rising. She hurried on and found the old woman's house. True to Angelica's word, she saw the raven perched on the thatched roof. The bird was black as pitch, save for its eyes which gleamed a strange red. Maeve drew her shawl more closely about her and called a hello at the half-open door. A hoarse voice from inside bid her to enter.

The old woman inside may have been the oldest person that she had ever set eyes upon. The face beneath the scarf was a mass of wrinkles, and the eyes had a vaguely familiar aspect to them.

"Ah... Maeve, so you have come at last," the old woman croaked. With one hand she idly stroked an old black cat. Maeve guessed the cat was blind, for its eyes had a milky sheen and it seemed not to notice her.

"You... you know me?" Maeve stood shaking in the presence of the old woman.

The woman let go a cackling laugh. "Precious, everyone in the village and about the village knows of you. So, at last there is a thing you want from old Mother Aram."

Maeve told the woman the story of her needs and the woman smiled, bearing teeth long and yellowed. She then held out a small pouch to Maeve. "Take this then, little Maeve, mix it with a drop of your own blood, then merely put it in the food or drink of the one you desire and he will be yours forever."

Maeve slid the coin across the table to the woman, not wanting to touch the parchment-like skin of her hand. The woman brought the coin to her mouth and with the tip of her tongue tasted of it. Maeve turned away in disgust.

"What of Ilsbeth, Mother Aram?"

The old woman stared at the girl and Maeve felt as if all of her secrets were being revealed. Then Mother Aram smiled at her. "Fear not, you shall have exactly what you deserve."

The old woman watched from the doorway until Maeve had disappeared into the forest, then quickly followed her down the forest path.

Angelica burst through the front door of the inn, causing Ilsbeth, the innkeeper's wife, to look up from the table she was serving. The younger girl approached the woman. Ilsbeth was much taller than the girl and quite a handsome woman with coal black hair and lively brown eyes. Those eyes were now fastened on the girl coming in from the gathering dusk.

"May I be of assistance?" Ilsbeth looked at the girl curiously. She had seen her in the evenings talking with young Maeve. They sat huddled together for hours it seemed. Seeing the girl up close, there was something quite familiar about her, but Ilsbeth was at a loss to put her finger on it.

"Ah, Goodwife, have you seen Maeve about?"

"Maeve? No, not this evening. I am surprised that you and she are not at your usual spot. Tell me, how does the courtship between Maeve and Wilhelm progress?"

Angelica smiled slyly. "Well, let us say that young Wilhelm is not the only iron in Maeve's forge."

Ilsbeth's brows drew together in concern. "What are you saying? Is there another who would court our village beauty?"

Angelica smiled at the woman. "I would be very surprised, good wife, if Maeve would be content ever to be a farmer's wife. What Maeve wants, Maeve will more than likely have."

She fixed Ilsbeth with a knowing look that chilled the older woman's core. "One way or the other." With that, Angelica turned and sailed out the door leaving Ilsbeth to ponder over what she had said.

Ilsbeth was leaning into the kitchen door when, from the corner of her eye, she saw Maeve herself enter the inn. The girl had a wild and wanton look about her. Her face was flushed, her eyes glittered and sparkled. Every male eye in the room turned to catch glimpse of her and none more quickly than Ilsbeth's own husband. He turned, watching the girl over the rim of his tankard. Maeve seemed to be looking at everyone, but Ilsbeth noticed that the girl's eyes strayed again and again to Eban's face. Watching her, Ilsbeth's eyes narrowed to slits.

Ilsbeth looked from the girl's face to her husband's and back. She was unsure of just what was transpiring here, but Angelica's words echoed in her brain: *One way or the other... what Maeve wants, Maeve will have.* She decided that she would see just what would happen if she were to move to a spot where Maeve and Eban could not see her, but where she could watch them.

From behind a hanging curtain, Ilsbeth watched as the girl approached Eban standing behind the counter. The girl raised herself on her tiptoes to lean across the board, tilting herself forward so that Eban had a clear view down the bodice of her blouse. Ilsbeth was shocked at this strange behavior from a girl who had always seemed so modest. Still, she remained hidden, watching as the scene played out.

Eban surely was not immune to this young girl's charms, though for the life of him, he was in the dark as to why of late she should be approaching him so brazenly. Still, she was beautiful, her body full and lush and bursting with the juices of youth. Were it not for his loving wife... he chuckled to himself. There were times, in the last week or so, as he lay in bed with Ilsbeth, that his mind wandered. It was not his wife's dear face he envisioned, but that of the wondrous creature he saw before him now.

Eban smiled slowly and leaned his own body closer to Maeve, affording himself an even better view of the soft curves of her breasts. "Now then, Maeve dear, what can I do for you?"

Maeve cast her eyes about the room as if looking for someone. "My mother sent me to see if Father might be here with Wilhelm, but I see they are not." She pouted prettily.

Eban reached out a hand to touch her chin, then quickly drew it back. "No, they are not here, nor should you be, Maeve. You know that it is not safe to be going about in the dark. Shall I get someone to see you safely home?"

She smiled coyly and lowered her voice. "I fear you are the only man with whom I would truly feel safe."

Eban blushed slightly and cleared his throat. He looked about to see if his wife had noticed Maeve's brazen behavior. "Let me see who I might find to escort you home." He quickly walked off, leaving his ale sitting before Maeve.

As Ilsbeth watched, Maeve subtly brought her hand to the bodice of her dress and withdrew a small cloth pouch. The pouch was still warm from where it had nestled between her breasts. She was amazed that, as closely as Eban had looked at her, he had not seen it there. Maeve's hand was shaking so badly that she feared she would drop the pouch and spill the contents that she had so painstakingly come by. Her finger still hurt where she had pricked it to mix the contents with her own blood. She had need to act quickly before Eban found someone to see her home. If only there would be some diversion to mask her actions. She hid the pouch in her sleeve, anxious to be done with this. Her eyes darted about, watching, waiting.

Just then, a raven came to perch upon the window ledge of the inn. It stretched out its ebony-feathered wings and let out an unsettling croak. Its eyes seemed to glow a burning red. All attention was drawn to the ominous bird. It had to be now. Maeve slowly reached out to empty the pouch into Eban's drink.

A hand came down hard and fast on her arm.

"What do you think you are doing, girl?"

Maeve looked up into the outraged and stormy eyes of the innkeeper's wife.

"Ilsbeth! Nothing, I swear!" Maeve began to tremble and tried to wriggle her wrist free from Ilsbeth's firm grasp.

"Nothing is it?" The woman turned the girl's hand over, prying her fingers apart. The pouch fell to the floor. The white powder, now tainted a rosy pink, spilled out onto the boards. Ilsbeth's breath escaped in a hiss. "What is this, then? Poison?"

"No, I would never... I swear before God it is not!" The girl struggled to free herself to no avail. "Release me!"

"No, what is this? Tell me." Ilsbeth began to shake the girl. "If not poison, then what?" Her voice grew louder attracting attention. "Is it some sort of spell? Do you think I have no eyes? I see how you are. You are a witch!"

"No!" Maeve shrieked. With one last burst of effort, she tore free of Ilsbeth's grasp. Like the wind, she ran to the door of the inn and escaped into the night.

Ilsbeth's voice rang out, "Maeve would try to cast a spell on my good husband. She has turned to the dark magics of the tower. Find her! She has become a witch!" She held up the pouch for all to see. "Here is the proof!"

The patrons of the inn erupted into the night, following the distraught girl. Their cries alerted more villagers who spilled into the square to join the hunt.

As a single body, the crowd made its way to Maeve's home. They stood outside clamoring for her parents to surrender their precious child.

"What is this you are saying?" Joseff cried from the doorway. Ester stood behind him, twisting her apron in her hands. "Have you all gone mad? This is Maeve you are speaking of."

Eban stepped forward. "Joseff, we have proof, Ilsbeth caught the girl making to put some potion or other into my ale. And for myself, of late I am bewitched when she is around. Yes. It is witchcraft pure and simple."

Ester standing behind her husband began to wail. "But why? For what reason would she do this? I cannot believe what you are saying. Not Maeve!"

Eban placed a hand on Joseff's arm. "I am sorry, my friend, but if she is here, we will have her."

Joseff shook the man's hand off. "She is not here. I know not where she might be. Even if she were, I would never give my beautiful child to such a mob as I see before me."

A voice called out of the darkness, "They hide the girl! Perhaps, they are all witches! Take them as well."

Eban turned, stretching out his hands to the mob. "No!" His voice raised over the angry muttering. "First, we must find the girl. If her parents share a part in this, there are ways to make her confess to their guilt. We need to divide into groups to see if we can find her trail. Then we shall see what we shall see."

Maeve ran blindly as the cries of the mob followed her down the forest paths. Soon they were lost behind her and she slowed her pace to determine where she was.

Maeve paused, breasts heaving, gasping for air, yet fearing to tarry too long. God above, she thought, what had she done? What had possessed her to behave in this way? She looked around her.

She realized that in her panic she had been climbing steadily. Now the dark woods surrounded her and she was hopelessly lost. She could not go back down, for even now the voices of the angry villagers were being carried to her on the rising wind. Worse yet, the ground mists were rising, obscuring her footing. Alone and afraid, she leaned against a tree and wept.

Her brief reprieve was interrupted by the sound of a fallen

branch snapping beneath a foot. Frightened to her soul, she pushed away from the tree to bolt again, when she heard a now familiar voice, "Maeve, do not flee, not that way!"

Maeve inhaled a shaky breath as Angelica stepped from the fog. "Angelica? But how?"

The girl gave a soft laugh. "The villagers stumble over their own feet so badly they could not track a mad boar. I, on the other hand, saw you run and simply followed." She paused and listened as the distant clamor of the village mob grew louder. "They are coming. We must go."

Sure enough, in the distance Maeve thought she saw the flicker of a torch. She moaned softly and turned to Angelica. "Where... where can I go?"

Angelica took her hand and once more a chill passed through Maeve. "Come with me, I know a place." With Angelica leading, they fought their way through the forest and even further up the mountain.

When she thought she could not lift her foot one more step, Maeve stumbled, falling upon hands and knees. Beneath her were rough stone cobbles. Slowly, she raised her head and through the mist, beheld the Dark Tower.

Her voice all but stolen, she whispered, "No, oh no, Angelica, we must not go there. We must get away from here, the queen, oh God, we are doomed!"

"Nonsense," the girl said, helping her to her feet. "Do not be foolish. She is not at all what you imagine her to be. She will help you. She would not let the villagers have you. She understands."

Maeve looked at her, unbelieving. "Are you mad?" She turned to go down the mountain. "She will kill us, then drink our blood for her feast."

Angelica slowly shook her head. "I know her. I give you my solemn oath, she will not harm you. She will not touch one hair of your head."

In the distance, too close for their own comfort to the tower, more and more torches lit the night. "Decide now," Angelica hissed into her ear. "If they do not tear you limb from limb, they will burn you for a witch. The queen will take care of you."

Maeve looked from the torches to the tower and back again. Her body shook in tremors of fear.

Together, the two began to walk toward the tower. They passed a gateway to one side of the path, which seemed to stand as a territorial boundary to the castle grounds. Maeve noted the watchtowers rising from the corners of the castle as it seemed to loom over her. The stone, ancient before she was born, did not reflect the moonlight but seemed to absorb it, gathering darkness to itself. High above, horrid beasts of stone leered down upon all who approached. Their chiseled faces stilled her steps for a second as they took on the appearance of a macabre jury, casting their judgement down upon her for the charges of witchcraft. Angelica tugged at her sleeve. They climbed the wide stone steps toward the heavy doors. Angelica went to the door and put her weight to it. Slowly, it opened enough for the two to pass.

Maeve paused before crossing the threshold. "Do you swear she will not kill me?" Her voice was barely a whisper.

"On my oath, she will not touch you." Angelica turned and stepped within.

Maeve followed. She was barely aware of the hall through which Angelica led her. Huge columns rose high, disappearing into the vast darkness above and staircases clung to the walls around her. Maeve became more disoriented with each step she took. Everywhere it seemed, there were the awful leering faces of stone. She brushed cobwebs from her face. Her trembling threatened to take her legs from her. She thought her heart would surely stop here within this stygian blackness.

At last they came to another archway where two doors

stood with great rings in them.

"Go through here, young Maeve. I must leave you for a time."

Maeve turned to her, grasping at her sleeve. "No, do not leave me here alone."

Angelica smiled and said, "Fear not," then pattered off into the depths of the castle.

Maeve opened the door and entered a chapel, though unlike any she had seen. Candles were lit, but they did little to illuminate the black marble. It was oppressive and frightening. Maeve tried to find a way out. She stumbled about and at last came upon another door. She exited the chapel and found herself in the keep's graveyard.

The night mist crept between the statues and gravestones. Maeve wandered throughout the cemetery, studying the markers and chiseled effigies, until she came upon a statue of an angel holding an open book. She dropped to her knees, gazing up at the face of this long ago guardian. From behind her came a voice, soft and lurid, "Welcome, sweet child."

Maeve rose and whirled to come face to face with the Dark Queen, Mara herself. Draped in black velvet, an ebony crown upon her head, Mara's austere presence caused the girl to gasp in horror. The queen's dark eyes glistened and seethed with malevolence. The mist seemed to part before her as she stepped toward Maeve.

"Oh, dear God, save me," Maeve whispered.

The Dark Queen laughed, the sound turning Maeve's pounding blood to ice. "Dear little Maeve, your prayers fall on deaf ears." She laughed again, though quietly. "My, but you have been a busy little one, have you not? Think, Maeve. You have tempted a man to break his marriage vows, you have lied, you have stolen..." She paused to hold up, for Maeve to see, a small gold coin. "Let us see... committed witchery, allowed your own vanity to overcome your reason, such little as you

may have ever had, and... oh yes, consorted with the most
unholy of the unholy."

"No, I never... what do you mean?"

"No, I never," the queen mimicked. As she spoke, she
changed.

Maeve gazed in disbelief as the queen's features shifted to
become Angelica. She watched in horror as Angelica grew old
and withered before her very eyes to become Mother Aram.

The old hag cackled, then her years fell away as she
returned to the regal form of the Dark Queen. "You have
amused me, little Maeve, but I fear that our time is now over.
The villagers are coming for you and I think that I will give
you to them. I grow bored with you."

"You deceived me!" Maeve cried.

"Only because you allowed me to do so. I all but told you
who I was. It is not my fault that you did not listen."

"You lied to me. You said you would not hurt me." She
stared at the small but dangerous dagger that had appeared in
the queen's hand.

"And I will not. I told you that you would have just what
you deserved and so you shall." She held out the dagger,
offering it to Maeve, then turned her head to listen. "They
come. You do know how they deal with witches and those who
practice the arts, do you not? Before they are done, you will
swear that your mother and father instructed you in the black
arts and you will all burn. I think you know now what must be
done."

With that, Mara was gone. It was as if she had not been
there at all, save that Maeve now held the dagger in her hand.
Although the walls of the castle were thick, she thought she
could hear the voices shouting her name. As Maeve paced
between the monuments, the blade dangled from her listless
grip. She imagined she could smell the pitch of the torches.
She knew that salvation was now denied her even though it

truly was not her fault. She had been tricked. The vile one was right, however, they would not be content to simply put her to the stake. They would implicate her mother and father and any others they might want her to name.

She made her way to stand before another angel. This statue stood with arms outstretched, yet seemed to offer no solace. She gazed at its stony, unforgiving countenance long and long, until at last she plunged the dagger deep into her own heart. Her body was found at the foot of the statue, her arms still embracing the angel's robes.

Brom leaned against the balcony, staring out into the night. "So, it is Maeve that I have seen roaming through the mist and the moonlight, cursed to wander eternally, never knowing surcease from the pain of damnation, all because she was vulnerable and open to deception for one instant of her life." He slowly shook his head.

"Yes, it would be she, though there are many others as well. Sometimes they share their tales to those who would listen. The dead do not rest easily here, my lord, nor do they find their sorrow's end."

Brom turned to look at the old woman, "No, they do not..." He stopped. As he watched, the old woman's form shimmered in the firelight, then she smiled wryly at him and was gone.

Around the ancient, craggy tower,
spirits swirl like pale moths
drawn to a dark and unseen flame
that flickers still so deep within these walls.
Wispy wanderers of the night, disembodied souls,
phantom messengers from otherworldly shores.
These apparitions seek always
something from the living,
crying out for vengeance or justice
so that they may know eternal rest.
No longer bound in flesh,
but unfulfilled desires made visible.
Mere shadows left behind, unquiet,
unable to forget the memories
of their own untimely death and fall.
Whether wrathful or pitiful,
they appear most clearly
to the guilty, lost and lonely.

Noctem Aeternus

ROBERT MICHAELS

Brom stood silently before Rianna's grave, bitterly cold and lonely, still remembering the lingering moment that they shared in their last kiss. Rianna was several years gone now. Her precarious moment of immortality ended on the point of Brom's own blade. She had been spared one immortality to preserve her claim on the other. He tossed the long, black cloak from his shoulders and ran his fingers across the cold granite of Rianna's gravestone. If only he could hold her in his arms once more.

It was a night for ghosts in the bleak field of stone monuments that was the graveyard of the tower. Brom brushed strands of his long hair back from his pale, thin face and looked out across the cemetery. The spectres that haunted the lands around the Dark Tower arose like tendrils of fog swirling in the crisp night air. When the insatiable need for blood welled within him, it seemed to intensify his sense of these lost souls, and the ghosts appeared to him with clarity as they roamed the castle grounds in their futile quests for what might end their plight.

Brom turned his attention from the grave of his beloved to one of the tower haunts. He had caught faint glimpses of this unknown spectre many nights before, however, tonight she appeared to him in sharp focus. She sat beneath the arch of a mausoleum gate, the words *Noctem Aeternus* inscribed

into the stone above. In her hands, the ghost held a book, which she read from with rapt attention.

She had been a lovely woman when she had died. Although she was little more than a pale, gray trick of the light now, the suggestion of what had been was still strong in her and Brom remembered the fires of flesh well enough to know that this woman would have inspired them.

A large cross adorned the wrought iron bars of the gate, and stone figures of winged angels were carved into the pillars that supported the arch. One angel stood tranquil and serene, the word *Somnus* inscribed below its feet. The other was cast in the likeness of the angel of death, and below this statue the word *Mortem* was chiseled. Sleep and death, Brom thought, were luxuries that neither he nor this lost soul would know. She sat before the gate and slowly devoured the words written upon the pages of her book. Brom approached her cautiously, wary of the darkness that was locked away beyond the gate.

She glanced up and looked at the keep, and Brom turned to follow her gaze. When he turned back, she was gone. Her book, though, rested against the stone angel, the one which stood to represent sleep. It had obviously been set aside with some care and Brom found himself drawn to it. He stood in the shadow of the arch and hesitated for a moment, then leaned down and snatched up the book.

It was a real book and not some extension of her apparition. Yet, she could hold open its heavy cover and turn its vellum pages, when all else of the world was denied her touch. Casting a wary eye to the east where gray was starting to gather at the edges of the night, he lifted the book and opened its cover.

I was watching her from behind the trough. I knew the sounds well enough to know what was coming. Steliana was being beaten about the shoulders and face by Carola, her mother. Sharp cracks of palm on cheek and dull thuds of fists were followed by sudden shrieks that escaped Steliana when her mother's fingers tightened in her hair. I heard the low grumbles of Vasile, her father, too sodden with his nightly drink to do much more than goad his wife as she inflicted their rage on their daughter.

"Demon-child," her mother yelled. Then the air filled with a harsh smack.

All was silent for a moment, then there as another unintelligible mumble from Vasile. Steliana came running across the yard, glancing anxiously back at the house as she ran.

She darted around a shed and leaned back against it, now out of sight of the house. The distraught look on her face vanished and her lips curled into a satisfied smile. There was blood running down her cheek and she brushed at it with the back of her hand. She moved the hand slowly to her mouth and placed her tongue gently against the blood. With deliberate care she licked the smear of blood until her hand was clean. Her chest rose and fell in a long sigh, the thin fabric of her dress slithering over her curves with the movement.

She lingered there for a moment, then pushed away from the shed and headed toward the tangle of dark leaves that marked the end of her father's farm and the beginning of the woods that surrounded the Dark Tower.

I stepped out from behind the trough and moved to intercept her.

She did not turn to see me, but let out a light, "Hello, Kalman."

Steliana was beautiful. Whenever she was near, I could feel my blood rage in my veins. She always seemed to be dancing. She would spin when she walked so that the loose folds of her skirt would twirl in the air.

"Your parents worry about you spending so much time in the shadow of the tower, Steliana."

She looked in the direction of the forbidden castle, as if she could see it through the thick clot of trees. "It cannot be helped. Something beckons me to the tower. I must see what awaits me there."

"Death, Steliana. That is what the demons breed at the Dark Tower."

"No, Kalman, it is not death, not as we know it. It is life, real life, unending life. A life of untold passion. You know what their kind can reap and sow. They stand beyond the power of death, Kalman. They can command the flesh. They can control life."

"Steliana, there is real eternal life to be found..."

"That is dry stuff," she interrupted. "It would blow away in any stiff wind. The Dark Tower, though is rich and heavy with blood. Imagine having that for an eternity," Steliana said. Her voice was a hurried, breathless whisper and her eyes were focused on some point in the distance. She took her lower lip between her teeth and furrowed her brow just slightly, as if she were contemplating the enormity of what she was doing, then her great, green eyes widened in wonder and her wide, full mouth curled into a mischievous smile.

Steliana walked backward a couple of steps. She cocked her head a little in mock admonishment. "Do not wander too near the tower, Kalman. There are demons there." She gave me a smile and I stopped in my steps to savor that moment. By the time I could breathe again, she was far ahead of me.

It was already late into the night and I had work at my father's shop that would demand me at sunrise. Of course, I had to follow her. I glanced back at the house before entering the woods. I could see the dark heft of her mother still sulking about on the porch and the larger silhouette that must have been her father slumped against the house.

I was bitter cold beneath the scant branches of the dark woods. The angry trees did not suffer much sunlight by day and chased away the heat at night, replacing it with cool, misty air. There were few animals in this dark region, so their sounds were rare. I was alone in a silence broken only by the faint creaks and moans that told of the battles waged between the branches and the night wind. I hated this wood even by day, for it was a place of evil even in bright sunlight. At night, though, it was like a dagger at the throat. There was little that could have drawn me in there at night. Steliana, though, was more than enough of a lure.

I heard voices before I saw her, and I slipped into the trees beside the path. She was in a clearing lit by dull moonlight. A tall man in a crude, wolfskin cloak was standing near her. Steliana would move close at times, leaning in to draw him near. Then she would back away a few steps and his body would visibly slump.

I knew this man. His name was Romik. He was a trader from a village over that bleak ridge of rock that marked the boundary of the desolate lands. He was one of the few outsiders who would come into our village. He knew that we were desperate for goods and he used Vasaria to his profit. My father coined whole new curses each time this Romik left the shop.

Romik was a lean, rough man who knew fear was a frequent tenant in Vasaria and used his dark eyes and scarred appearance to intimidate those with whom he traded. He never made a real suggestion of anything, but he knew a village of whipped dogs when he saw one, and the curse of the tower had beaten us hard with fear over the years. Yet, even this coarse man seemed enchanted by Steliana.

She started along the cobblestone path that led up to the Dark Tower. Romik hesitated. Steliana gave him a backward glance and, of course, he followed. So did I.

I could feel the tower before I could see it. Its weight and the darkness it held seemed to drain away the air from the night and left a stillness that was reluctant to be breathed in. Steliana stopped and waited near the edge of the cliffs. Romik joined her soon after. He put his meaty hands on her waist and pulled her in close. He leaned down to kiss her, but she had turned her head away toward the castle.

Romik craned his neck to the side and pulled her face back around with a rough kiss. She did not pull away, nor did she join in his kiss. She seemed almost lifeless in her lack of response. Romik said something, but Steliana turned her head suddenly back toward the tower. Romik turned his head to follow her glance, as did I.

I edged closer to them, careful not to rustle the carpet of twigs and dead leaves underfoot.

"What you promised, girl," Romik said as she looked back at him.

"I made no promises." She took a light, playful step away from him, but he yanked her back and pressed his body tightly against hers.

"You think you can lure a man out here and then change your mind? I am not one of the spineless boys of your little village."

He took another rough kiss. This time she struggled a bit and pushed herself away. I glanced at the sheathed hunting knife bound to his right thigh.

"You will not do that again," she said. Her voice rose a bit now, a hint of her mother's bite there.

"Much more than that, girl."

Steliana tried to slap at him, but Romik caught her hand. He raised his own hand high, ready to strike down at her. I rose from my crouch and was ready to yell out to distract Romik, then the air seemed to grow thick and heavy, as if a sudden storm was rolling in.

The shadows around the ominous keep seemed to be shifting, almost as if the tower were some giant tree swaying in a strong gale. When I looked back for Steliana, I saw that she was gone and Romik was now alone. He was hunching slightly to peer into the darkness amid the rocks where he thought Steliana was hiding. I heard a rustle and knew that she had already slipped around to the edge of the ancient road that led from the keep. Her bare feet had carried her silently. She stood at the edge of that road and in the dim light I could see her smiling slightly at the obliviousness of Romik.

The stirring of shadows had reminded me where I was. I had no desire to watch Romik search about for Steliana. I tucked my book away and followed her back toward the village. When I had traveled some distance, I thought I heard a muffled yell back in the direction where Romik was hunting for her.

I could not resist the desire to look back. In the dim light of the waning moon, I could see a dark figure holding Romik's limp body upright, pulling him close. The shadowed figure lowered its face to Romik's throat, then suddenly stopped and turned its head toward me. Although it was too far and too dark to see more than vague shapes, I knew that it was looking at me. I could feel an icy chill shoot through my body and tighten my muscles. I wanted to run, to hide, to scream, to pray, but I could not move from the line of that gaze.

A scattering of pebbles far ahead reminded me that Steliana was heading back to the village.

I turned, but it was like trying to drag someone else's body. Only by sheer force of will could I make my muscles move. I took a few plodding steps. I fought hard to resist the desire to look back.

Then I heard an anguished scream. Mortal fear was in

that cry and it filled me with the need to flee. I shot forward as if I had been straining against a rope that was suddenly released. I ran and would not let myself repeat the foolishness of Lot's wife.

Brom paused from reading the book and saw that the gray was edging further into the eastern sky. Dawn, his mortal enemy, was giving him fair warning. He looked out over the field of gravestones and could now see several wispy spirits wandering the mist shrouded cemetery.

"Yes," Brom thought aloud, "the savor of blood heated by desire is finer than any pleasure known to the living. I have tasted such impassioned blood myself, and though the cost was great, I could not resist quenching my thirst upon it." He glanced toward Rianna's grave, then looked back at the book in his hands and continued to read.

I reached the edge of Vasile's farm just as Steliana was approaching the door of their disheveled farmhouse. She paused for a moment, then slowly pushed the door inward. Although she entered silently, her entry brought with it the sudden sound of her mother's angry howls and her father's deep bellows. I turned and hurried to the shelter of my home, careful to stay far from the trees and their shifting shadows. There would be much to write of this night.

Several days later, Steliana passed outside the shop, gliding down toward the square in that sultry way she had. No one in the village moved with much life in their step, except for Steliana. I set aside my work and stepped out of the doorway to watch her. She had a basket in her hand and was heading for the market stalls. She would work her magic on the men and boys of the market and then make her way back.

When she returned, I tried not to let her notice my enamored gaze. As she strolled by my father's shop, she stopped suddenly, then turned quickly to catch me staring at her.

"Watching me, Kalman?" she asked. Even though her feet had paused, her body could not rest and she swung the basket around as she stood.

"Do you know what happened to Romik?" I asked. "I have heard this morning that he did not arrive for his usual trading day."

"No." She looked away toward the distant tower. "Perhaps he has tasted immortality."

I did not smile at her jest. "Do you know the tales of the Baron?"

"Yes, Kalman, of course, he is said to be the lord of the keep."

"I think... he killed Romik," I whispered.

Steliana scoffed, "Do not try to frighten me away. I have no fear of the Baron." She let the basket drop to her side and she sidled up to me. I stepped back and found myself leaning against the rough log wall of my father's shop. She pressed close and placed her left arm against the wall over my shoulder. I could see the smooth skin of her neck and shoulders plunging down into the swell of her dress. There was a light dusting of freckles on the skin of her chest. She did not say anything. I dragged my eyes upward over her pale neck, slightly lifted chin, full and parted lips, and freckled nose until I was staring into her large, dark-green eyes. Her eyebrows rose slightly when I finally met her gaze. She leaned in so that her body just touched against mine.

"Do not go to the tower, Steliana. Next time it might be you who is caught up by the dark lord."

"Yes," she whispered, and I could feel her warm breath on my face.

"Yes?"

"Yes, I will be careful, Kalman." Her face started to edge toward me, but then she stepped back and lifted her basket so that it filled the space between us. "I appreciate your concern, but you still do not understand what awaits in the tower." Her eyes held mine for a moment, then without another word she slipped away and hurried toward her home.

I was still pressed against the wall. I stepped away and a deep sigh escaped me, although I think she was already too far gone to have heard it. I watched her go. I knew that she would not stay clear of the Dark Tower. When she spoke of what dwelled there, her eyes would suddenly go wide with wonder and she almost seemed to rise on her toes in anticipation of some invisible touch, like a girl longing to be kissed by an impossibly tall man. I did not think she would sink back to the ground until that kiss was bestowed upon her.

The following evening, I once again found myself lingering at the edge of Vasile's farm while his wife unleashed her anger upon their daughter. There was no bellowing this night. Vasile had either gone to the village or was lost in the hard slumber of heavy ale.

I held back in the shadows though, because I saw that I was not alone. There was a boy waiting near the shed. It was Gheorghe, the butcher's son, pacing impatiently back and forth. One day he would be the dull hulk of a man that his father was, but now his broad shoulders and boyish locks of hair made many of the girls pause in their work when he passed by. Steliana, though, was beyond such things. I could not imagine why he would be lurking by her home.

Steliana darted from her house, leaving her mother's curses behind, and ran to meet Gheorghe beside the shed. He reached out for her, but before he could take her up in his arms, she slipped past him and into the woods. It was enticing to watch her as she ran barefoot down the path. I could feel my body wanting to follow and I held a tree to steady my senses. Gheorghe gave chase, following the sounds of her footsteps as they rustled in the leaves and snapped the twigs that had blown over the road.

I trailed them both at a discreet distance. It was reckless to venture into the woods at night, yet Steliana could make any man cast aside his fears. As we neared the castle, the stars overhead were blotted out by a dense tangle of serpentine vines that had overgrown the barren trees.

Breathing heavily, Gheorghe slowed his pace, then paused where the path emerged from the woods. Ahead of him, Steliana stood in wait at the edge of the cliffs, under the eye of the Dark Tower. Gheorghe swaggered forward and pulled her close. There was no struggle this time.

I watched Steliana with that brute and wished that I were he, that it was I she covered with kisses, that I could be the one to caress her soft skin. My heart wrenched inside me until finally I turned away. I sat and wrote by the dim light of the moon until they grew quiet.

Steliana lingered where Gheorghe now dozed, scattering the pebbles at his feet with the tip of her foot. She glanced around at the woods and started to back away from him, then spun and started to stroll with that light, swaying stride of hers.

I began to follow her when a chill swept over me. I glanced back toward the tower and once again felt the strange sensation of movement in the shadows. Gheorghe must have sensed it too, for he had begun to stir. He sat up, but before he could get to his feet, a dark shape descended on him. Gheorghe gave a yelp and his head snapped back and dangled from his body.

I let out an audible gasp and the blood-gorged face of the fiend turned to look in my direction. I took a step back and turned to run. My muscles were tight and I could barely move, but I scrambled toward the forest path that led to the village. I could hear the movement behind me, slow, steady, shuffling strides. I tried to hurry my own pace, but my legs only grew slower and heavier with each step. I stumbled over a twisted root and fell forward onto a sharp branch which tore through my shirt and stabbed into my shoulder. The sudden burst of pain released me for a moment. The book fell free from inside my shirt. I snatched it up and started to run again. I felt dampness spreading on my shoulder and could catch a faint whiff of blood. My eyes went wide in horror, for I feared what the blood would draw.

A shadow leapt over my head faster than my eye could follow. The dark shape rose before me and I beheld a tall man dressed in black robes. It was the Baron. Before I could move, he clutched my neck in a firm grasp. His cold, black eyes latched onto mine and held my head in place even more firmly than the hand on my throat. His skin was pale and gray with death. Not a single strand of hair marred his smooth skull.

"What is thy place in this?" the Baron asked. His breath in my face was as cold as a winter wind and it smelled of old and rotted blood. I had expected his words to come out in a hiss, but instead his speech was precise and learned, like that of a scholar or priest. I could not find a voice with which to answer.

"I shall have blood enough this night to slake my deepest thirsts."

Cool fingers slid along the sides of my throat. I realized that those sharp, yellowed nails were tracing the line of blood as it pulsed in my neck. The fingers trailed down to the gouge in my shoulder, touching it lightly and lingering there. A sharp nail dug into the wound and my body flinched although my head could not move from the firm hold of the Baron's eyes.

"Thou dost draw thy fire from the watching of this. Is

that how it is?" The Baron's lips twisted in a slight smile, then his eyes widened, and his grip eased. "No. Such is not what thou art about. What dost thou hold?"

"A book," I stammered. "It is about a girl, Steliana."

"The girl who just lay with this boy?"

"Yes."

"She hath inspired such in thee?"

"Yes," I said, lowering my eyes.

The Baron's clawed fingers sprawled across the book. "This girl hath roused a darkness within me. What she hath awakened shall not be put to slumber again. For that I shall exact a price." The fingers on my neck loosened. "Thou shalt return here on the morrow and bring with thee the girl."

The hand slipped from my throat and I slumped to the ground. Shivering with fear, I rose to my feet, tucked my book away and ran back to the village.

I could not sleep that night. The moment that my eyes closed, I was confronted with a vision of what the darkness held for me. The Lord of the Dark Tower has marked me and I was in fear for my soul. I should have run from the village in the daylight. I should have escaped before the darkness called me out again. I could not leave, though, as long as Steliana was in such danger. I had to warn her, to tell her what had happened.

I was waiting at the table when my father sat down for breakfast. He glanced at my heavy eyes and at the book in front of me and shook his head. He surely knew that I had been up deep into the night with my writing. I took up my book and headed out.

I found Steliana filling her father's jug from a keg in the barn.

"You should not be here, Kalman. My parents do not like to think that I know anything of boys. If they saw you here, my father might have to kill you."

"Steliana, the Baron killed Gheorghe. I saw him."

"Did he see you?"

"Yes. He spoke to me. He demanded that I come back tonight, with you. You must not go, Steliana. He wants you."

Her eyes went wide.

"Then I must go."

"You must not. He will kill us both."

"It is not death, Kalman. It is something so very much more."

"Steliana."

"He knows what I have offered him and he welcomes me. It is what I have wished for." She smiled and gave me a light kiss on the cheek. "Thank you, Kalman. Now you must go before my parents see you here."

She gave me a rough shove, but then flipped her hair back from her face and offered me a smile. She spun on her heel and left the barn. I did not see her for the rest of the day.

Later that evening, I returned to the farm and waited for Steliana to leave her house. There was no yelling or screaming from within; somehow she had managed to slip away quietly.

I stood before her on the path, blocking her way.

"If he has summoned us, we must go. Do you think we could hide from him?"

"We could leave and go over the mountains."

"No, Kalman. He awaits. I must go to him."

"I cannot let you, Steliana."

"Then catch me." She glided past me and stole into the woods. She was many strides ahead of me. She seemed to run with total abandon, while I was wary of shadows and limbs and vines and fell farther behind with each step.

By the time I reached the end of the woods, Steliana was standing in the clearing ahead of me, before the Dark Tower. Her dress shimmered across her graceful body in the cool, pale light of the crescent moon. I closed my eyes for a moment and burned that vision into my memory.

I started toward her, then stopped short.

A dark figure glided from the shadows and stood before her.

"I have come, as you have bid of me," she spoke, her voice quivering with nervous anticipation. "I offer my blood to you in exchange for your gift."

"Gift, girl? It is not a gift that I offer thee."

"Have I not pleased you? Have I not brought you blood?"

The Baron gave no answer to her question, but instead commanded in a deep voice, "Thou shalt follow me."

"Yes. Anywhere you will lead me, I will follow."

"Steliana." I heard the shout and almost wanted to look around for the fool who had made it, but I knew the fool only too well.

"Yes. Thou shalt also come with us, boy. This one must understand the consequences of her deeds. Thou shalt play thy part in that."

He beckoned and I felt my body pulled ahead. Within a few rushed strides I had fallen into place beside Steliana. She turned her head slightly and smiled at me.

"We shall experience immortality, Kalman," she whispered, then let out a contented sigh.

The Baron paused a moment, then continued to lead us toward the entrance of the keep. He lit a candle and led us inside. We passed through a large hall, blank and empty in the darkness beyond the pale sphere of weak candlelight. We followed him through twisting corridors and a dim, sinister chapel and suddenly came out into the night again. We passed through a plot of graves, most carved with figures that were ill at home in the darkness that now ruled the tower.

We approached an archway that stood amidst the graves. While the tower seemed to radiate death from its stones, the archway seemed to emit a shroud of darkness that threatened to engulf all hope or faith. I wanted to turn and flee, but the force of the Baron's will kept me advancing toward the arch. I tried to focus on the cross that had been cast at the heart of its wrought iron gate, but it was lost amidst the shadows that lurked beyond the iron bars.

The Baron stopped and beckoned Steliana forward. She came and stood before him, as close as a lover.

"I bestow upon thee, now, what thou hast earned," the Baron said.

Her body was not tensed back in fear, but was arching up in longing as the dark figure loomed over her. Her eyes were wide and her chest rose and fell in a slow, deep rhythm.

What happened next transpired too quickly for my eyes to follow. It was only that dull thud of flesh striking flesh and very slight recoil of Steliana's neck that told me that the hand of the dark lord had slashed across her throat.

A line of blood formed below her chin and seeped down her neck. Her lips twisted in pain and her jaw clenched with the effort of maintaining her focus. She turned her head to one side and tipped it back to offer the blood.

The hand that clutched the fabric at the bosom of her dress opened. Steliana dropped to her knees before she could catch herself. Her eyes widened in disbelief.

She lunged forward and grabbed at the Baron's robes.

He took a step back and Steliana fell into the dust at his feet.

She rose to her knees and looked up at him. I could see her mouth moving, but no words escaped. Steliana clutched her throat, then lifted her hand to her face and I could see that her palm was coated in blood. Her hand lingered there for a moment and I thought that she was about to lick the blood. Instead, the hand dropped to the ground and Steliana pushed herself to her feet. She swayed. The shimmering dress was now marred with blood and dirt. Her fists clenched with the effort of holding herself in place.

Although no sound escaped her lips, she mouthed the

word, "please," repeating it again and again.

I wanted to go to her, but I could not move. I could only watch as she struggled and pleaded.

The Baron looked upon Steliana without compassion and spoke, "It is no kindness to feed such poison, girl. I have drunk deeply from thy vile offerings, but have no gratitude for what thou hast done. Far from it. Thou hast bargained with the creations of the Fallen Ones, and thou shalt never know salvation. It is too late for thee to turn from the path thou hast chosen, but I shall grant thee one small token. Thou shalt have this book that chronicles thy downfall. It shall be the only thing of thy fading world that thou shalt be able to hold. Read it and know what thou hast brought upon thyself."

Even as her eyes closed, her lips still formed the word, "please." Steliana fell to the ground and the Baron then turned to me.

"Finish thy journal, boy," the Baron said, "for thou hast witnessed how the tale ends. Return with it to the tower and leave it here, before this gate, so that she may have the knowledge of thy book with her for all the ages to come. Then go from this place and never come here again." The Baron looked down upon Steliana as she lay lifeless at his feet. "She has awakened the fire of blood in me... I shall not spare thee again." The Baron turned and disappeared into the cemetery.

I fled through the castle and ran home as fast as my legs would carry me.

Now, as I write these final words, sadness engulfs me.

Steliana was beautiful. She danced when she walked, turning the head of every man she passed. Now Steliana wanders the night forever, only in death aware of the cost of her desires. I wish I could say that she was foolish, but I have felt a lure as strong as the one she felt. And I, too, felt death at my throat. And even having watched her blood rush away into the night, I cannot say that I would easily walk away if Steliana again danced barefoot ahead of me on her way to the Dark Tower.

Brom closed the book and set it carefully where the spectral form of Steliana had left it. He looked one final time at the arch, his eyes fixed upon the inscription chiseled into the rough stone above the gate, *Noctem Aeternus*. It was a solemn reminder of his fate and hers, for they were both cursed to haunt the night eternal. Many times he had contemplated letting the light of the sun put an end to his tormented existence, but could not force himself by act of will to let the sun's rays scatter the darkness from his heart. He could linger, but soon some primal instinct for survival would arise within him, and he would retreat into the tower to seek the sanctuary of shadows.

Brom turned from the arch and the blackness that lay beyond it. He paused a moment before Rianna's grave, thinking about the strange lure of the darkness and what it had cost him. The memory, though painful to endure, had suppressed the strong craving for blood that raged within him, at least for one more night. Brom lost himself in bitter reminiscence, then he strode off for the Dark Tower. Distant ghosts faded into the rising mist as the first rays of dawn cast a crimson glow across the eastern sky.

All night I reconstruct her rosary,

no prayer is in my soul —

The crimson beads and simple crucifix,

no prayer is in my heart —

A token of my one true love, now gone,

no prayer is in my chest —

An endless circle spanning naught and all,

no prayer is in my throat —

Restrung, restored, but not to be returned,

no prayer is in my mouth —

What has been grieved is gone, but not forgotten,

no prayer is on my lips —

All night I reconstruct her rosary,

no prayer is in my soul —

Nightwatcher

JAMES PIPIK

A howl rose, mournful and shrill, piercing the heavy granite and mortar of the keep. Alone within the sanctum of his library, Brom lifted his quill from the page and raised his head to listen. Even the candles flickered uneasily, sending shadows fluttering around the room like startled rooks. The sound of howling was not unusual in the mountains, but this was different, not a wolf or dog. Brom sensed something strange behind the cry, a sentience, as if the howl contained a word, if only he could make it out. It came from nearby, perhaps even within the outer ramparts of the castle.

Brom set aside his journal and followed the fading echoes down through the chapel, the eyes of the icons following him across the room, to the cemetery.

He came outside beneath a cold, starless sky. The moon sank low and heavy in the west, throwing uneven shadows through the rising mist. The gravestones rose through the fog like silent, pale islands on a gossamer sea. Brom's eye strayed to a particular stone, newer and straighter set than its neighbors. He stood before it, his hand reaching into his pocket and fingering the string of rosary beads there.

181

"At last, you have come in answer to my call," a raspy voice whispered from somewhere behind him. Brom turned toward the voice.

A single standing stone crowned with a gargoyle stood silhouetted against the swollen moon. The gargoyle bent forward, grasping the stone with both hands, and great, dark wings sprang from its back. Though such grim monuments had adorned the keep, inside and out, Brom had never before noticed one among the graves. Only statues of angels stood here amidst the tombstones. The moonlight blinded him to whoever was speaking. The voice seemed to emanate from somewhere behind the stone.

"Who dares intrude on my domain? Show yourself."

"Am I not plain to see here before you?" The gargoyle atop the stone raised its head slightly, its eyes seething and molten.

Brom stepped back and put his hand to his sword beneath his cloak, though he doubted that it would be of any use against the thing he now faced. It moved with the languorous ease of a great predator and its wings seemed almost to rustle in the faint night breeze, but it was as solidly stone as the marker it crouched upon, ponderous and heavy. "What manner of creature are you?" Brom asked.

"Fear not, my lord," the creature said. "I mean you no harm. Confined here, alone as you are, I should think you would welcome guests, even one such as I."

"Solitude is my lot," Brom said. "I desire no visitors, least of all those uninvited. I say again, what are you?"

"A mere watcher in the night," the thing on the stone replied. It sat back on its haunches as if making itself

comfortable. "I have come here often through the long years. You are not the first Lord of the Dark Tower I have known. Of old, kings ruled here, and once even a great queen, and I have called upon them all. I knew your predecessor well in his day. Yes, many times I have visited this place where you now live."

"I merely dwell here, I do not live, for nothing here is truly alive."

"This is not so, my lord," the thing said as if shocked at his ignorance. "There is a power in this keep that is yet alive. It merely sleeps, waiting like a seed deep in the soil for its time to grow and prosper."

"More like a plague, shut up in a temple of death with locks and wards upon the door, lest it wreak its destruction upon the world."

"An analogy more apt than you know, my lord," the creature said. "For once freed from its prison, nothing could stand against this power."

"All the more reason to leave it sleeping in its tomb," Brom said.

"Unless one were allied with such a power and could take part in its strength, in its wisdom, in its victory."

"Its victory would be the defeat of all men."

"Men?" It spat the word. "What are men to such as you, my lord? Poor, weak creatures, fighting amongst themselves over their tiny patches of ground, their pitiful illusions of empire, their crumbling crusts of bread. Men say, 'This belongs to me and no other,' and they hoard it and defend it until at last they perish and their lands, their wealth, their kingdoms pass on to others, until they too fade into dust. Men are beneath your least consideration, my lord."

"I am a man myself," Brom said in even measure.

"Nay, Lord Brom," it pleaded, wounded on his behalf. "You have outgrown mere mortality. You have grown powerful. Death itself holds no sway over you. How little it would take for you to make every knee in Vasaria bend before you! Vasaria, did I say? You could grind the continent itself beneath your heel, stride across the earth like a god! The Muhammadans that fought you in Palestine would feel the bitter taste of your sword! Asia and Africa and even lands undreamt of beyond the oceans would go up in flames before the fire of your wrath!"

"If men are beneath my notice, why should I want dominion over them? If a creature such as you even has breath, you waste yours. Such power interests me not at all."

The creature leaned forward, its eyes burning into him. "No, of course not. Not power." It paused again, its head tilted to the side, considering. "But love..."

"What of it?" Brom shot back.

"Love, yes. That is what you desire." The creature raised a taloned hand, the merest suggestion of a gesture, but Brom knew where he pointed and turned to the gravestone beside him. Brom read the single word carved into the marble: Rianna.

"There she lies," the creature continued. "Slain by your own hand."

"That which I slew was no longer Rianna," Brom said. "Though in form she appeared to be my love, her essence had turned dark and wicked, possessed by malevolence.

Taking her life was the only way to save all that was precious within her."

"Is that what he told you, the dark knight that stood in your chapel and counseled murder? Did you think it truth? Nay, my lord, she was not possessed of an evil spirit, but freed from the cruel bonds of human weakness. She was brave, my lord, braver than many a sworn knight. How could she have survived her bleak, plundered childhood? How else could she have defied the village elders to care for a wounded knight that brought his miseries to her doorstep? How else could she have dared to love him? How else could she have forgiven him for abandoning her?

"At last, she gathered the courage to come here, the place her short life had taught her to fear most in all the world, to seek you out again, to ease your loneliness, to carry your burden with you. And other trials she endured, other labors she undertook, other sorrows and affronts of which you will never know.

"And when the grief her courage had seen her through was at last redressed with strength and power, she did not fear her own strength, as you did. She stood ready to take the future into her hands, to join with you to forge a new destiny. But that was never to be. She was cut down within sight of her reward.

"And her spirit has not gone to some eternal paradise. She lingers here still. For though you wronged her greatly, she cannot leave you."

"You lie," Brom spoke over his shoulder.

"Nay, it is my words that are truth," the gargoyle spoke sadly. "That creature that moved you to slay your love, that hid behind a fair form, I know him. We are of a kind, he and I, though we have chosen separate paths. This harbinger of truth, as he would have it, deceived you. The spirit of your love remains nearby, longing for you still."

"I have seen other such spirits," Brom said, glaring back at the creature. "They are as beyond my reach as heaven itself."

"Do you think she cannot be brought back to you? Death is no obstacle. It holds no sway over you. Why should it bind her? You reck not the power that lies dormant here." It lifted its hand again, a movement even more subtle and small, but Brom felt his eye drawn away again, across the cemetery to the ornately gated archway that opened into the catacombs.

"That entranceway is forever sealed."

"There is another way," the creature said and leaned forward again. "You hold the key. You need only use it."

Brom thought immediately of the strange key he had taken from the lone trespasser who had invaded the keep long before. Even now it sat heavily in his pocket. He had never discerned its use.

"Yes, you know whereof I speak," the creature said, as if reading his thought. "It opens the way to your only hope."

"I know something of this 'hope' of which you speak. Lilith, she is called, mistress to demons and mother to monsters."

"So spoke your predecessor in his madness. So scribbled he in the insane ramblings he called his journals. He was too small for the greatness entrusted to him and he betrayed it. He ended on his knees before you, begging for release. Do you seek a similar fate, years hence?"

"He was a holy man," Brom said. "He sacrificed his humanity to keep that which waits below from rising again."

"His faith in illusion drove him to lunacy. Trust not his ravings."

"Better that I should trust you?"

"Trust your own strength. Trust your own wisdom. But know this: they come, in their beginnings, from Mara herself. She is the source of your power over men. She will restore your love and give you a place of honor. Or have you grown so fond of this wretched and solitary existence?"

Brom stood with head bowed, his eyes resting on Rianna's headstone, but his mind looking inward. "To me, my fate seems just. Perhaps all you say is true. I have no way of knowing. But all my life I sought only to serve my king and my God. If this is the lot to which such a life brought me, so be it."

The red seething of the creatures eyes flared a moment and a baleful light spread across its tortured features. "If such self-loathing be your nature, then I will trouble myself with your education no longer. I thought only to save you much pain and sorrow, but it is of little importance. Your submission is assured. You have tasted blood and relished in its sweet succulence. Your journey to Mara's embrace has begun. And when at last you surrender to your thirst, you will feel pleasures greater than any mortal could know."

If Brom heard the creature's taunts, he gave no sign.

The gargoyle stirred then and glanced over its shoulder at the moon, settling behind the western mountains. "Alas, this night grows old and I must take my leave."

"Then be gone and have done with it," Brom said quietly.

The thing laughed then, low and thin. "Have you resisted temptation, like your savior in the desert? Think not too highly of yourself, my young lord. For the long, empty years stretch out before you, more vast than any Sahara, filled with blinding days and hollow nights. And no angels will appear to wait upon you when I depart. In the years to come, you will be alone with your hunger and my words. And through all those years, she will be waiting for you."

"Who?" Brom asked, perhaps of himself, looking down at the grave and then further on to the arched gateway. "Rianna... or Mara?"

He turned back to the standing stone, but the moon had set and the creature was gone. As the sky behind him in the east betrayed the first flush of dawn, Brom wondered if the thing had ever been there at all.

He made his slow way back to the keep, his fingers seeking again in his pocket for his rosary. But when he drew it forth, he found the beads tangled and knotted around the strangely carved key.

With every breath
the air grows stale,
Deathly cold winds
howl and wail,
Raging thunder
pounds like drums,
When something wicked
this way comes.

Vesper Tolls

JOSEPH IORILLO

The threat of an autumn storm hung over the village of Vasaria as the gray afternoon gave way to evening. The twilight stillness was interrupted by the distant rumble of thunder, and those villagers not already indoors hurried to their dwellings to prepare for the storm's fury. The antiquated bridge over the stream near the village outskirts suddenly shuddered with a burgeoning violence; it was not the arrival of the storm, but something else entirely.

Out of the dark woods and across the bridge thundered a dozen armed marauders on horseback, riding with the speed of wraiths. They carried torches, and the firelight gleamed off their black helmets and plated armor. The invaders swept into the village, setting huts ablaze. Shrill cries and the clamor of steel filled the air, and within moments havoc ruled. Through the flames and the billowing smoke, the warlord, Walsegg, emerged astride a tall black horse, a heavy broadsword clenched in his gloved fist. His horned helmet bore the semblance of a ghastly, leering skull of some predatory beast.

Walsegg merely sat and watched from atop his steed as his dogs of war ran rampant through the streets, chasing down terrified villagers, trampling them beneath their horses and hacking at them with battle-worn swords. The invading horde moved with merciless efficiency. The warlord barked orders from his tall saddle, commanding half of his men to raze the poorer dwellings. The remaining six warriors began a swift and systematic plunder of the larger homesteads. The marauders' immense satchels of canvas and leather were quickly filled to overflowing with what meager trinkets and victuals the villagers possessed. Several men and women lay slaughtered in the dirt, their eyes wide open, still holding a gaze of astonishment as they stared up at the boiling, storm-laden sky.

Walsegg turned his attention toward one of his men stumbling out of a hut on the heels of a terrified and bloody young girl bereft of her clothes. She shrieked unceasingly at the violations she had suffered. The warlord yelled an order and her pursuer left off. Annoyed by her shrill screams, Walsegg reached out his sword as the girl ran by and caught her at the throat. Her cries silenced, she dropped to her knees in a cascade of blood, her face frozen in an expression of horrified awe as if she had gazed upon the landscape of Hell itself.

A small child, tears streaming down her cheeks, stood in the doorway of a nearby home, the butchered corpses of her parents at her feet. Her dress was spattered with their blood.

Another of Walsegg's armor-clad warriors rode to the warlord's side, dragging an old man behind him through the dirt road. The elderly man's wrists were bound together by a long rope which tethered him to the plunderer's saddle. Walsegg took the end of the rope and the old man rose to his feet, his knees and elbows bloodied and raw. He stood in defiance before the warlord.

"Have you no sense of justice? Of mercy? You are exiles from humanity!" the old man cried. "What proof of your courage is it to slaughter the innocent, to murder the defenseless? What testament of your cunning is it to plunder those who have nothing? Your mindless savagery is no virtue, wild animals have as much."

"Your words would be more cautiously chosen," Walsegg replied, "if you knew to whom you spoke."

"I know to whom I speak." The scorn in the old man's age-hoarsened voice was a challenge to all of the invaders. Many of the warriors stirred upon their mounts, looking uneasily at their leader, fearing his reaction. "You are Walsegg the Devil, Walsegg the Fierce, and the infamy of your repute inspires dread, but not fear. Only true strength deserves such an honor as fear."

The warlord's reply was calm, even genial, but imbued with as much potential ferocity as the cauldron of swirling, fitfully flashing thunderheads above. "If I strike down the weak and the defenseless, it is only because all who I have encountered in this world have chosen to be weak and to have no defenses. If I take from those who have little, it is because none who have crossed my path have had the ambition nor the intelligence to possess much. This world is full of the poor, the wilfully wretched, and the ignorant. But one can always choose to fight that destiny. Those who lie dead before you deserve your contempt more than I, for they could have resisted." The warlord's voice now returned to a harsh growl. "Tell me now, old man, have you a treasure-hold here in this village? Answer me truthfully, lest I drag you through the streets all night to loosen your tongue."

The old man's eyes scanned the warlord's battle-scarred face as he desperately weighed his dilemma. He knew that Walsegg's men had already taken everything of value, however meager, that this village had once held. Sadly he realized that any answer, whether it be truth or misdirection, would ultimately bring his own death.

Just then, a clamoring sound interrupted the turmoil as the Dark Tower made itself known by the tolling of its great bell. The tormented cries of the villagers now fell to a hush.

The old man's face no longer held a look of defiance as he began to plead, "You have taken all that we have. Please... show us mercy. If it is riches you desire, go to the tower. A thousand villages like ours together would not equal a fraction of what the tower holds." The old man did not have to gesture to the angular mass of shadows and dark stone that comprised the huge castle some miles away, rising high above them upon its mountain spire. Like an immense onyx idol, the tower was visible to all.

The warriors felt the first few drops of cold rain. The wind was stronger, and the storm was closer. Walsegg gazed for a long time at the castle, but there was no evidence of respect or disquiet in his eyes. If the tower held anything of value, he would have it. If anyone foolishly challenged him, that challenge would be met with the blade of his broadsword. The world had not yet offered him anything that equaled his strength; when Walsegg struck, the world yielded. The castle's size and aura of gloom did not move him. He was not afraid of shadows nor of any living thing.

A heavily scarred soldier bearing a gore-drenched sword glanced at Walsegg and then nodded to the old man. "Shall I dispose of this wretch?"

"No, Markov," Walsegg said. "Spare the old one. Living with the memory of this night's carnage shall be punishment enough for his insolence."

Markov struck the old man with the hilt of his sword, driving him into the dirt. Blood seeped through the old man's fingers as he held his hand to the deep gash that had opened below his eye.

Walsegg commanded Markov to remain behind in the village with two other men; they would form a garrison to watch over the town which now belonged to Walsegg. The warlord led his remaining troops out of Vasaria, toward the mountain, toward the tower.

It had begun raining in earnest now, a steady, chill rain that hissed through the thick forests and the tangled underbrush that obscured much of the serpentine path which climbed inexorably up the mountain's face. The entanglement of barren branches overhead offered the swiftly moving cavalcade of dark horses and grim men little protection from the downpour, and their torches fought to remain lit against the falling rain. The occasional flash of lightning lit up the mountain in a cheerless, mock daylight, rendering the streamers of tangled ivy and the twisted, skeletal branches as the ferocious limbs of nightmarish creatures reaching out above and around them. The thunderstrikes grew in frequency, evolving from low, groaning rumbles into ear-splitting clashes and shrieks, as if the mountain itself were crying out.

The warlord, still unmoved, slashed at the annoying overhangs of branches and vines with his sword, his disciplined mind focused solely on the tower above as it grew larger with every step, expanding in the mist like a great dark cloud. Soon the steep path leveled out somewhat, and the horsemen found themselves passing the marble ruins of an arched gateway. A sudden gust of frigid wind extinguished half of their torches, preventing a close inspection of the ancient structure.

Walsegg spurred his steed onward; the Dark Tower was before him, and another burst of bluish lightning illuminated it in all of its immense, monstrous elegance.

The castle's dread black towers and spires soared upward toward the jagged streaks of lightning and the pounding rain, and the ledges and battlements were encrusted with the hunched, leering stone figures of gargoyles and other assorted guardian beasts. Walsegg studied the castle's now-silent belfry, momentarily transfixed by it for reasons he could not explain.

A tall, central archway framed the tower's lone entrance at the top of a wide, crumbling staircase. The castle grounds were girded by an insurmountable stone parapet wall extending away from the sides of the keep. The warlord glanced briefly at his men and nodded curtly to the right and to the left. His men split up and galloped away to either side of the parapet while he continued his scrutiny of the castle.

He had encountered many fortresses in his time; his experience told him this castle's treasures, whatever they were, would not be held within the main tower, but would be secreted away in some obscure, well-hidden crypt or antechamber. Still, his eyes were drawn to the belfry. Another silent strike of lightning illuminated the gargoyles along the front cornices of the tower. He knew it was merely a trick of the chaotic light, but he had the impression that several of the mocking yet mournful figures had changed places.

Soon the sound of hoofbeats drowned out the hiss of the rain. His men returned. "There is no other way in," one warrior said breathlessly. "The wall extends all the way around both sides, up to the very edge of the cliff."

"Then this shall be the way we go," Walsegg replied, dismounting.

The warriors followed suit, drawing their swords and rekindling the dead torches with those still alight. Once their horses were tethered to the remnants of withered trees, they mounted the stone steps. Walsegg paused briefly to inspect the massive, arched double doors and the strange rune design inlaid upon them in metal. It was of no precious metal, merely iron, so he did not concern himself with it further. With two swift, practiced blows, the warlord shouldered the doors inward, their ancient hinges emitting a growling squeal and a gust of stale, dust-choked air issued from the dark corridor beyond. It was as if the tower itself had breathed. The airborne grit whirled madly, turning a glowing scarlet and orange in the torchlight and seeming to take on obscure, faintly menacing shapes. It dispelled quickly, however, as the armed band strode undaunted into the castle, their heavy boots sending thunderous reports throughout the cavernous interior.

No sentinels stood watch, nor did any guards await them. They were met only by darkness. It hung, thick and heavy, like an opaque cloud around them, overwhelming the meager light of their torches. They were able to see only a scant few feet around them. Suddenly, a blue-white flash of lightning lit up the keep's interior for a brief moment through narrow casements. Walsegg scrutinized his surroundings as best he could. Twin marble staircases on either side of the vaulted, cathedral-like hall swirled upwards to an ornate balcony above. Ahead of him, an archway seemed to lead only deeper into the black abyss. Near the base of the left-hand staircase, he caught glimpse of what he thought to be the face of a gargoyle sculpted in the effigy of some feral demon. The flash of lightning, however, was short-lived and the men were again left adrift in a sea of choking darkness.

Moments later, another, longer flash of lightning allowed them to see their way better. The gargoyle Walsegg had seen, though, was gone. More tricks of the light, he thought. Just then, a wind hissed through the hall and seemed to taunt them with whispers from the lofty shadows. The warlord tersely directed five of his men to the right-hand stairs while he led the remaining warriors to the left staircase. He thrust his torch at the area of the floor where the statue had stood, yet he saw nothing but an unbroken layer of dust over the cracked marble flagstones. He tensed his grip upon his sword.

From midway on the staircase on the opposite side of the hall, the lead man, a young warrior named Kulas, called out to no one, it seemed, "So, the voices within these walls were not merely the wind after all." Then the gust of a sudden draft put out his torch and there was nothing but blackness on the staircase. When another flicker of lightning lit up the keep again, the men on the right-hand staircase gazed dumbfounded at the place where Kulas had been, for the warrior was there no more. All that remained on the spot where he had stood was his extinguished torch. The last thing Walsegg saw before darkness overwhelmed them again was one of his men picking up the torch and studying it in disbelief.

"Kulas!" his comrades called out. Their voices echoed through the vast chamber, but there came no reply.

"It would seem we are not as alone as we might have thought," Walsegg announced. His bland but determined tone struck a calm counterpoint to the agitated curses and questions voiced by his bewildered men. A warlord to the heart, Walsegg understood the rules of engagement and knew that if their unseen enemy moved by stealth, it must be because that was his only advantage.

"Find him," the warlord commanded to the remaining men on the far staircase. Another flash of lightning found the warlord gesturing with his sword to the balcony above where both staircases met. There were suggestions of doorways there at either end as well as a larger arched doorway in the middle.

The warriors ascended quickly to the second level of the keep, their torches struggling in vain against the oppressive ebon shroud of darkness all around them. The air seemed to grow colder with every step. Walsegg's men seemed unnerved as they gathered on the immense marble gallery. Their faces revealed looks of concern, even distress, in the flickering firelight.

With a gesture of his broadsword, the warlord sent four of his men to the rooms at the far right side of the balcony.

In a low voice, Walsegg ordered, "Search every room... work your way toward the center and rejoin us here. We will then breach the central chamber at full strength."

Walsegg led his detachment of men to the distant rooms on his side of the balcony. Two of his men explored one chamber while the warlord, flanked by the two remaining men, stepped through the doorless threshold of another chamber. His torch seemed even weaker and more pitiful than before, illuminating only a few feet of cracked marble floor in front of him before impenetrable darkness reigned once again.

A searing, silent flash of lightning came to his assistance for a moment, allowing him to glimpse a featureless chamber, barren and cobwebbed, distinguished only by several narrow windows bereft of draperies.

The lightning succumbed to darkness again, and there was a majestic, rolling crash of thunder. The roar drowned out an exclamation from one of the warriors behind Walsegg, an exclamation that began with a cry to his god. Then the low, growling rumble seemed to carry with it a shrill shriek. It sounded as if nature herself had gone mad.

Walsegg turned to his men, but another lightning flash revealed that his two accompanying warriors were gone. He called out their names, but there was no response, only the moan of the wind and the hiss of cold, serpentine drafts over the dusty floors and casements. Returning to the balcony, he encountered one of the two men he had sent to investigate a nearby room. The man's face looked ashen and alarmed in the chaotic flicker of his torchlight, and his eyes formed the silent question of where his comrade had gone. Seeing Walsegg without his two escorts, though, only deepened the anxiety in his eyes.

The warlord nodded toward the middle part of the balcony; perhaps the men had gone to regroup with the others. But when Walsegg and his lone warrior stealthily made their way to the chambers on the far right side of the balcony, they found only silent darkness. Thrusting his torch into one room after another and waiting for the almost rhythmic flash of lightning to further aid his search, the warlord saw nothing in the chambers except the occasional hanging drapery or ornate chair, the faded traces of some ancient regal splendor. The four men Walsegg had dispatched to this part of the keep were nowhere to be found.

Upon the floor near the threshold of one chamber, the warlord caught the glint of bright metal. He crouched and saw that it was a golden crucifix. One of his men had snatched it from the corpse of a monk during their raid on a monastery some months ago and the warrior had worn it around his neck, though he held no reverence for this deity. The only significance it had for him was that it was made of gold. Now the finely woven chain had been snapped in half and the crucifix itself seemed twisted, as if it had been grasped by a hand of unnatural strength.

Walsegg stood and turned to his lone escort, but that warrior, too, was now gone. Walsegg whirled about, brandishing his torch and awaiting the lightning strikes, but the balcony, stairwells and entry hall were deserted. He stood still for some moments, hearing only the wind and the soft burning hiss of his torch. There was something gravely wrong here in the thick darkness and unearthly quietude.

The warlord made his way toward the middle chamber, the sinews of his sword arm tense and ready for battle. Though not visible from the balcony or from the entry hall below, the meager glow of candlelight could now be seen, emanating from deep within the chamber. He stepped across the threshold into a massive hall with an arched ceiling supported by twin processions of marble columns. At the far end of the hall, a small flight of stone steps rose to form a dais upon which sat a stark but beautiful throne flanked by a pair of candelabras in wrought iron stands. Next to the throne stood a pale man in the long, dark robes of a priest. His head was completely bald, as if shaven in some vow of servitude. The holy man appeared to be in silent meditation as he gazed upon the pages of a heavy tome in his hand.

"Welcome," the priest said in a low tone. "I have awaited thee." He smiled wanly and lifted his eyes to the warlord.

"You have heard, then, of Walsegg?" the warlord said.

"Nay, I know thee not... by name."

Walsegg stalked forward past the procession of marble

columns on either side of him. His torch and the light of the candelabras did not offer much illumination, though he did have the unsettling impression of shifting shadows in the dark spaces between the columns, which may have been merely breeze-blown draperies.

Walsegg stopped at the foot of the steps and examined the holy man closely. Around the priest's neck, a heavy, tarnished cross glittered in the dim, darting firelight. This crucifix represented only humility, passivity and suffering in the warlord's eyes, thus branding the priest as little more than another antiquated, powerless relic in this massive, stone tomb. His almost sickly pallor and solemn, deeply set eyes gave Walsegg the impression that he was a very old man, although the warlord's predatory instincts did not abate. This holy man alone could not have been the enemy responsible for the disappearance of his men.

"What army lurks here, cloaked in shadows?" the warlord demanded.

"I alone keep vigil here," the priest replied.

"You lie." Walsegg mounted the steps in two long, sure strides and stood towering over the priest.

The holy man said nothing, his eyes steady.

Walsegg considered the priest's maddening calm with annoyance. "We were drawn here, into this ambush, by the tolling of the tower bell."

"I rang the Vesper bell to summon the lost and the worthy. Though it has been long silent, this night I found reason to sound its toll, to summon thee to a higher court."

Walsegg studied the crucifix around the priest's neck. It was tarnished nearly to black. "There is no justice higher than what is proffered by man. Where in this world do you see the hand of your god dispensing justice? Or mercy? Your faith is a superstition in a world governed by strength alone."

"Faith is the greatest strength there is."

"Will it preserve you, then, from the cut of my blade?" Walsegg held up his broadsword thoughtfully, letting it catch the firelight. "It did not preserve the life of the last holy man I encountered, in the village of Kulvarak. I chained him to a post and stripped the flesh from his bones with my lash. He needed only renounce his god and claim me as his lord and master, for I alone held his fate in my hands. Though he screamed and pleaded beneath the lash, he would not abandon his faith. Do you see such pitiful obstinacy as strength?" Walsegg stared intently into the priest's dark and soulless eyes, but could gain no insight.

"Indeed, thou art a man hardened by the fire of battle," said the priest.

"There is no greater teacher in this life."

"And what hast thou learned from battles lost?" the priest asked.

"Indeed, you are not familiar with the name of Walsegg, for I have never known defeat." He held the tip of his blade at the priest's neck, staring hard at him all the while. If indeed he was the lone devil in the darkness, responsible for the disappearance of the warlord's men, then he had made a fateful mistake by coming forth into the light. He was now at a disadvantage to Walsegg, standing at blade's end, only inches from his death. "A man is only as good as his flesh and his steel. Do you feel the power inherent in this blade?" He pressed the blade against the priest's throat, on the very edge of drawing blood. "It is forged of the rarest Damascus steel. The metal is hardened by thrusting the near-molten blade into the body of a slave, then plunging it into frigid water, the weak serving the strong, even in their pitiful deaths. This sword has withstood all who have challenged me. It has served me steadfastly, while your god has served me not at all. Nor will he serve you this night. I claim this fortress as mine."

The warlord drew his broadsword away from the priest's

neck and lowered it to touch the empty throne in a gesture of possession. The blade came to rest upon a deep crack that scarred the smooth stone. The action seemed to disturb the priest's calm demeanor. The holy man's eyes narrowed briefly and he almost appeared to hiss, as if touching the throne were some kind of dark heresy.

Walsegg smiled slowly. "Your vigil is over, priest. When next the bell tolls, it will announce to all the land that I have taken my rightful place in the tower."

The priest's drawn face betrayed the calm hint of amusement. He shut his heavy volume and set it at the foot of the throne. "Art thou quite certain of such a declaration?"

Gripping his sword in both of his calloused hands, the warlord now prepared to dispatch this contentious nuisance. "As certain as I am of your wretched mortality."

"It is written that whatever one giveth, so shall he receive, measure for measure." With a smooth, almost careless motion, the priest's hand suddenly seized the warlord's cherished sword by the middle of the blade. With both hands, the priest snapped the blade in two as if it were little more than a stick of kindling. The sword's destruction made an explosive crackle, augmented by yet another rolling crash of thunder. The pieces clattered to the dais at the warlord's feet.

"My poor, lost warrior," the priest continued, "at this moment, I truly pity thee."

Walsegg could only stare at the priest as if he had strayed into some kind of waking dream. He gripped the short-bladed dagger at his hip, but could not draw it from his belt. The unholy creature before him had already seized him by the throat and Walsegg felt his once awesome strength and vitality draining away like rain through a sieve. He fought in vain for breath, but darkness engulfed him and his consciousness faded. The last image he was left with was the fierce red of the firelight reflecting off the shards of his sword.

It was the roar of the storm that brought him back into wakefulness after he knew not how long. His head aching terribly, Walsegg opened his eyes and allowed them a moment to focus on his predicament.

He found himself confined to sit upon the throne. His outstretched arms were lashed by several lengths of rope to a rough post that weighed heavily upon his neck and shoulders. A thick, choking noose had been coiled around his throat and bound him to the throne, the very throne that he had boasted would be his. Breathing became impossible except in shallow, hitching gasps. If he slumped in one direction or another, the noose was pulled taut and air was denied him completely; bursts of rage-red sparks would flood his vision as unconsciousness threatened. He had no choice but to sit as upright as possible, like a lord surveying a ceremony in his honor, his eyes addressing the diabolic, mad tableau before him in the hall.

The great room was now alight with torches atop the four iron cages before him in the spaces between the columns on either side of the chamber. Within the cages, dazed and silent, were the figures of his men, their wrists bound tightly before them.

"Markov," the warlord whispered, not quite believing the testimony of his eyes. He recognized his trusted adjutant in the nearest cage, his face pressed to the bars, his eyes wide and full of unspeakable dread. Markov was supposed to have remained in Vasaria with two others, but those other two warriors were here as well, huddled in the furthest corner of the cage. They no longer looked like the battle-tested soldiers Walsegg knew them to be. They now looked like whipped, cowed beasts who sensed their coming slaughter.

"Markov, what is happening?" he said in a ragged whisper, but Markov either did not hear him or was too beset with shock to respond.

The demonic priest appeared suddenly, coming up from behind Walsegg and putting his death-white face close so the warlord would hear every whisper. Walsegg tried to shy away from the nightmarish visage, but the noose prevented him. A sour stench emanated from the foul thing at his side. It reminded Walsegg of many of the tombs that he and his men had raided over the years. It was the odor of decay and death.

"Behold," the fiend said quietly. "Now thou shalt bear witness to a higher justice."

The pale creature strode purposefully away down the short flight of steps, his black robe flowing around him like a storm cloud. He stepped toward the cage containing Markov and unlocked it with a heavy brass key. The three men inside backed away from the door as if retreating from some encroaching fire. One man began to whimper and another began to howl in panic as the fiend entered and grabbed Markov by the hair, dragging him outside. Markov gasped and struggled against the fist that held him, but the fiend paid him little mind, merely shutting and locking the cage again with his free hand.

The demon dragged him to the steps leading to the throne. Markov gazed at the warlord, his eyes pleading for assistance. Walsegg struggled against his restraints, but his bonds were relentlessly taut. The pale demon leered at the warlord's immobility, his cold smile growing and becoming a grimace of unadulterated hate as he drove his long, taloned thumbs into Markov's eyes.

Markov screamed as if his soul were being torn in two, and his cries drowned out even the explosions of thunder outside of the dark fortress. The other caged men also began to shriek and weep as they threw themselves at the iron doors of their cells and kicked ferociously at the locks, trying to gain freedom. Markov's unending cry degenerated into the rasping, inhuman sound of imminent death as the cloaked monster suddenly wrenched his claws downward, tearing the lower half of the warrior's face and skull away. The demon tossed the flesh aside like a discarded mask. Markov had burst the bonds at his wrists in a final surge of strength, but he could only flail mindlessly at the priest, who tore the warrior's throat out with his loathsome fangs, drinking deeply at the spurting fountain of blood as if tasting some rare, life-giving wine.

Walsegg screamed silently, without breath. The fiend turned toward the warlord, offering him a blood-gorged smile. Markov's lifeless body crumpled to the stone floor, the dark, bleeding holes of his eyes affixed upon the warlord. Walsegg lurched against the ropes holding him fast. "What... what are you?" he finally managed to whisper hoarsely to the abomination in the form of a man who now picked up part of the blade from Walsegg's ruined sword. "What creature of hell are you?"

The fiend did not answer, but instead proceeded back to the cage holding Markov's two companions. He unlocked the door and flung the gleaming remnant of the blade inside. One of the warriors, terrified beyond screams, picked it up immediately and slit his own throat, the blood spraying forth upon his comrade. The fiend stalked into the cage, toward the cell's last living captive, with cold determination, his dark eyes glistening with a malice beyond reason. The warrior backed away from him, attempting to grasp the fallen blade, but it was beyond his reach. Cowering in the corner, the warrior could only gaze up at his executioner in childlike awe and terror as the shadow of the fiend fell upon him.

Walsegg shut his eyes against the atrocity and made another lunge against the bonds cinching his arms and chest. The noose only tightened itself more around his neck, and consciousness once again left him as the cries of his men reached the pitch of absolute madness.

His time in the blessed, dark pool of unconscious forgetfulness was short-lived, however; a searing, white-hot pain in his abdomen brought him awake, gasping like a man who has come close to drowning. Walsegg cried out, not fully comprehending his situation. His arms were still bound to the heavy post, but he was hanging upside down from an immense iron pendulum of some sort. His bleary eyes finally made sense of the scene, and he realized he was now dangling from the hammer within the tower's great bell.

The unbearable pain he felt stemmed from a bleeding pattern of lacerations across his naked chest and abdomen. He recognized the design as that of the rune upon the keep's entrance. As he swayed within the confines of the bell's blackened iron dome, he caught a glimpse of the dark-robed monster standing below him, gazing up at him with amusement. The fiend held Walsegg's dagger, still gleaming with the warlord's blood.

"What child of Lucifer are you?" the warlord breathed desperately. "Kill me swiftly and be done with it. Why do you torture me so?"

"Look within thyself for the answer, my poor, deluded warrior. Thou hast taken thy rightful place in the tower. Thou belongs to the hand of fate now." With an air of wistfulness, the fiend moistened one long finger in the blood adorning the dagger and made the sign of the cross upon Walsegg's forehead. The warlord squirmed away from the sickeningly cold touch of the creature.

The belfry resounded with the fiend's retreating footsteps, and the warlord found himself alone. He struggled against the ropes, crying out in agony as his struggles made the deep gashes in his flesh bleed hotly.

Suddenly, he detected a new, more ominous sensation, and he lifted his head to see the appalling sight of a dark, furred mass that had silently alighted on his blood-streaked chest. He felt the pricking of small, barbed teeth and the horrifying touch of a tiny, warm tongue devouring the blood. Walsegg cried out in misery and the sound startled the bat. The creature hissed and unfurled its broad, leathery wings in an attitude of attack, its miniscule red eyes glowing with blind hate. The warlord swayed madly, attempting to dislodge the beast, but his movements only made him bleed more profusely than before. Soon another bat swooped underneath the bell and latched onto his stomach, biting and licking.

Walsegg threw himself against the side of the bell, unleashing a concussive tolling that split his ears and shook his bones. He managed to lift his aching head again and saw several more bats darting back and forth across his flesh, maddened with hunger by the taste of his blood. Several more hovered, screeching in the air around him, their wings brushing against his skin, making him cringe in revulsion.

Within moments, the interior of the bell was filled with the beating of wings and the high-pitched shrieking of the bats. Walsegg's entire body was covered with a writhing, undulating layer of the creatures, their teeth nibbling efficiently at his flesh, drawing more blood, and the blood drawing more bats as well. Some of them tried to burrow into the open wounds along his abdomen, as if to submerse themselves in his blood in a mockery of baptism.

Beyond madness now, the warlord hurled himself against the sides of the bell again and again, and his gagging, agonized screams could be heard even over the storm, even after the last Vesper toll was sounded.

In arcane tomes, on crinkling pages,

I search for my future's key,

locked in the past.

Even the shortest night takes ages to pass,

as I do battle with the hunger in my soul.

No mirth can move a mind tormented thus.

For too long I have existed alone.

Yet, I dare not seek solace

for fear of awakening the darkness

which lies dormant within me.

Sanctuary

RUSSELL NOVOTNY

1 was lost, hopelessly lost, that much was sure. And it was my own fault, and I knew it.

I had been lost in the wilderness of the forest outside the village before, yes, many times. One does not grow up in this region without spending as much free time as one can in the woods. The children of the village all know the woods as well as we know our fathers' fields and workshops. But I was truly lost this time, and these woods did not feel anything like home. They were different, unfamiliar.

I know, I should have gone straight from Vasaria when I got my task from the elders. I should have gone right then, but I did not. Instead, my mind had wandered and I had forgotten about the errand until late after supper, and by then there was nothing I could do but wait until nightfall and then sneak away from the house to do it.

I cursed my own idleness the whole way, as I left my home and family behind, and then Vasaria itself. It was snowing heavily as I set out, not like the light and wispy flakes that had been blowing all afternoon and that I could have been walking in. No, I had waited, and so I was heading into the blackness of night and a thick, falling snow, and trying to keep warm.

I had thought I was going south, toward the river, but it was hard to tell. Though the moon was full, it was veiled by the heavy clouds of the storm. If it had been day, I could have guided myself using the sun or some familiar landmark. But it was not day, only night, and I was surrounded by a cold, howling storm. And I was utterly, hopelessly lost.

Even the ravens seemed to be taunting me, high up in the bare trees, invisible against the night sky. They croaked a mocking laughter. Even if I was slightly off course, I would eventually come across a stream which I could follow toward the river. Still, I kept plodding aimlessly along through drifts of white that got slowly deeper and hid knotted roots and rough rocks that tripped up my frozen feet.

What else could I do but keep walking? Turn back to the village? I could not even tell which direction it was. I would likely never again be entrusted by the elders, not if I failed at so simple a thing as this. Better to stumble on than go back, for you always come out somewhere, even if it is not where you set out to go, and then at least you are not lost anymore.

I paused near a tall, gnarled tree, not realizing until I stopped how heavily I was breathing. I watched each puff of breath turn to icy steam and then blow away with the wind. I waited until my breathing became regular again, and then turned completely around once to see where I was.

What I could see gave no comfort. Snow clung to blackened branches, giving the barren, winter trees the appearance of skeletal fingers reaching out from the dark woods. The wind howled fiercely, yet above it all I could still hear the beat of my own frightened heart pounding and ringing in my ears.

I had moved only a few difficult feet from that spot before I stopped once more. Had I heard something? A voice maybe? The wind made it so hard to make out any other sounds. I heard only its howling, and certain it was nothing, was about to walk on, when a chill, deeper than any winter storm, swept over me. I watched the crooked branches of a nearby tree cease their sway and come to a rest, but the howling I had heard continued, and grew louder. I froze in place. It was the cry of winter wolves. A pack of them by the sound of it, lean, cold and hungry. They were coming nearer, heading my way.

And now the wind rose again, the voice of the storm whispering cruelly as if to scold me. I took a step, then another, then started to run, faster it seemed than I had ever run, even in any village footrace, despite the roots and rocks and blinding snow. Only when you are chased do you find how fast you can truly run. When a wolf is at your heels, you will almost believe man can fly.

There was no sound, then more howling, then nothing again, and then they were upon me.

They struck suddenly, out of nowhere and everywhere, springing out of the night like demons, catching me in mid-stride. One hit me from behind. He leaped and caught me high up, sending me spinning like a cloth doll. I crashed down in a tangled heap of arms and legs. As I fell, without thinking I cried out, "Father!" As if he could even hear me, for he was most likely miles away and snoring in his warm bed.

I came to a stop with my head against an old rotted stump, my face partly in the hard dirt and ice. When I lifted my head, it swayed unsteadily and I had trouble focusing my eyes. I felt a warm trickle down the side of my face and tasted blood at the corner of my mouth. I rolled to my side and felt a fierce jolt of pain in my left shoulder and arm.

I rose from the twisted undergrowth only as far as my hands and knees. The pain in my shoulder was sharp and intense. I winced and nearly cried out as I struggled to rise. I put my hand to my shoulder and was surprised at how strange it felt, how it was warm, and at the same time so wet. I would have cried out, for every smallest movement of any part of my body sent waves of pain through me, but as I balanced awkwardly on my knees, I saw the dark outlines of three or four wolves half-hidden among the trees and falling snow.

My hands searched the snowy ground for a stone or branch which I could use to defend myself. Through a dizzied gaze, I saw the dim reflection of several pairs of gray eyes, and knew without needing to turn my throbbing head that other ghostly, floating pairs of eyes were surely behind me and to my sides. I did not need to see them to know it, I could almost feel their hot breath on my skin.

One wolf, large and lean, emerged out of the gloom, its savage features becoming clearer as it drew closer. Its mouth was open slightly and its moist tongue swept across its teeth, as if the beast were already tasting me. I found myself silently mouthing a prayer through chattering teeth and trembling lips. "The Lord is my shepherd, I shall not want..."

The words seemed only to keep time for the wolf as it slowly advanced. Now only a few feet directly before my face, the beast drew back its black lips in a vicious snarl and I stared into its drooling maw, jagged with long, white fangs. I was swaying back and forth weakly and shivering violently. I felt lightheaded and colder than I thought a human being could have been. I lost the power for words of any kind. The lead wolf's steady eyes stayed fixed on me as the others eagerly watched and waited.

How I wished and prayed that I might be back at home instead, that I was somewhere, safe inside, anywhere away from the wild world all around me.

Everything was so quiet and still and dead in time. This is the last sight I shall ever see on Earth, I thought, when suddenly, the wolf halted like a dog called to heel by its master. Its long snout snapped shut. Its eyes seemed to widen and get brighter, and then, still staring at me, the lead wolf began to back away.

I could not believe what was happening, it had to be a dream or delirium. I blinked quickly three of four times, but yet I saw it: the lead wolf retreated to rejoin the pack, and then, without ever breaking their gazes from me, their glowing eyes melted back into the woods, and the night, and the snow.

I tried to rise to my feet, but it was like moving in deep mud. I lost my balance and fell headfirst into the snowy ground. Just then, a shadow fell over me, blocking the moonlight. As I turned to look upward, my gaze was met by a lone pair of eyes towering over me as if one of the wolves were standing upright like a man. I felt my heart drop and then darkness rushed over me.

When I opened my eyes there was only blackness without form, and pain everywhere, and I had no doubt that I was in Hell. I was on my back on a hard, wooden surface and was too weak to move. I stared blankly into the nothingness. After a while, I was able to distinguish some of the features of wherever I was, and I decided that I was probably not dead after all. But where was I?

From around me there were lights, many small lights, that gradually became visible as candles, a series of red vigil candles, some near, others farther off. An occasional whistle of wind swayed the flames and made shadows dance over the walls.

In the faint light, I saw a vaulted ceiling above me. It appeared ancient and vast. Surrounding me were dark stone walls covered in busy patterns that were but dim blurs to me. Turning my aching head ever so slightly, I saw that farther down, and in fact covering most of the wall, were colorful pictures, large ones. I stared at them until I realized that they were stained glass windows, a row of them, shining faintly.

I was in a chapel. Thank God. Unlike the simple church in our village, this one was much more ornate and several times larger. I had heard the elders speak of such holy places, but had never seen one for myself.

I put a hand to my brow and touched a cloth wrapped tightly around my head. I crossed my right arm to my left shoulder, beneath my torn coat, and it too was wrapped, bandaged neatly. Both wounds ached powerfully as I struggled to sit up.

Now I could see what I took to be statues of saints and prophets standing upon pedestals, in niches throughout. At the far end of the room, there stood what must have been the altar, though it was heavy and black. No cross adorned it. A lone, red vigil light hung above it. On every wall were elaborate carvings and designs, and though I could not see them clearly, I imagined that they were beautiful and took some small comfort in the Godly tales they must tell for the faithful.

Where was I exactly? I knew of no such place within a day's walk of Vasaria, and though it now offered me safe haven, something about it made me feel uneasy. It did not have an air of holiness about it the way a place of worship should.

As I studied the chapel, I caught something move in the shadows near the altar, and I drew in my breath in fear. A figure stood there, hooded so that only part of his face showed. The feeble candlelight flickered and for a second I thought that whoever it was licked his lips as if in hunger before a meal. I shuddered as I was reminded of the wolves. Then the dark, cloaked shape began to glide noiselessly across the stone floor, coming toward me.

I tried to stand, but I was too weak and managed only to bring one hand to my face as if warding off whatever it was. As I peered between my fingers, I caught the glint of something around the cloaked figure's neck. It was a crucifix, though darkly tarnished. This must be the chapel's priest, my savior from the wolves.

I dropped my hand, relieved and feeling somewhat foolish. The priest stood several feet away from me. He was tall, dressed in a black robe so that I saw neither his feet nor his hands nor hardly his head, merely a bit of pale cheek and chin, a firm mouth, a pair of bright eyes peering from the shadow of his hood. Some kind of hermit or recluse, I guessed, always indoors in prayer or meditation.

"Rest," he said. "It has been a long night already."

"Is it still night?" I asked.

"Yes, it is midwinter's eve, the longest night of the year. But it will be over soon enough, for better or worse." He lifted an arm and pointed to a small wooden bowl on the floor beside me. "Drink. You have lost much blood and this will help you regain strength."

I reached for the bowl and pulled it across the smooth stone floor and took it in one hand to my dry lips. The liquid was lukewarm, salty and bittersweet, but I did not stop to ask what it was. I drank until the bowl was empty, then put it down. "Thank you."

"Good." He had not moved an inch closer to me the whole time, and I could see just the lower half of his chalky white face.

"Who are you?" I asked.

"I keep vigil here."

"Do you serve the Lord?"

He answered slowly, "We all do, in our own way."

"Where am I? Is this a chapel?"

"It is my sanctuary," he said, sounding both proud and sad.

"I am safe here then?"

"Yes. Now. While you are here."

I looked around at the strange carvings and sculptures, the designs and patterns that covered the walls and windows. "I have never been to this place before."

"Few come here but the lost."

"How did you find me in the storm? How did you know to come?"

"Let it be enough that our paths crossed in your time of need."

"You saved me, saved my life. Thank you... thank you. I would have died out there, frozen to death or a meal for the hungry wolves."

"We all die, eventually, for the wages of sin is death. What is uncertain is how we live, what good we manage to accomplish and what lessons we leave behind as guideposts for others." He paused, then asked, "Who are you?"

"Me? Me, I am no one, no one of importance, merely my father's son, a simple farm boy from a tiny village."

He seemed to scan my face, as if trying to place which village I came from without actually asking me. It is true that I do not look like most of the others in Vasaria, even my brother and sister, and so strangers sometimes think I must be from somewhere else, another village far off, like some changeling snuck in from the forest.

Then he broke his gaze. "No one? Everyone is someone. Everyone plays a part, for good or for ill, a part in the grand scheme. We may not be aware of it as we enact it, for we are mere players in life's drama, not its authors. But if you reflect on the tale of your life, you may yet discern the role you play."

As he was speaking I listened, not so much to the words, but how he spoke them. I was trying to place where he was from as well. He spoke fluently enough, but with an odd accent, not from anywhere close. The words sounded foreign in his mouth, despite his ease with them, as if he had learned them alone from a musty book.

"Tell me then, what is your tale?" he asked.

"My tale? I have none... nothing has ever happened to me, if that is what you mean. I have nothing to tell."

"Nothing? Indeed."

"Truly. I have heard it told that when you are about to die that you will see your entire life once more, yet when the wolves were circling in for the kill, I saw nothing, perhaps because there was nothing in my life worth reliving."

"How old are you, child?"

"I am not a child. I am thirteen, well, thirteen soon," I said, hoping my voice sounded like that of an adult and would not crack like a dry twig in the middle of my words. He hardly noticed.

"Thirteen... Ah..." A strange look clouded his pale face, as quick and as sharp as a bolt of lightning. He was lost in thought and did not speak for a full minute, until I asked, "Father?" and he seemed to shake off his thoughts like rainwater.

"Thirteen. A special age. I recall when I was that age myself. It brings to mind a tale. Since you claim you have no stories of your own, perhaps it will be to your benefit to listen to it."

I silently nodded.

"Very well," he said, then began his tale.

"Once, in a land far from here, over the gray seas, there lived a husband and wife, a nobleman and his fair lady. The man was a great lord, with a vast estate, and was the sovereign of many serfs. He was a just and wise man, and so those under his protection prospered as the land prospered, and were content with their place in God's great fiefdom.

The nobleman and his lady enjoyed the admiration of their peers and the loyalty of their vassals, and were happy, save for one silent sorrow of which they never spoke. A minor sorrow, really, with so much to be thankful for, but both longed for a child, an heir, to gladden their future years.

And so each one, separately, prayed to God for this one additional blessing, and that winter, not so many years ago, the wife came to her husband with the joyful news that she was with child. There was unprecedented merriment that holiday, dancing and song and wine and feasts and gifts brought from far and wide.

But the happy anticipation ended before the spring thaw. For, through no fault of her own, the fair lady lost her child before it was born. The sad lady mourned her loss for days, and her serving women wailed with her. The lord, whenever he did speak, barely choked back tears. A mist seemed to settle over the length of the estate.

On the Sabbath Day following the family's tragedy, the nobleman and his lady rose early and went to their private chapel. When the lord began to sing his customary hymns, he noticed an unfamiliar voice, low and smooth, harmonizing with his own. Still singing, the nobleman glanced at his lady, but she was silent, for she had not the strength or heart to sing then, not even to God.

'Did you hear someone singing with me, my wife?' he asked.

'I heard only you, my husband,' she answered.

The lord took up his hymn anew, and once more he heard two distinct voices, his own and another, deep and strange. And now the lady heard the second voice as well.

When the nobleman paused at his hymn, the other voice continued, and then the lord recognized it. It was the voice of Sorrow.

'Sorrow!' he called. 'Why do you accompany me?'

'I have come to reside with you,' said the voice. And from that moment Sorrow was with them, an unwelcome guest who could not be persuaded to depart. Sorrow sat with the lord in his long, silent hours and whispered in his ear, urging on him all manner of bad counsel.

'You have a plentiful cellar full of choice wine, do you not?' asked Sorrow. 'A fine bottle will make you forget that I am here, if I am such unpleasant company.'

'Perhaps,' said the lord, and he emptied a bottle of old wine that warmed him slightly. And so he drank another bottle, and another, and another, until all his thoughts were murky. And although Sorrow was still present to him, watching and whispering, the lord had to exert more effort to see him clearly.

Time passed, and the nobleman discovered that whenever he stopped drinking, Sorrow reappeared more clearly than previously, and so he occupied his days emptying one by one the bottles in his winecellar. This alarmed his lady, who attempted to reason with him, but Sorrow whispered in the lord's ear, 'She does not understand, for only I do,' and thus his wife's pleas went unheeded.

As more time passed, the lord began to neglect his duties, to God and to men. He spent all his time alone, drinking, and no longer attended mass, or oversaw the planting and harvesting, or ensured his serfs' protection. And so the lord's land began to suffer, and his manor house to fall into ruin, and the lord's serfs to grumble and become riotous.

At night in bed his lady often wept and Sorrow lay between the couple and gave them both foul and fitful dreams. One night the man dreamt that his wife and lands were a burden he could no longer bear and that he should leave them rather than continue struggling. When he awoke, he gathered a few meager belongings onto a horsecart and departed from his house, leaving his estate in his bewildered wife's care. 'Better to be rid of her,' Sorrow told him. 'Was she not there at the birth of your troubles? Come.'

And thus the man traveled, with Sorrow his only companion, and eventually came to a deserted hermit's hut outside a squalid village, where he begged for coins for drink and ate acorns and grass and gave no thought to anything except Sorrow.

One day, not far from New Year's Day, the man was roughly awakened in his hovel by a young boy.

'Do you have a wife, sir?'

'I had a wife. I have left her.'

'I have been sent to find the man who is husband to a woman in need. Do you recognize this?' He showed the man an ornate wedding band.

'Yes. It is my wife's. What of it?'

'Then you must follow me, and hurry. Your wife is giving birth this very night, and it is a far walk to where she waits.'

Sorrow started to speak, but the man leapt up so quickly and sped after the boy that Sorrow went unheard, though he trailed behind the two.

Winded and tired, the man reached where his poor wife lay, struggling to deliver her child to the world. The man handed his last gold piece to the boy, to bring a midwife from the village, and the boy hurried off.

While the man and woman waited, Sorrow caught up to them, and asked 'What is it?'

'Can you not see? My wife is laboring, about to give birth.'

'A birth! We must celebrate this. Ah, but we have no wine,' said Sorrow.

'Nor any money remaining to buy drink,' said the man.

'Sorrow indeed, for how will we celebrate properly?'

'Wait,' said the woman. 'I think that there is one silver piece in my jewelry box there. All the jewelry is long gone, but one piece of silver I have hidden in the very bottom.'

'Then go get it out,' said Sorrow.

'Alas, I cannot, for I am too weak from pain and labor,' said the woman.

'Nor can I,' said the man. 'I cannot abandon my wife's side now. But perhaps you can retrieve it. There is the box. Go inside, find the coin, and we will all drink heartily to my child's health.'

Sorrow grumbled, but drawn by the silver piece, he disappeared inside the small, wooden box. As soon as Sorrow was inside the coffer, the man leapt up, slammed shut the lid and locked it tightly.

'You stay there, false friend. Your absence is sweeter than any wine. I am done with you now.'

Sorrow could only listen and gnash his teeth inside his cramped jail as the midwife arrived and the lady gave birth to a healthy son who brought sweet joy again to the man and woman."

He paused as if for breath and I asked, "Is that how the story ends, then?"

I could not see his eyes, but he seemed to glare at me. "Do you know the tale of the boy who interrupted stories?" the priest asked.

"No."

"Then listen attentively, and be more like Job, whom God eventually rewarded for his faith and patience.

"Once, there lived a man and his son, a boy about your age, and they ran a simple country inn for travelers. All would have been happy for them, for travelers were frequent, except that the boy loved to hear stories. He demanded them from every guest who stayed in his father's inn, sometimes making them stay up late hours to tell them.

But after a time and many, many tales, the boy became so familiar, or thought he was so familiar, with the stories he heard, that he grew bored and began to interrupt the tellers and ask questions in the middle. He still demanded stories from all his father's guests, but now he interrupted so frequently that it was bothersome for travelers to try and get through any tale. Travelers began to avoid the inn, and without guests the father faced poverty.

Into this dire situation came a stranger, a foreign-looking man who arrived on foot carrying only a long, intricately-carved wooden cane. The father was overjoyed to have a paying guest, but his heart sank when he heard his son demanding a story from the man. Surely he would drive this traveler away in frustration too, and then what?

The stranger agreed to tell the boy a story, but with one condition to it, that the boy must not make a single interruption of the story until it was completed or else the stranger would give him a beating with his carved cane. The father was afraid of this bargain, but the boy assured him that he would say nothing and so the stranger began his story.

'Once a raven flew into a cemetery, perched upon on a gravestone, and waited. A raven flew into a cemetery, perched upon on a gravestone, and waited. A raven flew into a cemetery, perched upon on a gravestone, and waited...' And so the stranger continued, his voice full of feeling, but his words always unchanging. 'A raven flew into a cemetery, perched upon on a gravestone, and waited...'

After many long minutes of this, the boy became impatient. This was more repetition than he had ever heard in his life in any previous tale. Finally, his ears could stand no more and he shouted out, 'What kind of story is this? Nothing happens. A raven flew into a cemetery, perched upon on a gravestone, and waited... that is all.'

'The beginning is the most delicate part of any story, and now you have utterly spoiled it. The rest of the tale would have unfolded in time, but since you have interrupted me, I will not simply beat you, but I will never finish my story.'

Raising his sturdy cane high, he dealt the boy many terrible blows, a harsh and furious beating, until finally the father stayed the stranger's hand and chased him out of the inn. The stranger was never seen there again.

The father nursed his son back to health over many days, but the boy's legs had been so savagely beaten that for the remainder of his days he walked with a marked limp. He never interrupted another story, from anyone, no matter how lengthy."

He stopped, and looked at me. My face must have held a puzzled look.

"What troubles you, young one?"

"I am almost afraid to say," I said at last. "I do not want to interrupt your story... if that is not the end."

"You have a question? You may ask it without fear."

"What happened to the boy? I know he never interrupted another story again, but what else happened to him... when he grew up?"

"What do you think? What would be fitting?"

I thought, not long, and then smiled and said, "He grew up to be a great storyteller himself, traveling far and wide. And his first story was always the same, an answer to why he walked with a limp. And no one ever interrupted any of his stories, ever."

He almost smiled when I finished. "A clever young man. And now, if you allow it, I will complete my original tale."

I nodded and he started again.

"Time flew, as it always does. With Sorrow safely locked out of sight, the nobleman and his wife, with their new son, shouldered the hard task of rebuilding their former glory, restoring their manor house, reseeding the land, providing protection for their serfs, and recollecting their wealth. The son who had rekindled their happiness gradually grew up into a bright and curious young man.

One day, however, when the boy was twelve, while investigating an old and unused room in the manor house, he discovered in a hidden spot a dusty box which he could not open. This box he brought to his father, who snatched it away from the boy.

'You must never, never unlock this box.'

'Why?'

'Because it will bring you Sorrow. Tomorrow I must leave, my son, for my king calls me to fight for him in foreign lands. I may be gone a long time, and will not be here to watch over you. So promise me that while I fulfill my duty you will not open this box.'

'Yes, father.'

'Very well. I shall deal with the box. Put it out of your mind.'

Knowing his son's curious nature, the man slipped into the garden that night and secretly buried the box. The boy, however, saw his father do so, and he resolved to go and dig it up the next morning.

The next morning, though, was filled with noise and excitement as the lord departed on his mission, and with the entire household in commotion, and then with his father gone, thoughts of the buried box slipped out of the boy's mind for a while.

Then, on the eve of his thirteenth birthday, the boy

dreamt that the box was calling to him from the earth, telling him that he need not heed his father's advice, that he was now no longer a boy but a man, and should therefore follow his own path. And when the boy awoke moonlight was illuminating the garden outside, and the boy crept downstairs and swiftly dug up the wooden box.

He carried the box inside to his room, unseen, and debated with himself until dawn whether to actually unlock it or not. At last, his youthful curiosity won out over his duty to his father, and with a dagger he popped off the box's lock.

Sorrow burst angrily from the box and leapt onto the frightened boy's shoulders. 'I have you now,' Sorrow cried. 'Did you think that you could keep me in that jail forever? You will not get rid of me so easily this time, I tell you.'

The boy said, 'I did not put you into that box, someone else did.'

Sorrow examined the boy. 'It is true, you are not the one, but you look enough like him for my tastes, and I am certainly not leaving you now.'

Just then, there was a noise outside the room and a sudden knocking at the boy's door. There stood the boy's mother, ashen and shaking, supported by servants. She started to explain but was incapable of saying more than, 'Your father...'

Finally, one of the servants told him in a trembling voice, 'Your father... I am sorry... we have just received word by messenger... your father... is... dead...' He would have spoken further except that the boy's mother swooned and had to be carried to her chambers.

And so, Sorrow reestablished his presence in the manor house, whispering poison words within the walls. The boy, when not in the chapel praying to God for his father's soul, brooded alone. His mother became unhinged by this new grief, and withdrew into a lonely tower, never seeing sunshine or speaking to anyone, not even her son, and maintaining the bare minimum for physical life.

As his mother retreated into realms of gentle madness, and with Sorrow his lone companion, the boy would have succumbed to Sorrow's direst urgings, but that he had sworn a solemn vow that kept him alive, to become a knight in his father's likeness, and to bury Sorrow again, if possible."

He stopped suddenly, as if to check that I was truly listening, but then said nothing else.

Afraid to question him a second time, I waited a while before at last asking, "And did he become a knight, the boy?"

"Yes."

"How does the story end? Did he ever rid himself of Sorrow? Did he trick it into leaving, or trap it somewhere else?"

"I do not know," replied the priest. "Those events have yet to unfold, for Sorrow's tale has yet to run its course."

"I am not sure I understand."

"Is there still sorrow in the world, somewhere? Is there still sorrow in your own village at times?"

"Yes, at times."

"Yes, sorrow is most persistent."

The priest seemed almost sad now as he spoke, and so I questioned him no more.

After a few moments of silence, I said, "I did think of something, while you were telling your tale."

"Yes?"

"Something I remembered, that happened... not to me, but in my village."

"Tell me."

"It is not much of a tale, I suppose, not like the one you

told, but it is a legend in Vasaria. The village elders say that once, long ago, before I was born, a man, an outsider, came to Vasaria. He was a crusader, a knight of the Scarlet Cross, who had been badly wounded when he arrived. He was cared for in our village. For several days he lay between life and death, both forces tugging at his soul, until by the grace of God he eventually awoke. When the knight recovered his strength, he left Vasaria to fulfill a sacred mission and was never seen again."

"And what was this mission?"

"No one knows for certain," I admitted. "Certainly there is evil enough in the world for a man to find a just cause."

"What do you know of evil?"

"There are the Turks, of course, who would destroy us all. I have heard tales of barbarians who plunder mountain villages. And once a traveler told the story of the Bloody Prince of Moravia. Even in Vasaria, we live in the constant shadow of fear cast by the Dark Tower."

"The Dark Tower?"

"Yes. From the village you can see a tower of black stone. It is old, older than Vasaria itself, so say the elders. Its true name is long forgotten and now it is known only as the Dark Tower. I have never seen it up close myself. We are forbidden to go near it. You must have seen it, or at least heard of it."

He nodded and said, "Tell me more."

"They say that Lord Brom lives in the tower, though no one has ever seen him... at least no one alive. I have heard it told that no one who ventures to the tower ever returns, and so far as I know, that is true. No one knows exactly what happens to them, but they do not come back. Some say that Lord Brom kills them and carves their bones into his furniture. Others say he is an evil sorcerer who steals men's souls and turns them into ravens and wolves and toads.

They say..."

"Who says?" the priest asked. "Who told you these things?"

"Well, everyone. The other children, my friends. We hear what the adults say to each other when they think we are not listening."

"Ah... I see. Continue."

"It is said that on clear nights when the moon is full you can see Lord Brom walking at the top of his tower, looking for new victims. His fingers are as long and sharp as sickles, and his eyes alone can stop a man's heart, and his breath can freeze a man's blood into solid ice. When he stalks at night, he makes all the village dogs whimper in their sleep. And if the milk turns sour overnight, we know that Lord Brom must have passed close by.

"I have also heard some say that Lord Brom creeps into the village at night, looking for misbehaving children to steal from their beds and take back to his tower to feast upon. But I think that part is just something that parents made up to tell their young, to scare them into being quiet at bedtime.

"Stories like that are for children, like scarecrows to frighten little birds, and I am not a child. And besides, it does not matter whether I believe they are real or not, they are simply stories."

"Simply stories?" the priest said. "But stories are important, my son, more than you can imagine. God created the world with stories, did He not?"

I did not know what he meant, but the priest went on.

"God did not fashion this world as you or I would mold a ball of clay, physically. No, He merely said, 'Let there be...' and there was whatever He spoke of. He told a tale of how the world was to be and the world was born of His words. This world is made of stories, to its core. And because the world is made of stories, you must be very cautious which tales you believe, which ones you tell and which ones you listen to. The right story, or the wrong one, can change you forever."

"My father says that the only thing that can change a man's world forever is his children."

He seemed to weigh this in his mind. "Children. A wise man, your father. But to return to the legends you have heard, what becomes of the crusader and his sacred mission?"

"No one is really certain. People tell different ends to the story. Some say that the crusader went to vanquish some evil thing, but was instead slain by it, and now his ghost haunts the night with the souls of the fiend's other victims. Others say the knight was triumphant, that he still lives, but an evil curse befell him so that he could never return to his homeland."

"Both, sad endings," the priest mused, then asked, "What do you believe happened to this noble crusader?"

I stared at the priest, looking long into the shadow that veiled his eyes.

"In my heart, I like to think that he was not killed or cursed, that he yet lives and continues to fight battles to uphold that which is sacred." The priest considered my words, and after a moment, I went on. "That is what I think, or what I would like to believe happened. And if the world is made of stories, then that is the one that I keep in my world."

"Perhaps your heart leads you to what others miss," the priest said. "The battle against evil is seldom decided in a single foray."

He paused. Then he moved so suddenly out of the shadows that I flinched. He came toward me without a sound, and I pressed hard against the rough, wooden bench at my back. Just short of reaching me, he veered a little to the right and stopped just beyond my outstretched feet.

His pale face, still barely visible under his hood, was turned half away from me, so that he spoke more to the wall than to me. He stuck a thin finger out at something on the wall.

"Do you see this carving here?"

I had to wriggle in my seat a bit and crane my head to the side, and ached fiercely all over doing so, until, in the dim candlelight, I could scarcely make out an image. "Yes, I think so."

His hand dropped back to his side, disappearing within the folds of his cloak.

I gazed upon an image chiseled in the stone wall of the chapel. In the middle was a ring which held an odd symbol that I did not recognize. Spread out above it was a bearded man with a crown and great wings. Two angels seemed to issue forth upon his breath. The angels each held spears and thrust them downward at two winged demons. The demons, which seemed to come from the mouth of a serpent-tongued devil set below the central ring, raised swords against the angels' lances. It was not unlike some drawings I had seen in books, but I did not know what lesson this carving held, etched in stone.

"There are forces of virtue and forces of evil. With every breath they contend for the world, one human soul at a time. How do they gain entry into these mortal souls? They whisper sweet words, stories, and whichever side spins the more convincing tale, that tale the soul believes, and clings to, and is bound up with forever.

"Allow me to tell you something about the crusader you spoke of, the one who passed through Vasaria many years ago, for I know something of his tale. His is a story about a man, an ordinary mortal. All his life he had heeded destiny's

call, until at last it brought him to a mysterious and lonely place. There, he came upon a creature, ancient and dark.

"The thing challenged him, but before the battle was joined the knight was given a choice. He could leave the battle unfought and return unscathed to his homeland and know love and prosperity, or he could make his stand against the ancient one, and if he lost, suffer the grim consequences. The sweet voices of evil and virtue whispered long in his ears."

I looked again to the carving on the wall. The angels and demons encircled the central ring. I pictured the crusader there, trapped between them.

"At last," continued the priest, "he chose to engage in combat, little though he recked the dangers. Death is not the worst this world threatens, my son. The knight was enslaved to a grievous and dismal fate. Beyond darkness and loneliness, there were terrible new temptations, desires... hungers. His faith alone sustains him, though at times the righteous path is a difficult course to maintain. He keeps his solitary vigil still, balanced between two great forces at the threshold where they touch one another as lightly as a kiss."

He stopped, still staring at the chiseled relief. There, the weapons of the angels and the demons almost clashed, but did not.

"Do you understand now what has become of your legendary crusader?" he asked.

He turned his face slightly to me, and though I could not see much more of it than before, I thought I saw it more clearly. I waited a moment, then said with a small smile, "Yes, I think so."

"Do you? Truly?"

I was less sure when he asked again, but still said, "Yes."

He turned completely away from me and moved back into the shadows where he had been standing, and I thought

I heard him say as he did, "I am not certain that you do."

I now noticed for the first time that I could see the outline of the priest a bit better and that it had become easier to see the fine details on the wall carvings all around me. I looked at the windows and saw that the stained glass shone more brightly, and I could see more clearly the pictures there. They seemed wrong somehow. The more I looked at them, the less comfort they offered.

The window directly across the room from me portrayed a scene which I first took to represent the story of Abraham and Isaac. Clearly now, I saw that the sacrificial fire was burning thick and black on the altar, but Isaac was nowhere to be seen and Abraham was bent over as if weeping. To the left was another window, this one depicting a son embracing his father in a lane outside their home. The prodigal son's return, I thought, until I noticed something I had missed before: In the hand of the son was a dagger, as if he was not falling into his father's arms, but stabbing him in the back.

I scanned the other windows for some familiar stories, something Biblical, but nothing was as I expected.

I started to feel cold again, like the ice in the bottom of a well, and afraid of things that I could not understand or put words to. Without either of us talking, the chapel seemed to whisper doubts into my soul. After a long silence, I asked, "Do you not get lonely here? Is there no one else here with you?"

"There are other souls here with me, and some guide and aid me in my duties. Others are under my watch, lest they gain too much freedom and cause harm."

The priest must have noticed that I was looking at him more closely, because he pulled back into the shadows slightly and then quickly asked, "Can you walk?"

I felt less pain than I had since waking up, but was still cold and lightheaded. "Yes. I think so."

"Then stand and come with me," he said. It was more a command than a suggestion.

"Yes," I said, and slowly rose to my feet. Pain and ache shot through me, and my head seemed to sway as if it would tumble off, but I stood.

He strode toward the rear of the chapel, then turned and bade me to follow him. "Quickly," he said, sounding angry. "There are some things you can argue with, but a sunrise is not one of them."

With pain and fear knocking at my ribcage, I did as he said.

"Where are you taking me?" I asked, but he gave no answer, only kept walking ahead of me. I followed, perhaps more afraid of being left alone in the comfortless chapel than of what awaited me ahead, in the unknown place to which he now led me.

We went out a doorway at the back of the chapel and down a series of dim corridors and finally up a short flight of stairs into another room, larger and without candles. The only light shone in from several slitted windows high above.

As we came into this room, the priest, instead of walking directly across the floor toward the archway opposite, turned abruptly along the columned wall nearest us, and walked the shadowed edges. I stopped briefly, not sure if I should do the same, but the priest did not look back or say a word, so I did as he did, following behind until we came to the cobwebbed archway and passed through it, into a short corridor and to a smaller room, windowless and unlit, with two huge wooden doors at the end.

The priest put his bone-white hand to the immense doors but did not open them.

"Listen carefully, my son," he said.

I was as near to him as I had been since coming into the chapel, but the darkness was so thick here that we may as well have been miles apart.

"Heed my instructions. Outside these doors you will see an ancient stonework, a triple archway to the side of the road. Beyond the ruin, you will come to a cobblestone path leading away from here. Follow this path through the woods and it shall lead you home."

"To my village... to Vasaria?"

"Yes."

I opened my mouth to say more, but he raised a hand, palm extended, inches from my face, to quiet me before any sound came out. His nails were long and pointed.

"I have not finished. You must do one further thing. You must swear to me that you will do it."

"Yes, anything. I owe you my life."

"Do not look back."

"Do not look back, " I repeated dumbly.

"Yes. You will see the archway, the road, and the forest path. You must follow this path, steadfastly. Do not veer left or right until you are returned to your village. You must not look back, no matter what you see or think you see along your journey, for if you do, a part of you will be lost forever. You will never again see the things around you in the same light. Now, promise me that you will do as I ask."

"Yes, I will."

He seemed satisfied and pushed the heavy oaken doors open with barely any effort. The weak light of dawn flooded in and overwhelmed my eyes after being in so much darkness for so long. Before I could adjust my eyes, the priest put a bony hand upon my back and gently but firmly guided me out of the doorway, remaining inside himself.

I half-stumbled down some cracked stone steps, still squinting hard. It would be a clear morning. The storm was over. There was a quilt of snow covering everything and the air was crisp, but not unpleasant. Ahead I saw the gateway the priest had spoken of, and set off toward it.

I nearly turned back to thank the priest once more, but then I remembered his words, and so I merely paused a moment and then walked on. Just as well, for I heard the great doors close again behind me, almost before I was down the steps.

I walked the weathered, cobblestone path past the gateway ruins. Wrought iron gates closed off the outer arches, yet the central span stood open. Sorrowful faces lined with snow adorned the top of each gate. Not far from there, I saw a narrow path among the trees that led into the woods. I followed it.

I trudged on, once more not knowing exactly which way I was heading. Twisted branches of black trees laden with ice and snow were entwined overhead, choking out the rays of dawn. As I walked, I tried to see all that was around me, though daring not to turn my head too far to either side. Ravens sat perched among the thorny limbs and watched me pass in unsettling silence. Though the priest said if I stayed on this path it would lead me home, I felt uneasy and began to doubt his words.

The path began to snake downhill. Ahead now, even through the dense trees, I could see that the sky was brightening. I must be heading east. I reasoned that I should be able to spot the Dark Tower soon, on one side of me or another, through whatever woods I now traveled. Once I found that landmark, I would be able to regain my bearings, but I hoped that the path I was following did not venture too near the forbidden keep.

The longer I walked and looked for the tower, the more curious I became. The woods began to thin out slightly until the path widened and I saw some things that I recognized. Just ahead was a tree stump shaped like a spider, and beyond that I could see a tall, moss-covered stone standing alone in a clearing.

Wait, I must be near the main road to the village, I thought. And so the path I was on had to be coming from...

Suddenly, a thousand dread thoughts rushed over me at once. Of course, the mountain, the trees, the ravens...

I could not help it, I swear. I stopped dead in my tracks and, without thinking, turned around. And there behind me, just above the treetops in the breaking dawn, I saw the Dark Tower. Where I had come from. Where I had been. With the priest. With the crusader. With Lord Brom.

In Vasaria, whenever anyone tells the tale of the Dark Tower and whatever thing lives there, they always end by saying, "No one ever returns from there." But that is not the whole story, for I now see, the few that do return from there are never the same. And that much of the tale I know is true.

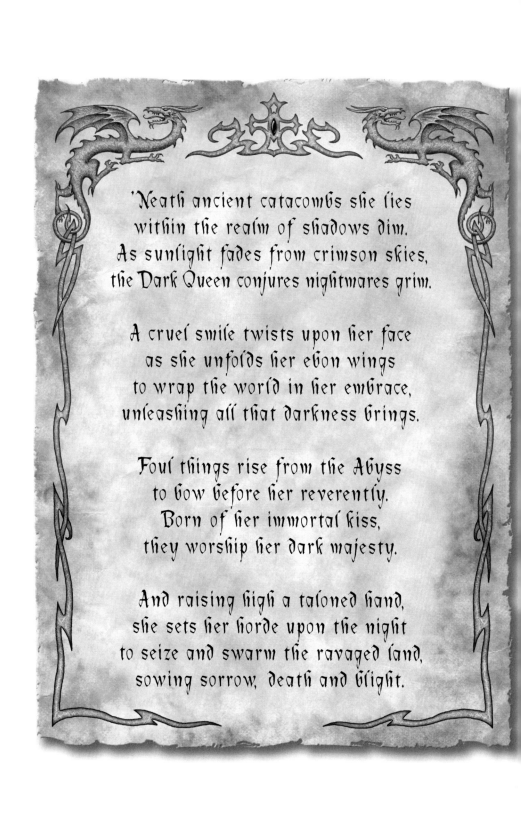

'Neath ancient catacombs she lies
within the realm of shadows dim.
As sunlight fades from crimson skies,
the Dark Queen conjures nightmares grim.

A cruel smile twists upon her face
as she unfolds her ebon wings
to wrap the world in her embrace,
unleashing all that darkness brings.

Foul things rise from the Abyss
to bow before her reverently.
Born of her immortal kiss,
they worship her dark majesty.

And raising high a taloned hand,
she sets her horde upon the night
to seize and swarm the ravaged land,
sowing sorrow, death and blight.

The Queen of Darkness doth reign as mistress to things most foul. She doth revel in wickedness, and Misery and Torment serve her as loyal subjects. She doth sate her hungers upon the sins of man, and slake her thirst upon mortal blood. She doth command the legions of the night, and her lot doth spread pestilence to mar the land. For she is the deliverer of woe and death upon all of God's creatures.

Lilith

Joseph Vargo

Though the tale is generations old, we preserve it intact still. We tell it just as it was told to us, as it was told to our fathers and theirs. When we are young, it is a dark secret kept shrouded from us, but when we come of age, we are made to memorize the story without embellishment or deletion. For this tale is that of our people and our land, the curse we struggle against and the one hope we hold for redemption. I tell it to you now, for it has become your tale as well.

None from outside knew the source of the darkness that spread across the mountains and vales of the Carpathians like the broad wings of Night. It first became known in small ways that might well have gone unnoticed had they not occurred in such proximity. Children went missing. Several once secure mountain passes were deemed dangerous for travel by night. Tamed forests that had been traversed in safety for centuries became dark and wild again. Though many grew uneasy, they but watched and waited.

But then the signs grew suddenly more ominous. Entire villages were emptied and abandoned. New rulers appeared as if from nowhere, establishing petty realms and reigning with an iron hand. A blight was upon the entire land, a shadow creeping steadily across this remote corner of the world, stretching its black arms across the Balkans into the light of civilized Christendom.

Twelve men came forth to stand against the darkness. Whence they came no tale now tells. In time, their journeys and their battles against the vile forces that ruled the land diminished their number, and only three remained to seek out the dark heart of evil. And it was those three that made their way into Vasaria, in the barren month of November, in the year of our Lord 959.

No one met them as they entered Vasaria beneath the night's dark veil. It was desolate, merely a hollow shell of the village that had once stood here. Tendrils of smoke rose from the splintered and charred remnants of wooden beams and the scent of fire still hung in the air. The wind moaned plaintively throughout the fallen stone and timber.

The three riders warily trotted their horses through the smoldering ruins, bringing them to a halt in the ravaged village square. Two of the men sat tall atop their steeds, unfettered by the heavy chain armor they wore. Imposing longswords hung sheathed at their sides. The third man wore the robes of a priest and rode hunched in his saddle, his head bowed in weariness as if burdened by the silver cross which hung from a chain about his neck. The knights dismounted and at once drew their swords. The holy man blessed and anointed each blade with oil he poured from a flask.

The two knights trod cautiously between the skeletal remains of mud-bricked hovels to search for traces of life, heedful and alert to even the slightest rustle of leaves. The priest stayed with the horses and lit a torch, then withdrew a heavy book from his pack. Opening the tome to a marked page, he began to chant aloud a Latin verse. His voice echoed throughout the fallen village as he recited his ancient prayer.

Not long after, the two knights returned.

"None remain," Stephon said solemnly.

The second knight, Thomas, shook his head to silently affirm that he too found no one.

"Then surely they are lost to the darkness," replied the priest.

"They could not be far. The embers still burn," Thomas said.

The holy man's gaze followed the cobblestone road which led through the village and into the darkened forest of surrounding trees. "There," he whispered.

Both knights turned toward Father Aldis. His face was frozen in a look of fear and awe as he stared above the treeline. Slowly, the two men turned to see what sight had filled the holy man with such dread. There in the distance, above the line of withered trees, stood a tower so black that it was barely visible against the night sky.

"Those who are not yet dead, soon shall be... or worse," said Thomas.

"There still may be hope for them if we act swiftly," Stephon urged.

"Nay," declared the priest. "This castle is no mere outpost, it is the lair of the Beast itself. We must wait until the dawn breaks."

Stephon paced helplessly. "It shall be too late by then."

"We are the last of our kind. Let us not fall to recklessness," warned Aldis. "Let us pray for them."

The three joined hands and bowed their heads in prayer.

The priest bestowed a blessing for the souls of the dead, then turned his gaze heavenward to deliver his benediction, "Lord, grant us the strength to smite the infernal legions, that we might reach those not yet lost, and deliver them from the depths of darkness, whatsoever deeds required."

The knights pledged the solemn oath, repeating the words, "Whatsoever deeds required." It was the oath that had bound them in their crusade. For years, they had fought side by side to battle the evil that had infected the land like a plague. They had slain demon spawn and vanquished all manner of foul things that arose from beyond the realms of death. What they had borne witness to had made them true believers in their faith.

As he swore the oath, the priest looked upon his comrades. Both were formidable warriors, strong and swift. He knew what the pact meant and he was bound to it; he was most likely to meet his death first. He was willing to lay down his life, a small sacrifice for this sacred cause.

The trinity kept their hands joined and knelt in silent meditation. They did not notice the approach of a mysterious onlooker.

"Whatsoever deeds required?" the stranger's voice echoed.

Stephon leapt to his feet, sword in hand. In the road before them stood a dark figure, blocking the path to the tower. The crescent moon cast a shimmering glow, giving the effect of a halo of blue light surrounding the stranger.

"Sheathe thy blade. I am no enemy," the figure said, holding his empty hands outstretched. "Whatsoever deeds required; dost thee take these words to heart?"

"Indeed, we have sworn this as the pact which binds us in our mission," answered Thomas.

"And, if that which is required of thee demands thee to go 'gainst thy moral principles or do harm to one of thine own, will thee do as such?" the stranger asked.

"If it be for the greater good, I shall, and without hesitation," Stephon proclaimed boldly.

"A noble sacrifice indeed, but thou dost now stand before the threshold of the Beast's domain. If thou art to venture onward, take heed to these words, good men, for they shall serve thee in thy mission." The figure paused for a moment, then continued, his voice now taking on a grave resonance, "When the serpent lies coiled deep within its lair, only one of its own might find way to strike it."

They stood, trying to make sense of the stranger's cryptic words.

"Thy mission is dire," the figure spoke again. "About thee, this small village lies desolate and dead. If this pox spreads throughout the lands, soon the entire Earth shall wither and be as such. Whatsoever deeds required, do not fail."

The trio looked about them at the blighted husks of buildings, then heard the flap and flutter of great wings as a cold wind fell down upon them. When they looked back, the dark stranger was gone, but not without a trace. A sword now protruded from the ground on the very spot he had stood only a moment before. No ordinary weapon was this; it was ornate, an exquisite relic. The pommel and hilt were adorned with dark jewels, and the sleek blade was etched with intricate scrollwork. Stephon plucked the sword from the soil. The long weapon felt light in his grasp. The moonlight shimmered and gleamed along the blade's edge. The three looked to one another. None spoke a word, but their faces revealed that the same conclusion was drawn by all; both the weapon and the mysterious messenger had come in answer to their prayer.

"We go now," Stephon said, "before the dawn."

"It is far too dangerous," warned the holy man.

"Nay," Stephon retorted, brandishing the relic sword, "we have been gifted, bestowed with the means to smite the beast, to vanquish all who would oppose us."

"It is not wise," Father Aldis begrudged.

Climbing atop his saddle, Stephon glared down at the

holy man, then looked toward his fellow knight.

Thomas mounted his steed, casting his vote without a word.

The priest watched as his comrades rode to the edge of the village and disappeared into the darkness that shrouded the forest path. At last, he followed.

Together, the three made their way through the withered and barren woods, ever wary of each shifting shadow, until finally they emerged before the baleful tower. The keep stood black as pitch, and all was still as death itself. They left their horses tethered within the trees and proceeded on foot toward the Devil's keep. At the base of a broad stone staircase, the priest stopped as if he had struck an unseen barrier.

"Dost thee feel the malevolence? It doth seep from this place to mar the land," the priest whispered. "It is the heart of darkness."

The castle stood silent and soulless, yet it cast a pall more dreadful than a thousand nightmares. The three ascended the steps which led to the towering entranceway of the keep. A cold wind rose as they stood before the massive doors and prepared to light torches. Stephon's eyes followed the black walls of the keep upward. Demons and abominations of stone held dominion in the furthest heights of the tower's facade. He stared at a row of macabre gargoyles. They sat motionless and silent, half-hidden in shadow, haunched upon a ledge above the castle entrance. One of the grim creatures held Stephon's gaze. As Thomas lit a torch, the gargoyle's eyes narrowed.

"They are alive!" Stephon shouted, but all too late.

Swift as arrows, four shadows leapt down from their lofty perches and set upon the trio of crusaders. Thomas was caught unaware; the torch dropped from his hand and he was in the clutches of one of the devils before he could draw his longsword. Stephon swung the relic blade, almost effortlessly severing the hand and head of one of the creatures, but before he could strike again, another fiend wrenched the sword from his grip. The priest held out his crucifix, but the sweep of a taloned hand tore the cross from its chain. Another hand, white and clawed, grasped the priest's throat. Leering into the holy man's face, the creature bared its fanged teeth and hissed dryly. The thing, once a man, had the look and scent of the grave. Rotting flesh covered its sullen features, and its glazed eyes were sunk deep into their sockets.

"Nay, my brother. The queen shall decide their fate," said the one who now held the relic sword. He stood taller than the others and his smooth flesh held an ashen pallor. Long, white hair splayed across the shoulders of his ebon cloak. He bore not the foul and loathsome mien of the others, but instead possessed an air of nobility. He laid a hand upon the heavy door and it opened with a resounding creak.

The three were led into the keep and were soon engulfed by the darkness within. Unseen hands reached out to harshly shove and drag them along as their nocturnal captors marched them through the castle. Surrounded, they stumbled through the shadows like herded cattle. Their footsteps echoed as if they were passing through a large chamber. From somewhere in the distance, a man's screams could be heard, drowning in a chorus of diabolical laughter.

They staggered blindly up a winding staircase and at last were led into the grand hall. The large chamber was dim, lit only by a few candles held by twin candelabras at the far end of the room. Heavy tapestries covered the windows with woven images of fierce beasts. All around lay dead and decaying bodies from which a putrid stench arose. Iron cages held captive the lost villagers. Men and women cried and screamed out for merciful release from their torment while small children cowered behind them. Foul creatures hissed and lurked in the shadows at the edge of the hall.

At the far end of the chamber, six stone steps rose to a broad dais upon which stood a single, tall throne. Reclining seductively in the throne was a woman who inspired both lust and dread. The three prisoners were dragged helplessly to the foot of the steps to stand before Mara, the Dark Queen. Her sleek, pale form was draped entirely in black. Her dark eyes glistened coldly as she looked down upon them with disdain.

"What have we, Dravek?" the queen asked, her icy voice casting a chill upon the air.

The white-haired one mounted the steps, then reverently dropped to one knee before the throne. He bowed his head and spoke, "Intruders dare to breach our stronghold. Our coven has been broken, my queen. Fenris is slain."

"Slain? By mortal men?"

"Yes, my queen," Dravek answered. Raising his eyes to meet hers, he held forth the sword and silver crucifix.

Mara fingered the dangling cross. "Holy warriors," she sneered, "this cause you serve is hopeless."

"Your legions have fallen before us," Stephon proclaimed defiantly. "Our crusade..."

"Your crusade," Mara interrupted, "has come to its end." She stood and stepped to the edge of the dais, glowering down at them. Though not imposing of stature, she struck an austere and frightening presence.

One of his captors effortlessly crushed Stephon to his knees before her. He lifted his head to face her cold stare. "You may strike us down, but more shall follow," he declared.

"Of a certainty," she said, a cruel smile twisting her lips.

"And I shall take them even as I now take you." She came down the steps toward them so smoothly that she might have been floating. Dravek followed her like a pale shadow. She passed slowly before Thomas and Aldis, meeting their eyes, a low, cool laughter rising from her. "Holy warriors," she mocked contemptuously, "your faith lies in fable and the ramblings of madmen." Holding the priest's gaze, she raised the crucifix and continued, "You foolishly worship the legend of a crucified mortal."

Stephon looked at Aldis to respond, but the priest appeared choked with fear. Stephon said, "Is it better to worship empty darkness?"

"Worship me!" Mara cried, her rising voice filling the great hall. "I am no vague promise of salvation made by prophets of submission to pious fools! I am power, power to defeat all the forces of light. In the fullness of time, a new sun shall rise over the Earth, a black dawn that shall allow those born of the night to live freely in this world and rule as befits our power and our nature. My darkness shall reign over all, and no light shall prevail against it."

Mara turned and took the relic sword from Dravek. She ran her hands along its smooth, polished flat admiringly. "Your deaths shall serve to amuse me and feed my hungry children." As she continued, her voice changed to a hypnotic purr. "Surrender yourselves unto me and I shall be merciful. Perhaps I shall bestow the dark gift upon the worthiest of you and embrace you into my fold." Now she lifted her eyes to theirs, and each felt his heart held frozen in his chest, trapped between beats.

Stephon forced himself to speak. "We desire not your dark curse, nor shall we beg for our lives. Our forces shall never succumb to you, for our strength is greater than yours."

Mara held out the sword, offering the hilt to the

crusader, the tip of the blade set against her breast. "Show me your strength, mighty warrior."

Stephon leapt up, reaching for the sword, and was instantly set upon by two of the queen's cadaverous minions, pinning him to the floor.

"Low dog, how dare thee raise a hand to thy master?" the queen condescended.

The hall filled with vicious laughter as Stephon struggled in vain.

Mara threw both the sword and the crucifix onto the floor before the priest, then spoke again. "Two choices rest before you."

The holy man's eyes fell upon the sacred relics at his feet.

"You may pick up your cross and summon forth its great powers against me, or you may pick up the sword and use the blade to do my bidding. Choose now, the path of your destiny."

Aldis hesitated, weighing his decision, the oath he had sworn to his faithful warriors and the words of the stranger echoing in his head. At last, he picked up the sword. The demon queen smiled, pleased by his decision. Vile creatures stood at each of her sides. Even wielding the holy blade, he would surely be struck down before he could reach the queen. Mara gestured a clawed finger toward Stephon, and the priest turned his gaze to his fallen comrade. The knight struggled against two of his captors who held his arm outstretched.

"Off with it," the queen said, coldly.

Aldis stared at his friend for a moment, their blood oath echoing in his head. The priest's eyes conveyed a silent apology, then he brought the sword down hard upon Stephon's wrist, severing his hand from it. The knight cried out as his life's blood pulsed from the stump. The priest's stomach turned at the sight of the ichor. A growing stain of crimson spread across the marble floor, and pale creatures crawled and slithered from the shadows to lap at the puddle.

"In the name of Christ..." Thomas uttered.

He did not speak another word before Mara was upon him. She clutched the knight by his throat and drove him to his knees. "How dare thee speak blasphemy in my presence?" She tore open his jaw, breaking it with her bare hands, then dug her black nails into his tongue and ripped it from his throat. Blood gushed from his mouth as he whimpered and gurgled, falling into a convulsing heap.

The priest was shaking as Mara turned her gaze toward him. He threw the sword away. It clanged across the marble floor, coming to rest somewhere in the shadows. As the Dark Queen slowly stepped toward him, the priest dropped to his knees, bowing his head before her.

"My only desire is to serve thee. Spare my life and embrace me into thy coven," he pleaded.

Mara approached him, and placing her hand below his chin, lifted his head with a single, sharp talon. Behind her, lustrous black drapes streamed down from the vaulted heights of the ceiling, giving the illusion of great ebon wings rising from her back. She smiled wide enough to show her fangs, then swiped the claw across his throat, tearing it open. Aldis clutched his neck, but his efforts did little to stop the blood which began to seep through his fingers.

The Dark Queen turned and let fall her black shroud to reveal a thin, silken gown, then ascended the dais to sit upon her throne.

"Bring him forth," she commanded.

Her minions dragged him to kneel before her seated majesty. She held a chalice beneath the gaping wound and let it fill with each pulse of his heart. She lifted the chalice to her lips and drank the blood, closing her eyes to savor it. "Thy blood is sweet. It is the untainted nectar of life itself. Its succulence is unknown to wretched mortals, relished only by my exalted subjects."

The priest slumped as he felt his life slowly fade.

Mara leaned over him as he lay at her feet. "I am the Queen of Shadows..." she said, pulling him to her. "I hold dominion over the night." Drawing the sheer fabric of her gown aside, she ran one claw lightly along the pale flesh of her breast. Mara sliced the nail through her skin, then cupped the priest's head and held his face to her bosom. "I am the Dark Goddess..." A trickle of blood ran down her white skin. He licked it, then sucked from the wound. Mara spoke softly into the priest's ear, "and I bestow you with life eternal." She lowered her fanged mouth to his throat.

A fever swept over him, torrid and charged, casting out the chill of near death that had gripped his body. His sight dimmed, and slowly his vision closed in until all was blackness.

Aldis awakened upon the cold stone floor. No longer assailed by the stench of decay, he was now invigorated by a sweet scent which rose from a pool of dark liquid. He tasted it, licked it, then crawled along the floor, lapping at it hungrily, until at last it brought him face to face with a ghastly visage. It was Thomas, his eyes frozen in terror, his mouth gaped wide, far beyond its natural extent, in a death scream. He was dead, and Aldis was now greedily drinking his blood. Savage laughter erupted from the queen's vile minions.

The priest brought himself to his feet as his strength steadily returned. Recalling the bloody gash which the Dark Queen had inflicted upon him, he raised a hand to his throat, but found no trace of the wound. The once dim hall now held a blue radiance. Aldis staggered past the cages which held the imprisoned villagers, and the people cowered in fear at the sight of him. He turned away and fled through the tower, the demonic laughter ringing through the halls behind him.

The priest wandered aimlessly through the twisting corridors, following the winding passages and stairways down through the keep until at last he came to a place where the infernal laughter could not penetrate. He now stood before the entrance to a chapel, deep within the confines of the tower. The doors hung open at odd angles, nearly torn from their wrought iron hinges.

Aldis slowly entered the forlorn sanctuary. Though cobwebbed and littered, the room still held all the trappings of ancient splendor. Columns rose to vaulted ceilings and the walls were lined with intricate stained glass windows.

Yet, even here, Mara's decadence held sway. The statues of saints and angels had been disfigured or cast down, and in their place, foul gargoyles glared out from the dark alcoves. The elaborately detailed windows held no hallowed icons, but instead depicted strange and cruel scenes of lost significance. The altar was a solid slab of black stone, covered with dusty candles. Discarded pages of parchment, torn and partly burned, lay strewn about like so many dead leaves. They stirred slightly as he walked by, revealing a mosaic maze set into the chapel floor, a prayer labyrinth.

The priest lowered his head in prayer as he began to follow the tiles of the maze, penitently walking the path of salvation, focusing intently on each whispered word, on each cold stone tile. He stepped over the scattered pages that littered the floor until he wound through the labyrinth and stood at its center. A solitary piece of parchment lay in the center of the maze. He picked it up to discover that it was a page torn from an ancient tome, transcribed in a fine Latin hand...

And from the dust and mud of the Earth, the Lord God formed a mate for Adam and breathed life into her. And her name was Lilith. And though she was graced with beauty and knowledge, she held reverence for neither God nor man and would not abide by them. She fled from the garden to the lands where no man yet lived.

And the Lord God called forth three Angels, Sanvi, Sansavi, and Semangelaf. And they were clad in armor and wielded avenging blades. And God sent His warriors forth so that they might return Lilith to the Garden to lay beneath Adam.

The Angels came upon Lilith as she joined in lewd revelry with the Watchers and the Fallen Ones. And the Angels would raise no sword against their dark brethren, so in turn, they placed boundaries upon Lilith's domain. The Angel's names would mark the borders of her realm.

And the Angels returned to stand before the Lord to tell Him all that had come to pass. And the Lord God declared, "Thou hast acted against the command of thy Lord God for the sake of thy rebel brethren. Therefore, thou art banished to the Earthly Realm. Thou shalt watch over the children of Adam. Guard ye the borders which thou hast set so that none of the brood of Lilith might trespass beyond."

And Lilith brought forth upon the Earth a brood of dark beasts and they dwelt in the night

The page ended in the midst of the sentence. The priest let it slip from his hand and lifted his eyes upward. There, painted upon the vaulted dome of the chapel, were the likenesses of three angels, winged and armor-clad, each wielding a gleaming sword.

The rays of the dawning sun streamed through the windows. At first, the light cast a warm glow, a wash of colors across the chapel, but soon the windows were ablaze with blinding and seething fury.

Aldis raised a hand to shield his eyes. Ardent rays ripped across his palm, instantly blistering his flesh. The priest reeled back and ducked away into a shadowed recess of the room. A thick, hooded cloak lay trampled on the dusty floor. Aldis quickly snatched the garment up and pulled it over his cassock, drawing the hood over his head. Cautiously, he stepped back toward the prayer circle which now shone brilliantly in the sunlight. He slowly entered the illuminated labyrinth and felt the sun's heat beating down upon him, even through the heavy fabric of the monk's cloak. As he stood, surrounded yet unscathed by the sun's light, the priest basked in revelation.

He left the forsaken sanctuary and ambled back through the dank and musty lower regions of the keep until he emerged in the entrance hall. Shards of sunlight streaked into the room from narrow windows above to fall upon a blood-red sigil emblazoned on the dark marble floor. Aldis hastened past the glaring rune and ascended a stone staircase which swept upward through the tower. The sound of wailing lamentations drew him to the threshold of the grand hall.

As he peered into the room, his vision returned to shades of azure. The tapestries which draped the windows allowed no light to enter the chamber, keeping the great room sequestered in cool shadow. The Dark Queen lounged in her throne and gleefully looked on as several of her undead minions dragged one of the captives from his cage and brought him to his knees before her. The man begged for his life, but his pleas went unheeded by his merciless tormentors. The ghoulish creatures surrounded him and tore at his flesh like a pack of feral hounds.

Aldis escaped all notice as he slipped into the room and concealed himself behind a row of great columns. He crept forward until at last he came upon the relic sword where it had come to rest amidst a pile of bones and skulls. He stooped to pick it up, concealing the blade beneath his cloak, then slowly walked across the hall, stopping to stand before the dais. His silver crucifix lay at his feet. As he picked up the discarded cross, a hush befell the room. Even Mara sat in attentive silence as he ascended the steps to stand before her throne. He threw back his cloak to reveal the sword in his hand.

"Thou shalt thrive on man's torment no longer," the priest spoke, his voice filled with defiance. "Thy day of judgement is at hand. Thou hast cavorted with devils and lain with the Fallen One. Whore of the crypt, thy offspring, spawned of all sorrows, hath suffered a plague upon mankind. Succubus, foul creature, thy true name be known. For thou art Lilith, Queen of Demons..."

She moved swiftly to quash his insolence, but the priest now matched her speed. In one deft stroke, he plunged the sword deep into Mara's chest. "...and I condemn thee back to Hell." He drove the blade clean through the queen and into the granite throne.

Heart's blood, dark and thick, ran down the blade's edge as Mara squirmed and writhed, thus impaled. He laid the crucifix over her heart, then leapt to the draped window. He tore down the tapestries which blocked the sunlight from the dais. Bright beams poured in upon the throne and its captive occupant. Mara's flesh blistered and seared as she screamed in agony. When her corpse was but a charred skeleton, the priest withdrew his sword from the throne.

Aldis turned now to face the queen's minions. As two of the devils lunged toward him, the priest tore down another tapestry. The creatures scampered to retreat, but were encircled by the light. They wailed in anguish, trying to escape the sun's scorching fury, but before they could reach the sanctuary of shadow, they collapsed to the floor in smoldering heaps.

Aldis lashed out with the relic sword again and again, slaying one after another of the unholy creatures. Their vile blood stained the walls and pooled upon the marble floor of the great hall. The priest kept to the light, safe beneath the cover of his heavy cloak. He forced the remaining creatures down into the entrance hall where light streamed in, blocking their retreat into the cool darkness of the castle depths. The final three creatures fled out the castle door to escape the priest's wrathful blade. Two cast themselves, shrieking, into the blazing sunlight, while the last one, Dravek, hesitated in the shade of the alcove. As the sunlight crept toward him, he turned to face the priest who now held him at bay with the end of his blade.

"Holy man," Dravek screamed. "Thou art no longer mortal! We are brethren, thou and I."

"Immortal? Brethren, dost thou sayest?" Aldis spoke, inching him backward with the tip of his sword. "Then let us go forth together into the light and embrace the sun's sweet caress, my good brother." Aldis stepped forward into the alcove, then stripped off his cloak, letting it drop at his feet. The priest advanced, and Dravek retreated to the edge of the waning shadow.

"She shall arise from the ashes," Dravek cried. "That which you have slain shall never rest. She shall return, even from beyond death."

The priest paused, staring coldly into Dravek's eyes.

"Then I shall await her," Aldis said. He stepped back into the confines of the keep, then slammed the castle door shut, throwing its great bolt. The last thing he heard was laughter before beams of sunlight broke beneath the door.

The people of Vasaria recognized their debt to the priest, who had saved them though it cost him dearly. Even as he freed them from their cages and cells, the captives saw his hunger, the same hunger that had meant the savage death of so many of their kin and kind at the hands of the Dark Queen's minions. Yet, somehow, the priest resisted this dark temptation and spared them.

Mara's remains were interred deep in the catacombs below the keep. Above the crypt, the name Lilith was inscribed to warn of the horror entombed within. The tomb was consecrated and the gateway to the tunnels was sealed with stone and mortar.

At last, the priest warned the villagers away. They knew well the terrible vigil he maintained over the years on their behalf as the new lord of the Dark Tower. Throughout the region, Vasaria became a name of darkness, and few came here thereafter.

In time, the surviving captives died off, and as the years took them, the truth died away. The tale of the tower and its baron grew in legend, and the priest's true name and calling was all but forgotten, remembered and passed on only by the elders of each generation. Our ancestors owed him a life's debt, as do we who have descended from them.

The Baron struggled long in his lonely vigil, again and again becoming entangled in the strange history of our village, a history heavy with tragedy and blood. His part is now over, but the tale of our people and our land, and the curse we struggle against, continues. This is the legacy you have inherited.

I know now of the vigil that the Baron kept here, the one I must maintain. What shall be suffered upon me through the long years as I carry on this watch? Solitude, madness, damnation. There are fates far more wretched than death.

'Tis said that a man cannot stray from the course of his own destiny. Am I then ever fated to remain here in this accursed realm of shadows? Even now I feel the call of that which waits below.

How shall I resist, and endure?

Watcher at the Gate

JOSEPH VARGO

The castle loomed before us as we emerged from the forest canopy. Behind us, scores of nocturnal eyes watched our every move as our horses proceeded slowly up the road to the keep. The tower appeared as a gigantic shadow, silhouetted by the full moon behind it.

Gregor rode just ahead of me as we ascended the narrow cobblestone path. "Not a single torch lit," he shouted, barely turning his head toward me. "It is forsaken!"

"Forsaken?" I responded. "More likely sacked and plundered of all its worth." Whether he did not hear my disparaging remarks or simply chose to ignore them, I cannot say, but Gregor steadily progressed on his course and, as usual, I followed. The keep appeared desolate, yet there was a pall that permeated the place, an overall sense that made me think of the tower as some huge mausoleum or forbidden crypt. "No doubt haunted and cursed by the souls of the fallen," I said beneath my breath.

"Haunted, cursed and bedeviled as well, least that is what the townsfolk would have us think," Gregor replied, then let loose a bold laugh, all the while staying his course.

To one side of the road ahead stood the remains of an ancient structure. Marble columns supported three lanceted archways, and heavy stone blocks, crumbled and weathered by the ages, lay to either side of the path. The arched wall appeared to be all that remained of some larger edifice, long ago fallen, perhaps a sentinel gate which would have stretched across the road, forbidding passage to the keep. It was here among the standing columns that something strange first caught my eye.

From a distance, it appeared only as a wisp of white mist with neither form nor essence, between the central pillars of the gate. Gregor noticed nothing. His gaze was firmly fixed upon the tower, but I had the keen eye of a scout and was thus more wary of our surroundings. As we drew nearer, I could see that the wisp of white was no mist, but instead a fine silken gown which shrouded the form of a young woman.

"Gregor..." I whispered, then again, louder, "Gregor, look."

The girl stood within the open central archway, looking toward the castle and the moon beyond. Atop the gate, a row of ravens sat perched and watched our approach. We brought our horses to a halt just before the standing columns.

"Are you lost, milady?" I asked. The girl gave no response. She made not even the slightest gesture to acknowledge our presence.

The outer archways were closed off by elaborate gates of wrought iron. The twin gates were crowned by sculpted heads of court jesters entwined within the intricate ironwork. Their faces bore woeful grimaces that invoked a sense of dread and despair. Their lifeless eyes cast a somber gaze and stared blankly into the darkness.

Gregor now addressed the girl, "Surely you must be far from home, perhaps in need of a chaperone or escort. If need be, my fellow traveler and I would gladly avail ourselves to you." His beguiling words did not surprise me, for though he was ordinarily brutish and crass, Gregor could charm a serpent if it suited his needs.

Just then, the distant howl of a wolf broke the night's calm and fell to join the rising moan of the wind, creating a long and mournful wail.

Curiously now, the girl spoke, not in answer to our questions, but instead reciting a cryptic rhyme.

"Wolves and ravens share the night,
an omen for the morrow,
The wind carries the banshee's cry
to foretell coming sorrow."

She turned her head and looked toward us. Her face was young and fair, her complexion pale, almost white. Her gown, like fine gossamer, flowed and floated upon the breeze.

"What brings one so lovely to this forlorn place in the midst of the night?" Gregor inquired, still keeping a charming lilt to his voice.

Turning once again toward the castle, she leaned her head far back to bask in the glow of the moonlight, then answered simply, "The moon."

The girl seemed distant, as if lost in deep reminiscence. Gregor watched her intently, sizing his prey, then turned a sly eye toward me and said in a low voice, "If this be the only treasure we take from this place, then she shall make this trek worth our while."

"That would not be wise," she said, overhearing his remark, "for it would only serve to anger Lord Brom."

"Lord Brom?" asked Gregor. "Is he your Sovereign?"

"He is my love. I come to him here when the moon is full."

"Why is he not here then?"

"Alas, tonight the ravens announce your arrival. He awaits within the tower.

"He awaits? Let us not disappoint our host then." Gregor said, then started his horse toward the castle.

"Stop!" she cried out, her voice echoing through the night.

Gregor's horse halted at her command.

"Do not test me child." Gregor's patience had quickly worn

thin. "Though you be a sweet morsel, many such as you have met their fate at the end of my blade."

"Yes, I know your kind all too well," replied the girl.

"Do you now? Tell me then... of my kind," he goaded.

The girl looked at Gregor, silent and contemplating for a short while, then spoke, "You are strong and proud, relentless and unyielding. You let nothing stand in your way. A warrior to be reckoned with. Your sharp blade, the emissary of your wrath. Your thirst for blood is matched only by the rage that courses through your veins. Unburdened by guilt for the sufferings you inflict, you do not know the weakness of mercy. You give no quarter and expect none in return. Many have fallen in your wake." She paused, then said in a lowered voice, "Lord Brom has need of men such as you."

Gregor smiled, his vanity quenched.

She then turned her gaze to me, silently surveying me for a moment, then said, "A follower only, no great warrior, nay, merely a soldier. You have not the stomach for the tragedies of war. Your sword lays heavy in your hands, weighed down by your own conscience. Hindered by grief and remorse for the few lives you have claimed in battle, you can recount each one, their faces forever haunting your memories. You try to hide your true nature beneath a cloak of false bravery." She stopped, looking me slowly up and down, then said at last, "There is only death for you beyond this gate."

The meaning of her words sunk slowly into my heart.

"We shall see what awaits us within," Gregor said, then turned to me. "Come, let us go forth."

But I had no desire to follow, for I took heed of her warning. The abysmal pall that marked this territory had crept over me and I knew beyond a shade of doubt that I now stood at the threshold of death's domain. "No," I replied.

Gregor glared at me, his brow furled with disfavor, then he smirked and said, "So be it."

"Leave your steed here," the girl said to him. "You will have no need of it beyond this gate."

Gregor dismounted and handed me his reins. "Watch my horse," he sneered, "and perhaps I shall give you a copper piece when I return, boy." He withdrew his sword from its sheath, then proceeded toward the tower on foot.

The ravens upon the gate took wing and followed him to the castle. I squinted and watched him stop before the entrance to the keep. He put his shoulder to the heavy door, and with a great creak it swung open. A moment later, he lit a torch which illuminated the castle's grim facade.

For the first time, I beheld the Dark Tower in all its sinister glory. The place made my blood run cold. The ravens, which had disappeared into the darkness of the tower's shadow, had come to take roost upon several gargoyles above the arched doorway. They began to croak and caw down at Gregor. He ignored them and entered the tower. The glow from his torch emanated through the open castle door.

Still calmly gazing at me, the girl stood in serene repose, her arms outstretched between the pillars of the central arch. The silken material of her gown was aglow with soft, radiant light. Her ebony-black hair flowed in sharp contrast against the moon which now hung low in the night sky behind her.

"Think back upon this night," she said, her voice now strangely hollow. "Remember the decision you have made here."

Just then, I heard another creaking sound, followed by a heavy slam. I looked back toward the keep. The castle door now stood closed, and all was once again dark within. The ravens shrieked and croaked their ghastly caw until it reached a crescendo in what sounded like a tortured scream.

The unrelenting chorus of the raven's cries caused Gregor's horse to stir. It tore free of my grip and bolted down the forest path. As I turned to give chase, I looked one final time toward the watcher at the gate.

She was gone. Only a swirling mist remained where she had stood.

With desperate haste, I spurred my horse to pursue Gregor's runaway steed. The thorny bramble caught my clothes and tore at my flesh as I fled through the dark wood, but I dared not slow my steed until that accursed place was far behind me.

I never laid eyes upon Gregor again.

Long ago, I am told, a village maiden ventured to the tower one moonlit night. She went to meet her love, but met her fate instead. It is said that she still visits when the moon shines full, this ghostly watcher at the gate, granting passage only to those who may serve some purpose within the tower. For the lord of the keep still has his needs.

Journal Entries and Poems

Index of Artwork

JOSEPH VARGO resides in Cleveland, Ohio where he has been conjuring fantasy artwork professionally since 1986. His gothic images open a gateway to the darkside and dare the viewer to venture within. Joseph's haunting visions of fantasy and horror have appeared in numerous publications, and his lithographs, printwear and Gothic Tarot deck are distributed worldwide.

TALES FROM THE DARK TOWER

This book is dedicated with appreciation to those who have enjoyed my artwork.
This project would not have been possible without your support.

When my friend, James Pipik, approached me with the idea of collaborating with various authors to tell the stories depicted in my paintings, I was at first hesitant. I had created a menagerie of haunting and sinister characters throughout the years, all the while harboring my own basic ideas about their origins and the stories behind them. I envisioned this book as a collection of tales which would expand upon my early conceptions and fit together as a whole. I outlined several stories and worked closely with the writers to keep continuity throughout the anthology. After nearly a year of dedicated perseverance, these talented authors have brought my visions to life.

Joseph may be reached through Monolith Graphics at:
goth@monolithgraphics.com

CHRISTINE FILIPAK lives in Parma, Ohio where she works as a professional graphic designer. She holds a Bachelor of Fine Arts degree from Kent State University. Using a combination of computer skills and classic art techniques, she creates elegant and timeless imagery for numerous corporate clients. As art director for *Tales from the Dark Tower* and *Dark Realms Magazine,* Christine has utilized her talents in design and layout, as well as writing and editing.

MASQUE OF SORROW

In writing the origin of the curse that haunts the Dark Tower, I began by wondering how the queen's mortal seduction and transformation into a creature of darkness might have taken place, and what might have precipitated it. The visual elements of a slain king, a dark queen, an evil court jester and ominous ravens stirred memories of the classic tales by the Brothers Grimm. The Dark Queen's name was derived from the ancient legend of the *Mara,* a beautiful night-creature, a succubus, that seduces men in their dreams. The maniacal jester in the painting, *King of Fools,* portrays the embodiment of rebellion taken to the extreme. But what if something far more sinister lurked behind the harlequin mask? The result is a dark and delightfully wicked fable.

Christine may be reached through Monolith Graphics at:
goth@monolithgraphics.com

JOSEPH IORILLO is a freelance writer living in Cleveland Heights, Ohio. He is a *Summa Cum Laude* graduate of John Carroll University and holds a Bachelor of Arts degree in English. Joseph is a staff writer for *Dark Realms Magazine* and has also written several contemporary mystery and suspense novels. His most recent project is the psychological thriller, *John Threesixteen*. Though his excursions into gothic fiction are rare, he holds a lifelong interest in all things supernatural.

VESPER TOLLS AND SHADOWS

Writing these stories offered me the opportunity to explore two sides of this tormented, gothic villian. Though he harbors the potential to be savage and cruel, the Baron struggles against surrendering to the emerging beast within, and seems to possess a dark nobility. Yet when pitted against the mindless, unfeeling brutality of the warlord in *Vesper Tolls*, the Baron unleashes his vengeful wrath, even at the cost of relinquishing the last shreds of his humanity.

Joseph may be reached at: *JoeIorillo@cs.com*

JAMES PIPIK lives in Amherst, Ohio with his wife and daughter. In addition to being a freelance writer, James is also an accomplished illustrator and musician. *My work on this book is dedicated with gratitude to Joseph Vargo.*

SENTINELS AND NIGHTWATCHER

Gargoyles have always held a dark fascination for many people. Traditionally intended as guardians of many old castles and churches, they have come to represent manifestations of our own fears. In Vargo's paintings, these ancient beasts appear as though they could move or speak just as one's attention is turned elsewhere. What knowledge would such a creature gain during the centuries as it kept its silent vigil? What might they do or say if they were not made merely of stone? Would they be good or evil, or simply indifferent to mankind?

James may be reached at *jimandee@aol.com*

Eric Muss-Barnes lives in California. He founded the publishing company, *Dubh Sith Ink*, and released his first novel, *The Gothic Rainbow*, in 1997. Eric also established *Dreamdancer Motion Pictures* in 1994, producing several video projects including the gothic/industrial program, *Shellsongs*. His photography and digital artwork have been showcased in art galleries and his writing has appeared in numerous magazines such as *Outburn* and *Industrialnation*.

BORN OF THE NIGHT

My story would be dedicated to my precious friend, Michelle LaRock, but she blesses my life with far too brilliant a joy to devote unto her such a dark tale. So, I shall simply mention that I am thinking of her fondly...

Many years ago, the first Vargo painting I saw, and the one which made me a fan of his work, was *Born of the Night*. Therefore, I was greatly honored to write a story which centered around it. Joseph's artwork is very story-like. His paintings seem to breathe tales behind them and appear like photographs of surreal nightmares. *Born of the Night* is an exception; the image is akin to fragments of a strange and elusive memory. It is more poetry than prose, more like a talisman or a symbol of an event than an image of an actual occurrence. So, I spun a story which draws from the artwork in metaphor and flows in the same sort of dreamlike manner.

You can write to Eric at *eric@wyndfeather.com*
Visit *www.wyndfeather.com* for more information on his various projects.

JALONE J. HAESSIG lives in Grafton, Ohio with her husband, Hans and their two children, John and Suzanne. Jalone is a homemaker and freelance writer who loves a good ghost story. She is a staff writer for *Dark Realms Magazine* and is currently expanding one of her short stories, *The Hollow*, into a full-length novel. Jalone majored in Journalism at Marshall University in West Virginia.

SORROW'S END

This story is dedicated to my husband, children, mother and siblings who, while they may not always understand what drives me, always support and encourage me. Without them, nothing else matters.

Creating a story from a painting is an enticing prospect. With both the *Sorrow's End* and *Lector* paintings, I was led to wonder what had bound this woman's ghost to the angel monuments in this forsaken cemetery. I questioned further what had brought her to the Dark Tower and whether death was truly the end of her sorrow or the beginning.

Jalone may be reached at *hhaessig2@juno*

Russell Novotny lives in Cleveland, Ohio with his wife, Lisa, and his daughter, Yulia. He is an adult education teacher and stay-at-home father. Russell holds a Bachelor of Arts degree from Cleveland State University. His favorite author is William Shakespeare.

Child Rowland to the dark tower came,
His word was still, 'Fie, foh, and fum,
I smell the blood of a British man.'

SANCTUARY

— King Lear

With loving thanks to my wife, Lisa Kastor, for keeping the worst of the wolves away.

My idea for *Sanctuary* began by wondering about Brom's isolation. Wouldn't he be incredibly lonely after years of keeping his solitary vigil? Would his need for human companionship outweigh his thirst for blood? What stories might he tell if he had someone just to listen? What wisdom would he wish to impart upon an impressionable young visitor to the Dark Tower? The illustration, *Good Versus Evil*, appealed to me because of something subtle that it suggested: the power of the spoken word. The manner in which a story is perceived depends on who is telling the tale. The angels and demons depicted in it appear to stream forth from the open mouths of their creators, as if they had been fashioned from words alone, like stories come to life. The tale of *Sorrow* was adapted from an old Russian fable.

Rᴏʙᴇʀᴛ Mɪᴄʜᴀᴇʟs lives in California with his wife and their four children.

Nᴏᴄᴛᴇᴍ Aᴇᴛᴇʀɴᴜs

I could not help but assume that there must be a story written in the book that the ghost holds in the painting, *Noctem Aeternus*. I began by wondering what held this apparition to the Dark Tower and what might have lured her to this dreadful place when the rest of the village cowered in fear of it. A young girl's fascination with the escape that darkness offered would be the reason. I then realized that the only story which might matter to a ghost would be the tale of her life and that it would take someone who loved her to scribe in detail the events leading to her bitter end.